THE WING WARRIOR
– Book One of The Legend Riders –

By Kevin Outlaw

This is a book about heroes, and as such it is dedicated to mine: my dad.

Also with thanks to my wife and mum, for their constant support, and to my daughter Isabella, whose smile makes everything worthwhile.

CHAPTER ONE

The woods on the east side of the village were out of bounds. The trees there were old and tall and grew thickly, so that only occasionally could a beam of sunlight penetrate the gloom; and the paths were overgrown and broken, leading off to dead ends and deadly drops. If you didn't have your wits about you, it was all too easy to get so lost you would never find your way back out.

Untamed animals lived in the woods – wild pigs and hungry wolves – making it dangerous to walk alone. The old men of the village even said there were goblins hiding in the deepest places where humans rarely went, hunched in the wormholes of rotting tree stumps and waiting for lost children to walk within snatching distance.

Of course, nobody had ever really seen a goblin, but what they had seen was a large stag whose immense, twisted antlers were evidence of considerable stature and age. This stag swaggered around in a self–important kind of way, butting any lost travellers with those dangerous antlers whenever he got the chance; and for most people, that was more than enough reason to give the woods a wide berth.

Things, though, are rarely as they seem, and really this stag was not the bully people thought he was.

Four seasons ago, three vile and brutish men had gone hunting; and for a day and a night they terrorised the woods. Such was the devastation they caused, with their black–barbed arrows and ugly knives, that all the animals – except for the hedgehogs, who were a surly bunch and not the kind to get involved – called a great council. The animals asked Sage, the mighty stag, to protect them from the intruders.

What Sage did next, nobody really knows, but only one hunter ever returned from the woods, and he was part–mad, raving about a cruel stag that waged war against humans without cause, and animals that seemed to have human reason and held meetings to discuss plots against humankind.

The story quickly spread, but people chose only to believe the parts they wanted to believe, and disregarded the rest. So Sage got lumbered with a reputation as a vindictive, foul–tempered, unpleasant sort of a creature, while not one single person believed that a squirrel and a badger once had a heated debate about how to dispose of two hunters' bodies.

For his part, Sage really had no argument with humans, and he often helped them out. Most people who accidentally ventured into the woods and became lost were casually directed to the nearest exit with some gentle antler–prodding. But there was a certain group of children who needed no such assistance, and were regular visitors. As long as they behaved, and didn't start doing anything stupid like poking the badgers with a stick, then Sage saw no reason to chase them off. He did like to keep an eye on them though, just in case.

After all, they were only human.

The boy with brown hair, who Sage knew was called Nimbus, was standing knee-deep in the gurgling water of the Forbidden River and holding a sharpened stick like it was a spear. He was an ungainly–looking boy, part–way to becoming a man but with still plenty of growing to do, and he gave the appearance he didn't quite fit into his body yet and hadn't quite got the hang of how all his limbs were supposed to work. Sage could tell the boy was going to become a handsome and powerful man one day, or at least as handsome and powerful as any man could be expected to become; but by the way he hunched, it seemed doubtful the boy had any idea of his own potential for greatness. Much like most humans.

There was a second child sitting on the riverbank, a girl with brown hair that came almost to her waist. Her name was Glass, and she was Nimbus's younger sister. She reminded Sage of a rabbit, or perhaps a field mouse. She was so small, so fascinated by the world, so eager to understand everything and hurt nothing. It was such a shame they were all traits that most people seemed to grow out of.

As Sage watched the children, he couldn't help wondering what the future held for them. Would they become like the hunters he had been forced to hurt, and return here one day as his deadly enemies, or would they learn to live a different way? He had little time to think about it before one of the squirrels scampered down a nearby tree to warn him that the wolves were out, and he decided to go to make sure they weren't causing too much trouble.

As for the children: They were completely unaware of their silent observer's departure, just as they were completely unaware that they would have been eaten by wolves by now if they hadn't been under Sage's protection. They had far more important matters to concern themselves with.

'You'll never catch one,' Glass said, splashing her feet in the water.

'Of course I won't,' Nimbus snapped. 'Not if you keep scaring them away. Quit splashing.'

'I don't think it will make any difference. We've been here all day. I'm bored.'

Nimbus waded deeper into the river, and stared intently through the foaming water until he could see the pebbles of the riverbed. If he was very still, he knew the fishes would start swimming around his feet; then he would be able to spear one. It would flip and flap and try to escape, but if he was quick, he knew he could do it.

'Nimbus?'

'What is it, Glass?'

'I'm bored.'

'Wait a minute.'

'Why?'

'Just wait a minute.'

There was a big, silver fish splashing towards him.

'But...'

'In a minute, Glass.'

The fish swam nearer. Nimbus remained motionless, poised to strike.

Just a bit closer. That was all.

Just a bit closer, and he would have his fish supper.

He was so tense he could feel his muscles shaking, his hands trembling, his heart pounding in his chest.

Just a bit closer.

The fish circled around, just out of reach, its single shining fin breaking the surface of the water for a second. Nimbus held his breath.

Just a little bit closer.

'What are you doing, Nim?' someone above him said.

Nimbus almost jumped out of his skin in fright. Something wet and slippery flapped over his bare feet. He squealed, lost his balance, and tumbled backwards with a splash.

Glass started giggling behind her hand.

Chest–deep in the river, Nimbus just caught sight of his fish supper's tail disappearing under the water with a plop. Only an expanding circle of ripples proved there had ever been a fish at all.

'You let it get away,' the voice from above said.

Nimbus scowled at the girl who was sitting among the tree branches. 'That was your fault, Sky,' he shouted.

She smiled mischievously. 'Don't be so grumpy.'

Nimbus stood, shaking water from his tangle of curly hair. 'That was my supper,' he humphed. Glass was still laughing, and he glared at her angrily. 'It was going to be your supper too, Stupid. Now we'll have to eat that horrible stew Mum was making.'

'Get over it,' Sky said, dropping into the water. Her yellow hair billowed around her shoulders. Standing in the river, she could almost have been mistaken for a mermaid. 'You should have asked Tidal to help.'

'Shut up,' Nimbus said, stomping over to the bank where his boots were. 'Tidal always catches fish. I wanted to catch one for myself. Like my dad does.'

'Nim, wait up.' Sky splashed after him. 'I'm sorry.'

'Leave me alone, Stink Witch.'

'Oh, you don't even know what a stink witch looks like.'

'No. But I bet it looks a lot like you.'

Nimbus climbed out of the river and sat in a dark recess under a tree. Just the kind of recess a hungry goblin might have lived in, if the stories the old men told were true.

'Nim?' Sky said.

Glass plucked a smooth, orange stone out of the water. 'He's going to sulk now,' she said. 'He won't talk to you. He does this to me all the time. You're lucky you don't have to live with him.' She turned the stone over in her little hands, examining it thoughtfully. 'Do you think Daddy would let me have a pony? I'd like a pony.'

'Nim?' Sky said, again.

'Shut up,' Nimbus growled.

'Fine.' Sky crossed her arms, turning her back on him to stare at the surrounding trees. 'You are such a girl sometimes, Nim.'

'Am not.'

'Yes you are. You're a bigger girl than your sister is.'

'Am not.'

'And you've got a girl's name too. Nimbus. That's so silly. A silly girl's name.'

Nimbus sat bolt upright. 'Well... Well... Sky is a girl's name too.'

'I am a girl, Nim.'

Nimbus put his boots on. 'Yeah, well. It's stupid. I'm going home.'

'Home?' Glass dropped the orange stone. The rushing river swallowed it with a glug, sucking it back to the bottom and jolting it along with the current. She stood, brushing the dirt off her knees. 'We're going home?'

'Come on,' Nimbus said.

Sky was still looking at the trees, studying them as if she expected them to come to life. There was no breeze. The air was heavy and still. 'You know what? I don't think I like it here,' she said.

'Don't be silly,' Nimbus said. 'I've been coming here all my life. There aren't really goblins.'

'Says you,' Glass muttered, under her breath.

'I've never even seen a wolf.'

'Doesn't mean there aren't any,' Sky said.

'Scaredy Cats. You're both frightened, aren't you?'

Sky looked at Glass; Glass looked back. Maybe they were scared, but neither of them would admit it to Nimbus.

Suddenly, there was an explosion in the middle of the river, and a huge fish shot out of the water. The fish seemed to hang in midair for a long time, caught on an invisible line, and then it arched its body, plunging back out of sight.

'That was my dinner,' Nimbus said.

'It's okay, Nim,' Glass said. 'You're just not meant to be a fisherman.

'You're probably right. I think I'll leave the fishing to Tidal from now on.'

'Good,' Sky said. 'At least then we won't go hungry.'

'Shut up.'

'Shut up yourself.'

'Scaredy Cat.'

'Grump.'

'Stink Witch.'

'Troll King.'

Nimbus grinned. 'That's a good one.'

'I've been waiting all week to use it.'

For a moment they stood silently, watching the river, waiting to see if the fish would leap out again. It didn't.

'Let's go,' Nimbus said.

He held Sky's hand, put one arm around Glass, and together they left the riverbank, heading into the darkness of the trees where the goblin myths seemed a little truer.

'There's one,' Glass said excitedly, pointing out a white ribbon tied to the branch of a nearby tree.

'I see it,' Nimbus said, sounding more than a little bit smug. He had been marking paths through the woods with coloured ribbons for years, and it had definitely been one of his better ideas. White ribbons plotted the route between the village and his favourite fishing spot, green ribbons went to a small clearing in the heart of the woods, and red ribbons led to the cave. Nobody ever went to the cave, though; not even Nimbus.

'Nearly there,' Glass said, skipping ahead.

'Don't go too far,' Nimbus said. 'It's starting to get dark.'

'You know she doesn't like the woods, don't you?' Sky said.

Nimbus shrugged. 'I know, but it's not my fault. I don't ask her to come with me.'

'She's your sister. She wants to spend time with you.'

'She's a pain.'

'Look at her. She's got scabs on her knees from scrambling over rocks, bruised arms from climbing trees, cut hands, scratched cheeks. All from chasing after you.'

'So?'

'She'd follow you wherever you went. There aren't many people who would do that.'

'Tidal would.'

'Tidal is a brat. He'd only go with you if he was going to get the chance to show off.'

'Maybe. What about you? Would you follow me?'

'Nope.'

'Why not?'

'Because you're so slow, you'd be following me.'

Sky dashed off after Glass, whooping gleefully. Nimbus watched her until she was obscured from view by the trees, then he shook his head and sighed.

He and Sky had been friends for almost as long as either of them could remember. She had always been there – an important part of his life – and it was impossible to imagine a time when she wouldn't be.

But recently, mainly in the last few months, things had started to feel different between them, and he didn't know why. Now, when he thought about her pretty pink smile, the pine–needle smell of her hair, or her almost musical laugh, he got a funny sensation in his stomach. He was old enough to know what that sensation meant; he just wasn't sure why he should have it when he thought about Sky. After all, Sky wasn't like other girls. Sky was just Sky.

Just a friend.

He was still contemplating this when he heard the voice.

'Nimbus.'

At first he thought he must have imagined it, then he thought it must have been the wind rustling through the leaves. But it wasn't the wind, and his imagination had never been that good. There really was a voice, very faint and very weak, saying his name.

He looked around, listening carefully.

On his right was a tree with a white ribbon tied to it; on his left was a tree with a red ribbon.

With a growing sense of unease, he realised the cave was nearby.

Three years ago, when he had been much smaller and not nearly so brave, he had got lost while exploring the woods. After stumbling around for many hours, and running at one point when a stag tried to butt him with its antlers, he eventually found the cave. It was a horrible place, but he had no choice other than to spend the night there. He had tried to light a fire, but it had been raining and nothing would burn; so he had huddled in a tunic, shivering, too afraid to sleep in case he got eaten by wolves, or bears, or a really angry stag.

At first light he had left the cave, telling himself he would never spend another night there, and since then he had returned only once, in order to mark the route with red ribbons. He had used red for danger, and even during the day – never getting closer than a hundred paces – that terrible place had sent a chill running down his spine.

The voice called out his name again.

He swallowed hard.

'What do you want?'

The leaves rattled and chattered like witches discussing the best way to cook a small boy. The red ribbon flapped, and in the dimming light it looked like a slobbering monster's tongue.

Nimbus strained to hear the voice again.

'Hello?' he called.

The voice said his name, but seemed farther away this time, farther along the path leading to the cave.

'Tidal, is that you? I'm going home, so don't think I'm going to chase after you.'

There was no response, except for the rustling of bushes and plants.

Nimbus peered through the gloom. He couldn't see anybody, but he could sense there was someone – something – there. Something that wanted him to follow. Something that wanted him to go to the cave.

He could think of only one thing that lived in caves and

attempted to lure children away from woodland paths.

Goblins.

Despite being almost fourteen and a half years old, and quite strong and brave for his age, he couldn't help thinking that perhaps he wasn't ready to meet a goblin just yet.

'Right. I'm going home,' he said.

He turned. Stopped. Looked for a white ribbon. Couldn't see one.

He listened for sounds of Sky's laughter. Nothing. All he could hear was that voice calling his name, trying to draw him into the very heart of the woods.

A breeze blew around him, and leaves bustled over his feet. He was totally alone.

'Sky?'

Alone, and lost.

'Glass?'

The path seemed to stretch on forever. Mist was creeping against the tree trunks. Night came down on the wood ever more quickly. It would be totally dark soon.

'I'm not going back to the caves,' he whispered, clenching his hands to stop them shaking. 'I'm not going back there, and you can't make me.'

A flash of yellow lightning briefly lit parts of the path, revealing everything that had been hidden by shadow.

Horrid shapes sprang up in the stutter of brief illumination, and in that last second Nimbus saw a frightful figure looming out at him from the bushes. As he was dragged to the floor in a tumble of flailing arms and legs, his screaming was drowned out by the crashing of thunder.

CHAPTER TWO

Nimbus closed his eyes tightly, and hoped being eaten by a goblin wasn't anywhere near as painful as the old men of the village had made it sound.

For a long time he stayed that way, waiting to feel sharp teeth gnawing away at his skin. He waited, and waited, but nothing happened.

Eventually he risked opening one eye.

His friend Tidal was standing over him, a grin splitting his grubby face from ear to ear. Glass and Sky were standing nearby, looking equally pleased with themselves.

'Who's the scaredy cat now?' Sky said.

'Can I help you up, Old Chum?' Tidal asked. A fork of lightning illuminated the four friends. The shadows of the trees wrapped up and around them fleetingly as thunder boomed.

'I knew it was you,' Nimbus said, regaining his feet and brushing leaves out of his hair, his relief only slightly outweighing his embarrassment. 'I could smell you.'

'Smell me?'

'You smell of fish.'

'At least I can catch fish.'

Nimbus flushed red. 'You shouldn't go jumping out on people like that, or you'll end up getting a thump.'

'Who from?' Tidal's grin widened, and he shoved Nimbus in the arm. 'From you?'

'I didn't say that.'

'But that's what you meant, wasn't it?' Tidal shoved Nimbus again, hard enough for him to lose his balance and almost fall. 'Are you going to give me a thump, Nim?'

'I meant...' Nimbus looked over Tidal's muscular frame, at his wide shoulders and strong hands. He was the tallest, brawniest fifteen–year–old Nimbus had ever met, and in all the time they had been friends Nimbus had never been able to beat him at anything.

'Come on,' Tidal jeered. 'I'll let you hit me first. One free punch, right in the face. Give it your best shot.'

Nimbus stared at his feet. He had already been embarrassed in front of Sky once today, and he had no intentions of getting into a fight he had no hope of winning. 'I'm not going to thump you, Tide. I'm just saying you should be careful. And it's not funny taking down my ribbons. They're the only way we've got of finding our way out of this place.'

'I haven't touched your stupid ribbons.'

'Then where are they?'

Tidal shrugged. 'I don't know what you're talking about.'

'We didn't take any down,' Sky added, helpfully. 'We came right back here after we met up with Tide. We thought it would be funny to scare you.'

'Very funny.' Nimbus looked at the dark arches of the leaves. Fireflies were drawing smiling faces in the gloom. 'But if you didn't take the ribbons, where have they all gone?'

'Are we lost?' Glass asked.

'No.' Nimbus smiled his most convincing smile and ruffled her hair. 'No, of course we aren't lost. I just seem to have misplaced some of my ribbons.'

'There's a red one over here,' Tidal said.

'And there should be a white one on the opposite side of the path,' Nimbus snapped. 'But it's not there, is it?'

Sky and Glass sat together on a tree stump while the boys continued to bicker. 'Do you think they know what they're doing?' Glass asked, picking up a handful of brown and yellow leaves and letting them fall through her fingers.

'I'm sure they'll get us home,' Sky said.

Glass started to sort the leaves into piles, based on colour, shape, and size. 'Boys are silly,' she said.

Sky watched Nimbus dashing up and down the path, creating swirls in the thickening mist as he searched for the missing ribbons. 'They certainly are,' she said.

'I just don't get it,' Nimbus said, hopelessly. 'Someone must have taken them down. There's no other explanation.'

'But why would anyone do that?' Tidal asked. 'You must be looking in the wrong place.'

'But...' Nimbus made his hands into fists. It was getting cold. 'I'm sure the ribbons were here,' he said.

A bolt of lightning sliced a jagged trail through the sky, briefly cutting out nightmarish shapes from the crowded mass of trees. Every shadow was a witch; every hollow was a black eye watching. There was another crash of thunder.

'Nim?' Sky called. 'Nim? What are we going to do? We'll get soaked through if we stay out in this mist.'

Glass continued playing with her leaves. She was deep in concentration.

'Yeah, Nim. What are we going to do?' Tidal said.

'We'll have to keep moving. We're bound to find a white ribbon sooner or later. These woods are full of them.'

'That's your plan? You want us to walk around aimlessly in this mist? We'll never find a ribbon like that. We'll just get more lost.'

'Well, I don't know what else to suggest. What do you think we should do?'

Tidal flicked his hair out of his eyes. He was smiling, but it looked false, like he was more afraid than he was letting on. 'We could go to the cave,' he said.

'Be serious. No–one goes to the cave.'

'It would be dry.'

'It's horrible. It's dark, and full of strange things, and...' Nimbus's lips seemed very dry, his palms particularly sweaty. 'There's something up there.'

'Like what?'

'Like something you wouldn't want to meet.'

Sky stood. She had come without a cloak, and she was uncomfortably damp. 'Nim,' she said. 'We can't find our way out tonight, and we can't sit here. The cave is our best bet.'

'But...'

Glass squashed a handful of leaves into a brown–red pulp. 'We should go to the cave,' she said.

The fireflies were gone now. The dark of night had lowered thickly over the woods. Owls hooted and flapped from branch to branch. Other things snuffled and snorted in the mud beneath the bushes. The world was alive with things that couldn't be seen.

'There may be goblins,' Nimbus said, reluctantly.

'There's no such thing,' Tidal laughed, slapping Nimbus on the shoulder. 'Now come on, I don't want to stay in the cave any more than you do, but maybe there we can start a fire and we can keep dry for the night. What do you say?'

Nimbus sighed heavily. What could he say?

'Okay.'

'Good man.'

Glass dropped the last of her leaves. She looked so small, surrounded by the massive woodland trunks; so fragile and delicate. 'I'm ready,' she said.

Sky took Glass's hand and set off along the path of red ribbons. Tidal chased after them.

Nimbus watched his friends leaving, took one last look behind him at the tree he was sure he had marked with a white ribbon, and then reluctantly followed.

As they got nearer to the cave, the mist dropped away completely, and the night didn't seem so dark. Even the growling of the thunder was left behind them. Rain began to fall, and the air was filled with its soft patter.

'I don't like it,' Nimbus said, his hands wedged firmly inside his tunic to keep warm. 'Someone has obviously taken down all of my white ribbons. They want us to go up to the cave for some reason. I don't like it.'

'So you keep saying,' Tidal grinned, leading the way confidently. 'And we've all heard your story about the time you were lost here. But nothing ate you then, and nothing is going to eat you now.'

'But I was lucky last time,' Nimbus muttered.

Eventually the trees thinned out, and the children reached a small area of scrubland where the weeds clawed their way hungrily over oddly arranged standing stones. There were eight stones in total, each as tall as Glass, and crows were perched on four of them, fluttering their wings and cawing mournfully.

On the other side of the clearing there was an imposing rock face, and beyond that the craggy outline of Sentinel Mountain sliced up through the clouds like a broadsword.

As he emerged from the trees, Nimbus pointed to a large opening in the rock face. 'There it is,' he said.

'This place is creepy,' Glass said.

They stopped outside the cave, exchanging nervous glances in a way that made it obvious they were all thinking the same thing. The cave didn't look any more welcoming than the woods did.

'So this is where the goblins are,' Tidal said, ducking inside. 'It's not very homely, is it? Wait here.'

Glass and Sky looked at each other, shrugged, and went straight in after him.

Nimbus was overcome by the feeling he was watching his friends being eaten one by one as they disappeared inside, and he shuddered uncontrollably. 'You shouldn't make fun. Something might take offence,' he said, as he followed them inside.

Tidal had already vanished into the back of the cave, and occasionally he could be heard muttering to himself as he explored the darkness. Sky and Glass sat close to the entrance. They were shivering, and rainwater was dripping out of their hair.

'Is this where you stayed last time?' Glass asked, quietly.

'That's right,' Nimbus said.

'It's not very nice here,' Glass said. 'I like it at home, in my bed with my dolls.'

Nimbus looked at Sky. She was bravely trying to disguise her concern. 'Are you okay?' he asked.

She nodded, but her eyes told a different story. She was scared to her bones.

'I'm sorry,' Nimbus said. 'I didn't mean to get us lost. I was sure we were on the path.'

'Never mind being sorry,' Sky said. 'Let's just get a fire started before we turn to ice.'

As Nimbus headed out in search of firewood, Sky held Glass's hand tightly. 'Are we going to get eaten?' Glass asked.

'I shouldn't think so,' Sky replied. 'Nim was on his own the last time he was here, and he was okay. And there are four of us now. Anyway, you don't believe in goblins, do you?'

Glass looked at Sky with big eyes that said she very much did believe in goblins. 'No,' she said.

'You don't have to worry. Even if goblins are real, they only snatch babies. You're almost eight years old.' Sky pressed Glass's nose and she giggled. 'You'll be too tough for them to eat.'

Glass seemed happy with this explanation for a second, but then her forehead creased with confusion. 'How will they know I'm too tough to eat before they've tried?'

Sky hugged her tightly. 'I'm more worried about my dad. He doesn't like not knowing where I am.'

'Will he be mad?'

'No. Hungry. I'm supposed to be making his dinner.'

There were footsteps from the depths of the cave. Tidal reappeared carrying a dusty oil lantern. He looked excited. 'Hey, guess what,' he said.

'What?' Nimbus asked, rushing back in with an armful of wood.

'It looks like this cave goes on for miles,' Tidal said. 'Gosh, Nim, didn't you even go back and explore when you were here?'

'I wasn't in the mood for an adventure,' Nimbus said, dropping his firewood. 'Now stop worrying about exploring and help me. I got lucky and found some dry twigs and grass in the hollow of a tree. We should be able to have a good fire.'

'Fire? That's a great idea. We can light this old lantern I found.'

'I meant a fire to stay warm. I don't intend leaving the cave mouth all night.'

'Are you joking? There could be something great back there. We might find goblins, or a stink witch, or anything.'

'I don't like witches,' Glass mumbled, sitting on the floor beside Nimbus and watching him intently as he stacked the wood in a ring of stones.

'Drop it, Tidal, you're going to scare everyone,' Nimbus said.

'We have to go and look,' Tidal said.

'We don't have to do anything.'

Nimbus began rubbing two sticks together. He had watched his dad make fire this way. Of course, his dad made it look easy.

'Okay then,' Tidal said. 'Put it this way, Nim. If you don't come back here and investigate, you'll never know what might be hiding in the dark. Anything could sneak out and get us in the night. Wouldn't it be safer to have a look?'

Sky touched Nimbus's shoulder gently, almost apologetically. 'It makes sense. If we went and looked now, it would help us all sleep a little better.'

'I don't like witches,' Glass repeated.

'It's okay, Glass. There aren't any witches in this cave.' Nimbus was starting to sweat from rubbing his two sticks together. 'If there were witches we'd all have been turned into frogs by now, wouldn't we? There's no need to worry.'

'Aw, come on.' Tidal stamped his foot. 'We have to at least take a look back there.'

Nimbus's branches finally started to smoke, and his face was illuminated as the dry grass and wood he had found burst into flame. 'Aha!' he exclaimed, triumphantly. 'We have a fire.'

Glass and Sky clapped, and even Tidal looked impressed.

The fire glowed a deep orange–yellow, crackling and popping as it cast odd shadows on the rutted walls of the cave. Every pocket of darkness where the light of the fire could not reach, every small hollow and crack in the stone, seemed horribly sinister and able to conceal all manner of monsters. Even the children's own shadows were alien and scary.

'Right,' Nimbus said. 'That should keep us warm until morning.'

'Nim?' Tidal said.

Nimbus looked at Tidal, then at Sky, and then finally at Glass. His sister was watching him in that way she always did when he was about to do something stupid; like she was proud of him and scared for him at the same time.

He felt his mouth drying out as icy fingers touched his heart. 'Okay,' he said. 'We'll take a look. Tide, hand me that lantern, and I'll see if I can get it lit.'

'Great,' Tidal said.

Nimbus crouched next to Glass and ruffled her hair. 'Hey, I'll be right back,' he said.

He didn't sound entirely convinced.

The Wing Warrior

CHAPTER THREE

In his life, Nimbus had been wrong about many things. He had been wrong about the number of plums he could fit in his mouth at once, he had been wrong about the number of times he could bunk off his reading classes before getting in serious trouble with his dad, and he had been wrong about which girl in the village had left him a love note at the beginning of a particularly embarrassing day a few months ago. But never had he been so completely off the mark as he was on that night in the cave when he had told Glass he would be "right back."

All night, Glass and Sky huddled together for warmth beside the guttering fire as they waited for the boys to return; and they were still waiting when the first rays of daylight crept over the treetops.

'Do you think a stink witch got them?' Glass asked.

'I shouldn't think so,' Sky said, smoothing Glass's hair. 'Witches like gingerbread and sweet things. Not smelly boys.'

The sun got higher and stray beams of yellow warmth cut through the leaves. Where those beams touched the ground, steam rose up like white wood spirits dancing in the morning light.

'Boys are smelly,' Glass agreed, poking at the glowing embers of the fire with a stick. 'If I was a witch, I certainly wouldn't want to eat one.' She continued poking the fire, sucking on her top lip thoughtfully.

'Is something on your mind?' Sky asked.

'I was just wondering if you ever get good witches.'

'I suppose so. If you knew how to use magic, and you helped people, then I suppose you would be a good witch. But nobody uses magic these days. I'm not sure if anybody even knows how magic works any more.'

'Leaf says magic was banned.'

Sky smiled. Leaf was an old woman who had travelled all over the world studying ancient lore before settling down in the village. The children would always gather around to hear her stories, and she even taught some of them important skills like how to read and write. If there was something about history that Leaf didn't know, then it probably wasn't worth knowing.

'Apparently, once all of the legends were gone, magic became quite dangerous,' Sky said.

'What are legends?'

'Oh, legends are wonderful things. They're magical creatures that existed a long time ago, so long ago that lots of people don't even believe they ever existed at all.'

'Do you believe?'

Sky watched the steam rising from the ground. The day was getting warmer and brighter. 'I think you have to believe in some things. You have to believe in your friends, in your family. But there are other things that it's nice to believe in, whether they're true or not.'

'Like legends.'

'They make the world seem better.'

'I'd like to meet one.'

'You have to be careful, not all legends are nice. You wouldn't want to meet a leviathan. They were giant creatures that lived in the oceans and rivers, and they would smash boats and eat fishermen. It was said that some of them were so large they could almost wrap around the whole world, and if they did that, they could crush it like a tomato. But the dragons were good. They protected all the people across the land. And there were other good legends too. Unicorns, and mermaids, and a very special horse called a pegasus.'

'Why was it special?'

'Because it had wings, and it could soar above the clouds like a bird.'

'I'd like to do that.'

'Me too.'

Glass fell silent, prodding the fire with her stick. She stuck out her tongue so far it touched the tip of her button nose. She was thinking again. 'So where did the legends go?'

'They just went. First the dragons, then everything else. Nobody knows why. I guess, sometimes, things just have to die.'

'Oh.'

The fire sizzled defiantly, and then went out. Sky wrapped her arms around Glass.

Where was Nimbus? He wasn't supposed to have gone all night.

'Did the legends do magic?' Glass asked.

'No. The legends were magic. They kept all the magical forces in the world balanced.'

A small, brown rabbit bounced out from under a bramble bush near the cave mouth. The two girls watched him as he twitched his nose, hopped around, and then eventually scampered out of sight behind the trees.

'If I knew magic, could I turn myself into a bunny?' Glass asked.

'I don't see why not.'

'I think it would be nice to be a bunny.'

'Maybe.'

'What would you like to be?'

Sky looked up. Strips of blue showed through the leaves of the trees like tears in green fabric. 'I'd like to be a bird,' she said. 'I'd like to fly away from here.'

'Why?'

'Just because.'

'Leaf says there was a battle. Lots of magicians all decided to fight, and they turned the skies silver and gold with magical fireballs and lightning bolts.'

'That's true. They say that happened when the dragons disappeared. Some people got scared, and others got greedy, and they all called on different wizards and warlocks and witches and magicians, and even a thing called a necromancer. The fighting was terrible, and in the end the use of magic was banned.'

'I would use magic for good things.'

'I know you would.'

There was an echoing thump from back inside the cave.

Sky's heart began to race, and she hugged Glass tightly. 'Nimbus?' she called.

There was no reply.

'Nimbus?'

Another thump, then the sound of footsteps. Tidal appeared. His hair was thick with mud and spider webs, and his clothes were soaked through.

'What happened to you?' Sky asked.

Tidal stomped straight past her and out into the woods. He didn't even stop to speak.

Nimbus emerged from the darkness. His clothes weren't ripped, and he was no muddier or scruffier than he had been the previous night.

'Hello,' he said.

'Nim!' Glass leapt to her feet, throwing her arms around his waist. 'I was beginning to think you weren't going to come back.'

'Good to see you again, Nim,' Sky said.

'We got a bit lost,' Nimbus explained.

'Did you have an adventure?' Glass asked. 'Did you find a legend?'

Nimbus glanced over his shoulder, almost as if he expected a dragon's head to loom out of the darkness, all fiery eyes, billowing smoke, and chomping fangs. 'No,' he said, quietly. 'No, don't be silly. Of course I didn't find a legend. All the legends are gone.'

'What happened to Tide?' Sky asked.

'He got a little bit more lost than I did. I don't think he's in a very good mood.'

'And I'm not the only one,' Tidal said, reappearing at the cave mouth. 'We're in big trouble. Your dad's in the woods with a search party. They're looking for us.'

Nimbus's head sank. 'I'm for it now. We all are. Sorry guys.'

Glass grabbed his hand. 'It's okay. At least we didn't get eaten by a goblin.'

Nimbus's father, Cloud, was a very large and very serious man with a very serious face, serious grey hair, and very serious ideas about children doing what they were told. He had spent the whole night looking for the children, accompanied by three other equally serious–looking men, who were equally likely to agree with his serious ideas.

When these men saw the children emerging from the cave, their serious expressions, just for a moment, gave way to expressions of excitement and relief. However, when Cloud spoke, his voice was just as angry as Nimbus had expected it to be.

'What's going on here?' Cloud demanded. He waved his big, callused hands in the air to emphasise his words. This was totally unnecessary as his booming voice was emphasis enough.

Nimbus hung his head, and kicked his toe in the ground. 'Sorry, Dad. We got lost.'

'Lost! You should never have been here in the first place. Especially here.' Cloud waved his arms at the cave mouth, at the jagged white rocks sticking out of the ground, and the hunched trees with their horrible clawing branches. 'I've told you so many times about coming into the woods.'

'We're sorry,' Glass said, desperately trying to hold back her tears. 'We just wanted to go fishing, but then somebody took down all the white ribbons, and we were lost, and we couldn't go home. And we really just wanted to go home.'

'What are you talking about? We've been finding white ribbons everywhere.'

Nimbus swallowed, kept his arms behind his back, kept his eyes down. 'We must have missed them in the dark and the mist,' he muttered.

'But you were sure somebody had taken them down last night,' Sky said.

'I must have been wrong.'

'But...'

'I was wrong,' Nimbus snapped.

'Well, never mind that now,' Cloud said. 'Let's just get you all home and warm. Everyone is worried sick.'

'Everyone?' Sky asked, winding the sash of her dress through her fingers nervously. 'You mean... My dad too?'

Cloud's stern face softened considerably. A lifetime of wrinkles and worry lines melted away. He suddenly seemed more youthful, and not nearly as intimidating. 'He's waiting for you.'

'How is he?'

'He's... concerned. I told you, everyone is. Come on.'

Glass allowed herself to be picked up in her father's huge, strong arms. He was wearing a travelling cloak, and he wrapped it around her shoulders as she clung to his chest. 'You should be ashamed of yourself,' he said to Nimbus. 'Bringing your sister to a place like this. It could be dangerous.'

Nimbus nodded, looking back at the cave. It receded into the darkness like the long throat of a terrible monster. And only he knew what was down there.

CHAPTER FOUR

The following morning was sunny and bright, and much nicer than the morning Nimbus and his friends had been found at the cave. In the village of Landmark, children were playing in the dusty streets, chasing each other and pushing each other over. In the fields that skirted the boundaries of the village, farmers were ploughing the earth and planting seeds. The twelve soldiers, sent from the city of Crystal Shine to keep law and order, were sitting in the garrison building playing cards.

As far as anyone was concerned, it was just another ordinary day. The parish minister was in the churchyard, weeding the graves. The cows and sheep were grazing peacefully. Several men and women were down at the river washing clothes, and farther on, where the water opened up to the wide expanse of the Everlasting Ocean, fishermen sat on the shore fixing nets and discussing the early–morning catch.

All in all, everything, and everyone, was normal.

Everything, and everyone, except Nimbus.

Nimbus hadn't been normal since he had emerged from the depths of the cave in the woods. He had been thoughtful and withdrawn, unable to sleep, and unable to concentrate on anything.

Both his father and mother had noticed, but whenever they asked him what was wrong, he would say, 'Oh, nothing,' and amble off in a dream. It was peculiar indeed.

On this particularly ordinary morning, Nimbus was sitting at the kitchen table, pushing uneaten eggs around his plate. His mother, Strata, was busy with the housework, her greying hair tied back from her face with a length of frayed string.

Cloud was eating lumpy porridge, lost in his own thoughts.

'Dad,' Nimbus said, prodding a piece of bacon with his fork, 'what do you know about Wing Warriors?'

'Wing Warriors?' his father humphed, spooning porridge into his mouth. 'Nonsense and children's stories. Is that what Leaf has been teaching you instead of how to read?'

'Um... Not exactly. I was just interested.'

'Well, never you mind about old stories and wives' tales. They're for people with too much time on their hands. I've never seen a dragon, or a Wing Warrior, and I don't believe in anything I haven't seen for myself.' He sounded very convincing, but there was a look in his eyes that suggested he might not be entirely telling the truth.

'But...'

'No buts. I don't want to hear another word about it. Let me eat in peace.'

Nimbus looked to his mother for support, but she simply shrugged.

When Cloud had finished eating, he stood, kissed Strata goodbye, told Nimbus to behave himself, and set off for the mill.

'Mum?' Nimbus said.

'Yes?' His mother was washing dishes in a bucket of water she had drawn from the well outside.

'Why is Dad so unwilling to believe in all that dragon stuff?'

His mother looked at him carefully, searching in his eyes for the reason behind such a question. Eventually she smiled, a slightly awkward smile, and poured herself a cup of tea. 'Your father is a very brave man, a very serious man. You shouldn't question him.'

'Is he still angry with me?'

'No. He isn't angry with you. Your father worries. The wilderness is no place for a young boy.'

'I'm not young. I'm almost fourteen and a half years old.' Nimbus puffed out his chest hopefully, and tried to ignore the fact his mother was taller than he was.

'You're growing up quick, Nim, but you're still a boy to me, and you're still a boy to your father. The wilderness is a dangerous place, full of animals and bandits.'

'There aren't any bandits in the woods.'

'Maybe not today, but who knows what tomorrow will bring? And your sister certainly shouldn't be playing there.'

'She follows me.'

'As you well know, so why not lead her someplace else? Someplace safer?'

'She's not my responsibility.'

His mother blew steam from her tea and took a sip. The sun was streaming through the window, filling the kitchen with a warm honey–roasted light. 'One day,' she said, carefully, 'your father and I may not be around. Then you will be responsible for your sister.'

Nimbus was suddenly aware of Glass standing in the doorway. It was impossible to tell how long she had been there, and Nimbus wondered how much she had heard.

'I'm ready,' she yawned, grabbing an apple from the fruit bowl.

'Good,' Strata said. 'Now off you go. Leaf is waiting for you.'

'But, Mum...' Nimbus protested. 'Why do I even need to learn how to read? I'm bound to end up farming or working in the mill like dad. Reading is just a waste of time.'

His mother frowned. She formulated her next sentence carefully. 'No–one knows what the future will bring, Nimbus. I would rather you faced such uncertainty with as many talents as possible at your disposal. Including reading.'

The children headed off, but they only got as far as the end of the garden path before Nimbus stopped. 'I'm not going to Leaf's class today,' he said.

'Why not?' Glass asked.

'I can't really say. There's just something I need to do. Tell Leaf I'm feeling ill, but tell her I'd like to borrow her book on legends.'

'You'll be in trouble.'

'Not if you do as I say.'

He looked long and hard at Glass. Eventually, after a good deal of thought, she nodded. 'Okay. I'll say you're sick. But you have to tell me where you're going.'

'Not yet. I will, though.' He ruffled her neatly combed hair. 'Now run on or you'll be late. And don't forget to ask Leaf if I can borrow that book of hers. Okay?'

'Okay.'

'Good girl.'

Glass saluted playfully, then scampered off down the road. When she was gone, Nimbus's gaze was drawn to his little one-storey house, and he was overcome by an odd sensation. Suddenly, he found it almost impossible to look away. It was as if he was seeing his home for the very first time, or perhaps the very last time, and he wanted to make a mental note of every single detail while he had the chance.

The thatched roof was starting to look patchy, the stonework was solid but uninspired, and the chimney was a little bit on the wonky side; but for all its faults, this was his home and he loved it.

A rustling in the bushes in the front garden startled Nimbus out of his daydream, and he looked up and down the street before once more returning his gaze to the house he had been raised in.

The Mayor of Landmark, the innkeeper, and several of the richer farmers, including one retired businessman who had moved from the North to invest in cattle, lived in far grander homes than Nimbus's. Those wealthy few could enjoy the luxury of two storeys, tiled roofs, balconies, beautiful gardens, stable blocks, and even indoor toilets. But such extravagance was rare in Landmark, and sometimes even frowned upon.

Landmark was, and always had been, a simple and ordinary

place, full of simple and ordinary people who lived in simple and ordinary homes.

But as Nimbus stared at his house, gripped by a sudden desire to perfectly remember every little fault and eccentric angle, he got the impression that nothing would ever be simple or ordinary ever again.

A shape moved in front of the lounge window. His mother.

Time to move.

He followed the main road north, not even the slightest bit concerned that this course took him straight past the soldiers' garrison. He had learned a long time ago, the soldiers rarely bothered watching the road. After all, Landmark was a rather insignificant sort of a place where almost no–one ever visited, and where there was never any trouble.

Sure enough, as he approached, he could hear the soldiers having a heated argument about the card game they were playing. As distracted as they were, they never noticed him slip past and make a hasty dash for the woods.

Once he was safely concealed by the trees, he slowed to a leisurely walk.

It was such a lovely day, even the woods seemed less gloomy. There were tiny blue and yellow birds flitting through the branches, strange bright flowers blooming in the hedges, and there seemed to be more sunlight than usual filtering down through the leaves.

Even the stories about wolves seemed like fairie tales on a day like this, never mind the stories about goblins; but even so, a shiver ran down his spine when he found the first of his white ribbons twitching in the breeze. A silent, formless dread crept up behind him to breathe down his neck, and his insides felt like they had turned to water.

He gritted his teeth and forged ahead.

As long as he kept the ribbons in sight, he knew he would be at the river in no time.

But, of course, he wasn't really heading to the river.

There would be no fishing today.

After ten minutes or so, he left the path of white markers, and began following the dreadful route marked by red ribbons instead.

The cave looked much the same as it had the last time he had been there. Endless. Cold. But this time something was different

This time Nimbus wasn't just afraid. This time he was excited too.

The oil lantern was where it had been left, and he lit it using oil and flint he had taken from his father's store earlier that morning. For a moment, the cave's black interior seemed to breathe quietly; then oily fingers of yellow light sprang out from the lantern and cut bright swathes through the gloom. Spiders and other crawling bugs scurried to find better hiding places.

Nimbus took one last look at the trees and the sharp white stones that stuck out of the earth around the cave entrance, and once again he had that feeling: The uncomfortable feeling that, after today, nothing was ever going to be the same again.

With the lantern at arm's length he moved cautiously into the cave. The trembling light probed ahead of him, inching over oddly shaped rocks and glimmering on fine veins of metallic ore in the walls.

One stone in particular caught Nimbus's attention, and he paused to look at it more closely. In the dark, it had the appearance of a monstrous skull, with deep eye holes that were certain to be home for slithering, crawling creatures. Apart from its odd, strangely unsettling form, the stone was also of interest as Nimbus recalled that it marked a point where the floor dropped away in a steep slope. He chuckled to himself as he remembered how Tidal had slipped down there, squelching and splashing through slime and mud to land in a bone–jarring mess.

Poor Tidal. He had been furious. But what else did he expect if he was going to blunder around in the dark like a dumb ox?

Nimbus inched around the skull–rock, careful not to turn his back on those vacant, staring eyes for even a second, and then he headed down the slope. The light from the cave entrance disappeared behind. Now, it was just him and the lantern. And the lantern really wasn't all that bright.

The tiny flame spluttered, projecting frightening shapes against the walls; and suddenly Nimbus didn't feel quite so brave and confident. After all, just because he didn't meet goblins last time he was here, that didn't mean there were none to meet.

'Goblins aren't real,' he muttered to himself, and he pressed on, determined not to let his nerves get the better of him. He had done this once, with Tidal, and he could do it again. Alone. Even if there was a strange sound coming from up ahead that put doubts in his mind. A babbling, gurgling sound: The sound of something terrible, being feasted on by something even more terrible.

He pressed himself against the wall and held his breath.

But he was being silly. Of course he was. He had been here before; he had heard this before.

Gradually, he realised that the sound he had imagined was the giggling of goblins slurping their way through a meal of little boy stew was actually just the sound of running water.

He remembered now. There was an underground stream here, fed by icy water that ran down from fissures in the walls.

With much grunting, and a few words he had heard some drunken men using outside the tavern one evening, he manoeuvred himself rather awkwardly between two rock spikes and onto a bridge of stone that reached across the foaming water.

He crossed with caution, aware that this was where Tidal had slipped the second time. He had toppled into the water with an echoing splash and had floundered like an octopus trying to climb out. By that time he had been beginning to think investigating the cave had been a bad idea. Nimbus hadn't said anything, but by that time, he was beginning to think it was one of the best ideas they had ever had.

Down even deeper, beyond the stream, the cave narrowed into a tight tunnel. Tidal had been too broad across the shoulders to go on, so Nimbus, who had been scared but too proud to admit as much, had made the final part of their expedition alone.

That was why it was Nimbus, and only Nimbus, who had found the vast underground cavern hidden on the other side.

That was why it was Nimbus, and only Nimbus, who returned there now.

As he puffed and scrabbled through the narrow tunnel, the lantern–light gradually revealed the epic expanse of emptiness beyond, and he was breathless with wonder as he cast the lantern back and forth.

The area was so big that even with the light held above his head the ceiling remained an unfathomable mystery, shrouded in total darkness. But Nimbus did not need to see the upper reaches of the cavern to know it was full of bats. He could hear chirping and squeaking, and the leathery flutter of wings.

For a moment he remained close to the wall, wondering if he had come all this way for his courage to fail at the last minute; but then, limbs trembling, palms sweating, heart pounding, he thrust himself out into the void.

As he walked across the great expanse of empty space, taking each step carefully in case the floor should suddenly disappear into a gaping chasm or goblin hole, he held the lantern as high as he could. The flickering glow it gave off seemed terribly ineffective in the creeping blackness, and the dark was so heavy he was not sure there was any light strong enough to penetrate it.

He counted his steps to measure the length of the cavern.

At one hundred and six steps he started to wonder how much oil was left in his lantern.

At two hundred and four steps he started to wonder if he had miscounted.

At three hundred and twenty–nine steps he started to wonder whether he was still walking in a straight line or if he had accidentally turned in a circle.

At three hundred and sixty–one steps he decided to stop counting.

The tiny, choking flame in the lantern sputtered and flared, hungrily consuming the reserves of fuel. What if it went out? This cavern was massive, and he would have no way of finding a way out. And nobody knew he had come.

He would never be found. He would just wander around down here, lost in utter darkness, until he starved to death. Maybe one day, hundreds of years from now, somebody would find his crumbling bones and they would wonder why a boy had come down into the depths of the earth by himself.

They would probably decide it was because he was really, really stupid.

He paused. Looked ahead, looked back. Everything was the same. There were no landmarks. It was just nothing stretching on in every direction.

What if he had turned back on himself? If he turned around again, would he be heading in the opposite direction to the way out? There was no way of knowing.

'Calm down,' he said. 'Think.'

He had to get to a wall; that's what he had to do. If he could find the edge of the cavern, he would be able to follow it around until he reached the exit, even if he didn't have any means of illumination. It was the best thing he had – the only thing he had – that was close to a plan.

He moved on, ignoring the voice in the back of his head that told him the cavern might be hundreds of miles around its perimeter with lots of little tunnels that were dead ends or ways deeper under the ground.

He didn't like that voice. But that was okay. It was only a little voice. And if he concentrated on putting one foot in front of the other, if he concentrated on not falling over, then the little voice was almost too quiet to be heard at all.

Left foot, right foot. Left foot, right foot. On and on, until the grey surface of the far wall came into sight.

Tears of relief sprang into his eyes, and he wiped them away quickly, feeling stupid and embarrassed even though there was nobody around to see.

The bats were silent.

The lantern–light danced across the wall inquisitively, almost playfully, picking out every nook and crevice to form an intricate pattern of light and dark.

As Nimbus moved nearer, marvelling at the way the darkness seemed to exist both inside and between each flare of light, a glimmer to his left drew his attention.

He moved the lantern around, instantly dispelling the illusion of patterns in the walls. The light enveloped and caressed the smooth edges of a beautifully polished suit of armour that was so shiny he could see his reflection in its surface.

It was truly magnificent armour, with red plates and metal gloves over a shimmering set of silver chainmail rings. The helmet had a face protector of iron bars like a dragon's clenched teeth and was decorated with a crest shaped into outstretched dragon wings.

Nimbus had once seen a drawing of a suit of armour much like this one. He had never thought he would see one for real. His father didn't even believe such armour existed.

'Wing Warriors,' he whispered.

His reflection smiled.

Nimbus had first found the armour the other night, and for some reason he had decided to keep his discovery a secret, even from Tidal who had been waiting for him back in the narrow tunnel. But it was a secret that had gnawed away at Nimbus ever since. Coming back – seeing the armour again – was the only thing he could think about; but having done so, he realised it still wasn't enough. He wanted to take the armour out of the cave completely and hide it somewhere only he knew about.

But how?

There was the sound of a bat unfurling its wings, only louder, and something large and scaly moved in the dark. Nimbus turned around, but there was nothing there, only the vast empty space of the cavern reaching out of sight.

Something hissed.

Probably just his imagination.

He looked again at the armour, wondering how much it weighed, and whether he would be able to fit it in the narrow tunnel he had crawled through to get here. As he was thinking, the lantern–light fell on a second object: something he hadn't noticed before.

His breath caught.

It was a diamond – the biggest diamond he had ever seen – and trapped within its many–faceted surfaces was the biggest, heaviest–looking sword he had ever seen. The end of the handle was carved into a growling dragon's head, and the hilt and finger–guard had been shaped into a curled dragon's tail. It had clearly been fashioned as a companion to the armour, which stood guard in stern, eternal silence.

Nimbus set the lantern on the ground. 'This is incredible,' he said.

It was by far the most exciting thing he had ever found. More exciting than his woodland fishing spot; even more exciting than the ruined castle beyond the woods.

He ran his hand over the smooth face of the diamond. It was warm.

How could it be so warm?

He leaned closer, and as his breath fogged the surface of the diamond a jagged crack appeared through it. The perfect shine of the blade inside grew brighter.

Nimbus stepped back, watching in awe as the crack got longer, zigzagging across the diamond and branching off in different directions.

'This can't be good,' he said.

The diamond started to shake with invisible energy, and a huge line crazed down through its middle.

Nimbus backed up a little farther.

'Not good at all.'

The diamond shattered, sending shiny flecks pinging and ricocheting off the walls as the sword hit the ground with a deafening clang.

'Oops,' Nimbus said.

Something huge shifted its weight in the darkness. 'I was thinking the same thing,' a deep, rumbling voice said.

'Who said that?' Nimbus squeaked, moving so his back was to the wall. His gaze darted around, trying to pinpoint the source of the voice. It was impossible to see anything beyond the faint glow of the lantern–light, but he could sense something moving heavily. There was the sound of a ship's sail flapping in high winds, and a rush of cool, stale air.

Nimbus reached down and grabbed the handle of the sword. It was so heavy he could barely lift it.

'Who's there?' he demanded.

No response.

He held the sword out, waving it threateningly – or at least as threateningly as he could – in the direction he thought the voice had come from.

'Who's there?' he repeated.

The cavern suddenly seemed very full, as if something had sneaked in behind him through the narrow tunnel, and then expanded to occupy all the available space.

Two large, yellow eyes opened in the darkness.

Momentarily, Nimbus's gaze flicked to the dragon–shaped handle of the sword he was holding.

'Oh dear,' he said.

The eyes started to move closer.

CHAPTER FIVE

People have always had great difficulty describing a dragon, probably because very few people have ever seen one; but Nimbus knew, as soon as the huge lumbering thing heaved its weight into the light, a dragon was exactly what it was.

It had a large head, fringed with jagged fins, and a pointed mouth of razor–sharp teeth from which a black, forked tongue would occasionally dart.

A glittering armour of red scales covered the dragon's muscular body from the tip of its snout, down its long neck, and even to the end of its monstrous tail. Only the dragon's folded, twitching wings were free from scales, and more than anything else it was the wings, so obviously immeasurably wide when they were fully extended, that made Nimbus feel so small.

And so terrified.

'Stay away from me,' he said, trying to sound brave even though his voice had shrunk to match the way he felt.

The dragon came closer. The five sharp, grasping digits of its two forward limbs were similar to fingers, suggesting this was a creature with two arms and two legs; but it used all four limbs in order to manoeuvre its immense bulk, moving in a way that was horribly similar to a gigantic lizard.

Nimbus tried to swallow, but realised he couldn't. The air had started to smell like something was burning, and he had the feeling that any second now the something would be him.

'You're alone this time?' the dragon rumbled, and the whole cavern shook.

'I...' Nimbus's mouth was totally dry. The sword was shaking in his grasp uncontrollably. 'Stand back.'

'You are the one who was here the other day, aren't you? The one the armour called to?'

'I... You...' Nimbus licked his lips. His back was pressed hard to the wall, and he wished he could sink right through the stone. 'Where did you come from?'

The yellow eyes of the dragon flickered as its gaze turned upwards. 'It's a high ceiling.'

'Don't even think about eating me.'

The dragon tilted its head slightly. Ridges of scales moved in the light, and Nimbus could see that while the scales had at first appeared red, they now looked green.

'I have no intention of eating you,' the dragon said. 'I don't eat humans.' The head moved closer, so it was only inches away from the point of Nimbus's sword. 'The bones get caught in my teeth.'

'Well,' Nimbus said, beginning to edge along the wall. 'I can see I've interrupted you, and I'm sorry about that. So, if you'll excuse me, I'll be on my way.'

The dragon moved one of its huge, clawed limbs, blocking any escape attempt Nimbus might have thought to try. 'Going so soon? I'm not sure that's entirely polite, after breaking my things.'

Nimbus looked at the chunks of glittering diamond scattered over the ground. 'That was an accident,' he said.

'I think not. You are the one who came the other day, aren't you?'

Nimbus nodded.

'You are the one the armour called to.'

'What do you mean?'

'You heard its voice, in the woods.'

'No. That was just my friend, Tide, trying to scare me. That was all.'

'It was the armour. It called your name. It wanted to be found.'

'It's just a suit of armour.'

The dragon laughed; a deep, booming laugh. Nimbus had the impression that from the tip of the dragon's nose to the bottom of that laugh was surely a great distance indeed. 'There is no such thing as just a suit of armour. All things have memory, and this armour has more than most. It wanted you to find it. I suppose that also means it wanted you to find me.'

'Why?'

The dragon's claws, each of which was almost as large as the sword Nimbus carried, scraped on the ground. 'I was hoping you could tell me that.'

'I didn't even know dragons were real.'

'Dragons? What is a dragon?'

'Well...' Nimbus paused, a smile creeping into the corner of his mouth. 'You are. You're a dragon.'

'I am?'

'Surely you must know that.'

'I've lived in this cave my whole life, just me and the bats, and they've never told me what I am.'

'Aren't there any others down here?'

'There is only me.'

Nimbus relaxed a little, lowering his sword. 'Haven't you ever been outside?'

'What is outside?'

'Outside. The opposite of inside. Haven't you ever left this cave?'

'No. I have to stay here.'

'Why?'

'To guard the armour.'

'Why?'

'I don't know.'

'Then why do it?'

'I'm not sure. It's not clear. Nothing more than a dream. Just a voice in the eternalness of slumber. I was put here to guard that armour, and to wait for someone.'

Nimbus swallowed. 'Me?'

'Perhaps. You are Nimbus, aren't you?'

'I am. But how can you know who I am, when you don't even know who you are?'

'I have lots of memories. They are like old books in a library, covered in dust and long unused. Sometimes I can read the pages in those books, but other times the pages are smeared, or ripped out completely.'

'Do you have a name?'

'I am nameless.' The dragon sounded sad, and its scales seemed to change colour once again. They shone pale blue in the dim lantern–light.

'Everybody should have a name,' Nimbus said.

'Perhaps...' The dragon paused. 'Perhaps you could give me a name.'

Nimbus put down the sword. Not because he wanted to, but because he didn't have the strength in his arms to hold it any longer. 'Can you fly?' he asked.

'I have wings, and I do have some recollection of what the sky tastes like, although I am sure I have never seen it.'

'Then I will name you Cumulo.'

'Cumulo? I like that.'

'Good. That's settled then. Cumulo and Nimbus. Two friends.' He looked carefully at Cumulo and his many sharp teeth. 'Two friends who don't eat each other,' he added.

CHAPTER SIX

'So is this Wing Warrior armour?' Nimbus asked, examining the suit carefully.

'Yes. It is the last surviving armour of the Wing Warriors,' Cumulo said. 'And the sword is the last surviving sword of the Wing Warriors.'

'Who made it?'

'The Wing Warriors. Obviously. Many years ago, in a very different time. All the crafts of men and dragons went into the armour's creation.'

'It's magnificent.'

'It is.'

'So why's it here? Why isn't it in a museum or something?'

'I don't know, just as I do not know why I, myself, am here. I guess we were to be kept secret until such time as you were ready to find us, or we were ready to be found.'

'Do you feel ready?'

'No more so than I ever have, but something tells me that now is the time to be found. Something, some kind of spirit, has awoken in the armour. It knows who its master is. For whatever reason, you are destined to wear it.'

Every muscle and fibre in Nimbus's body shivered, and something loathsome – a pit of fearful emotions – opened inside of him. He suddenly felt as if he was surrounded by dark phantasms that whispered of terrible adventures to come.

His mother had always said that when she was nervous she got butterflies fluttering around in her stomach. Nimbus didn't have butterflies. Nimbus had flapping dragon wings.

'Me?' he said, his voice nothing more than a mouse–squeak.

Cumulo nodded.

'No. Not me. Whatever you're thinking, think again.'

'It's not my decision.'

'No. It's mine. And I'm not wearing that armour.'

'We are the same, you and I. Until today, I did not know I was a dragon, but now I know, I cannot say I'm not.'

Nimbus ran his fingers over the armour's breastplate. There were no dents or scars in the metal; it was almost as if it had never been worn before. 'Who was its previous owner?'

'I do not know.'

'Did they... die?'

'I do not know.'

'Whoever they were, they were bigger than I am. This armour will never fit me.'

Cumulo chuckled, in his deep, echoing way. 'Size isn't always about how tall you are. I think it will fit you better than you realise, when the time is right.'

'And how will I know when that is?'

'I think you will know well enough.'

Nimbus shook his head doubtfully. 'Maybe what you're saying is right, maybe it isn't. Either way, the first thing we have to worry about is getting you out of here.'

'Why?'

'Because it's dark and cold.'

Cumulo swung his great head left and right, his unblinking gaze seeing everything perfectly. 'My eyes are very good. I am not sure I understand dark.'

'Well, take my word for it. It's dark in here, and I don't think it's a nice place for a dragon to live.'

'Why not?'

'No room to stretch your wings, for a start. No maidens to eat, villagers to terrorise.'

'Terrorise?'

'I'm joking. You do need a better place to live though. Somewhere where you can...' He gestured with flapping arms.

'You know? Get up in the sky, feel the wind on your face.'

'I guess I've never really thought too much about what a nice home for a dragon would be. But then, I never knew I was a dragon, which is probably part of it.'

'Well, now you know, and it's time for a change of scenery. Can you breathe fire?'

'I've never tried. There has never really been any great cause to. Not in here.'

'Exactly. We'll find you a nice place where you can blow fire without roasting yourself to death. Somewhere with some open space. It'll be great, a real adventure.'

Cumulo's breath plumed in a billow of white steam. 'I don't think I'm allowed to leave here,' he said. 'I seem to be remembering something from before.'

'Before when?'

'Just before.'

Nimbus sat with his back to the wall and the lantern between his feet. There was only a small amount of oil left, and the flame was spluttering weakly. It would not be long until he was plunged completely into the terrible underground darkness of this place.

'What do you remember?' he asked.

'Wise men in conversation, talking about a great evil. They said the dragon must stay hidden.'

'Do you think they were talking about you?'

'Yes.'

'Then we find you another hiding place.'

'But...'

'Don't you want to see outside? Don't you want to know about the things beyond this cave?'

'Yes, but something tells me terrible things will happen if other people learn of my existence.'

Nimbus grinned. 'Well, I can keep a secret if you can.'

Cumulo's scales reflected a deep, ruby red. It was not as if they changed colour, it was more as though they had always been that colour, but the angle of the light had made them appear different. 'Sometimes I feel as if I keep many secrets,' he said, 'some of which I even keep from myself, locked away in my mind.'

'More memories?'

'Sometimes it's like the memories are not my own, and somebody gave them to me for a reason I don't know about.'

'What makes you think that?'

'Because I knew who you were. And I knew of humans long before I ever saw one.' The dragon grinned a toothy grin in the dark. 'And I knew I wasn't supposed to eat you.'

'I'm glad of that, at least.'

'But don't you see? I have lived here all my years. I can't possibly know of humans, or Wing Warriors. Yet I have these memories. They are like visions seen through the eyes of someone else, and I do not know what they mean.'

'Well.' Nimbus stood. 'Maybe one day you'll find someone who can help you understand, but I'm sure you won't find them in here, so let's try to figure out a way to get you out. I can't think you got in through the same narrow tunnel as me, so there must be another way. Any ideas?'

'I think they may have brought me in as an egg. I would have been smaller then.'

Nimbus put his ear to the wall. He could hear the trickle of water on the other side. 'So you even hatched down here?'

'Yes. I don't think they ever intended for me to come back out again. Maybe I'm dangerous.'

Nimbus saw the sadness in the dragon's eyes. 'Maybe they were just trying to protect you. Nobody has seen a dragon for hundreds of years.'

'Why not?'

'Because...' Nimbus stopped. Swallowed. Cumulo watched him steadily. 'Because there are no dragons. At least, none that anybody knows about. You're the only one.'

Cumulo nodded, and his tongue flicked out through his teeth. 'I thought as much. What happened to them all?'

Nimbus put his ear back to the wall. 'Nobody knows. One day there were dragons, the next day they were gone. Some people say there was a dragon war, and all the dragons were killed, but a lot of people don't believe they ever really existed.'

'Guess they were wrong.'

'Guess so. I think there's another cave on the other side of this wall. How strong are you?'

'I don't know.'

'Do you think you could break through?'

'I don't know.' Cumulo pushed on the wall with one claw. When the rubble had finished falling, and the dust had finally cleared, he turned to Nimbus. 'Yes, I can,' he said.

Where the wall had been, there was now a huge hole. A cool breeze came through the opening, carrying with it an unsettling drip–drip–dripping sound.

Nimbus held out the lantern to illuminate the empty space beyond. He had been right, there was another cave.

The walls here were crusted with valuable–looking stones that winked and glimmered. The ceiling was an angry jumble of pointed stalactite rocks that dripped water in the same way a snake's fang drips venom. There was no ground, only an expanse of oily, stinking water that rippled with each drop of moisture from above.

'What is this?' Nimbus asked. 'An underground lake?'

'No. There is a breeze up ahead. This is a river, leading to the outside world.'

'But the waters are still.'

Cumulo sniffed the air, and stared intently at the river. There was no way to gauge how deep it was, or what things might lurk below the surface. 'I fear there is something foul in there, something old and evil. A creature of the ancient times.'

Nimbus caught a glimpse of something slimy and shimmering

in the river. A glimpse was all he needed to know he didn't want to see any more. 'We shouldn't go this way,' he said.

'I agree. I do not trust the look of these waters, or the way they smell. We will find an alternative route.'

There was a plop as something in the cave was dislodged and rolled into the water, sinking without trace. The surface of the river instantly came alive, as though many fishes had started to move, flipping and splashing their fins to cause mini whirlpools, waves, and ever–expanding ripples.

'We may have woken something,' Cumulo said. 'I would hold on if I were you.'

Before Nimbus could react, the river thundered into life, exploding with a fury that blasted him off his feet. White spray and the echoing rush of speeding water filled the air, and the bats screeched, dropping from the ceiling in a storm of clammy wings.

Then, as suddenly as it had started, the torrent of water stopped. Everything was silent again.

'What happened?' Nimbus asked, rubbing the water out of his eyes.

Cumulo was still watching the river. It appeared to be flowing normally now. 'I think,' he said, 'a very long time ago, something much older than I am came here to hide, and to wait.'

'What sort of thing?'

'I'm not entirely sure. It followed this stream from the sea, swimming against the current all the way, until it found the dark cool waters beneath the mountain. Then it curled itself up and went to sleep.' The dragon lowered his head, sniffing the river tentatively. 'It's awake now.'

Nimbus held the lantern out over the water. 'But it's so wide, and so fast. What kind of creature could block up a river like this?'

'The kind of creature it's not a good idea to wake up, I should imagine.'

An unusual object glimmered below the surface of the bubbling water.

'What do you think that is?' Nimbus asked.

'I don't know, have a look.'

Nimbus raised an eyebrow. 'Are you serious?'

'Whatever was here is gone now. It's quite safe.'

Cautiously, Nimbus reached into the freezing water. When he eventually removed his hand, he was holding a tooth the size of his fist.

'That's a big tooth,' Cumulo said.

'My dad's going to kill me,' Nimbus said.

CHAPTER SEVEN

Tidal lived in a little wooden hut just outside the village of Landmark, near the sandy shore where the Forbidden River joined the sea. His hut had only one room, in which there was a small mattress for him to sleep on, a chair and a table where he could eat, and a stove where he could cook. It was a very simple house, even by Landmark's standards, but that was because Tidal was not particularly complicated.

For as long as he could remember, he had loved the water, and he could sail a boat almost before he could walk. His mother had always said he was as much a child of water as he was of flesh and blood, and there was no denying there was a grace and flow to his movements that whispered of the ocean. He even had his own fishing boat, and on most days when the weather was good he could be found bobbing up and down just off shore, with a line in the water and a net full of fish, exactly as the people of the village had found him on the morning of his parents' boating accident.

Even now, there were villagers who commented on how strange it was for him to love the ocean so much, considering what had happened. But Tidal knew how dangerous the sea could be, and he did not blame it for taking his parents away. The ocean was wild and unruly; it was a friend to no–one. He couldn't hate something for being true to its nature.

Besides, just as surely as the ocean had made him an orphan, it had also saved him from growing up in the orphanage at Crystal Shine. By displaying his capabilities as a fisherman, even though he was only twelve years old at the time, Tidal had proven to the mayor of Landmark that he could look after himself. If he could put food on his table, and he was happy, then there was no need for him to leave the house he had grown up in.

Some people asked if he would be upset living so close to the place where his parents had died, but to those people he always said the same thing: 'My parents are gone. But the sea is always here.'

At the moment, he was sitting on the pier outside of his hut, with his feet dangling over the murky waters of the Everlasting Ocean. He was fixing his best fishing net, which had been snipped through by some overenthusiastic lobsters during the night; and as he worked, he would occasionally look out at the distant horizon where two fishing boats were being bounced around. Tidal would have been out there himself, but he had to get this net repaired.

Everything was quiet – peaceful – except for the occasional creak of the wooden pier as water slapped around its supports. Seagulls circled in a perfectly blue sky, weaving and ducking, plummeting into the foam of the sea before rising up again. Their silent dance was enchanting.

Out on the boats, strong men with broad chests and hairy beards threw their nets and reeled in hundreds of madly flapping fish. The bright sun painted everything golden.

Tidal sighed contentedly, but suddenly a memory of the time he had spent in the cave beneath Sentinel Mountain fluttered like a black crow through his happy thoughts, and he felt a chill despite the brilliance of the sunshine.

He couldn't help but shiver as he thought about his journey with Nimbus into those foul tunnels, and he was gripped by a peculiar sense of unease as he recalled the events of that night.

He and Nimbus had been exploring for what seemed like an age, and they were both tired and frightened, although of course Nimbus was more tired and frightened than Tidal was. They were even thinking about turning back, especially as Tidal was soaked through from falling in the river; but then they found a narrow tunnel which was just too tempting.

'What do you think?' Nimbus had said.

'I think you should go in,' Tidal had said.

'Really?'

'I'd go myself, but it's too narrow. Go on. I'll wait for you.'

'But... I'll have to take the lantern.'

'Go on, go on.'

'I'm not sure...'

'Nim, get in there. We can't go back to the girls without checking it out.'

'Can't we?'

Tidal had given him a shove. 'Hurry up, before we run out of lantern oil.'

Nimbus had not looked particularly happy about the idea, but he had squirmed his way through the tunnel anyway, and was quickly swallowed up by the darkness beyond.

Almost immediately Tidal began to have second thoughts.

It was pitch black, and scarier than he would ever admit to the others. The cave did not seem anywhere near as quiet as it should have been. It was almost as if the brooding dark was breathing. Horrible scuttling noises came from all around, and the whole time Tidal had the unnerving feeling he was being watched by something that didn't want him to be there.

He was more than happy when Nimbus finally wriggled back through the tunnel with the lantern.

'What did you find?' Tidal had asked.

Nimbus looked over his shoulder, and paused before he spoke. 'Nothing. Just more caverns. You could really get lost down here if you weren't careful.'

Tidal caught a glimpse of Nimbus's eyes in the faltering light, and for just a moment he thought he saw the flicker of a lie in his friend's expression. 'There was nothing down there at all?' he pressed.

'Not that I found. But this place is huge. I think we should leave before the lantern goes out. I'd hate to be scrabbling around here in the dark.'

Tidal had to agree, and they left the underground caverns, swearing to each other never again to return. However, while Tidal had every intention of sticking to his word, he couldn't shake the feeling that Nimbus had other ideas.

He tied the last knot in his net and gave it a good, hard tug to make sure it wouldn't come loose. He was finished, and there was still plenty of daylight left to get out in his boat.

At that moment, he became aware of a distant rumbling sound, as though a thousand horses were charging on the village of Landmark. The pier trembled beneath him, and the water along the shoreline began to splash and froth.

Fishermen on the beach were shouting and pointing. A gigantic wave, as high as a city wall, was rushing down the Forbidden River.

Before Tidal even had a chance to fully appreciate what was happening, the torrent of angry water crashed into the pier and smashed him off his feet. It was like being punched with a stone hand, and all of his breath was knocked out of him as the wave carried him off the pier and out into the ocean.

He was completely swallowed by the swirling water, and he could feel the terrible drag of an undercurrent trying to pull him down. He attempted to swim back to the beach, but the water was moving too fast and he was disorientated, unable to tell which way was up and which way was down. Frightened fish, nothing more than tiny flecks of gold in the dark, darted past him as he spiralled and twisted in confusion, his lungs screaming for oxygen.

Suddenly something huge, bigger than anything he had ever seen in the ocean, swam out of the gloom. In the dark and bubbles, he could barely make out what it was, but he could see sharp teeth in an open mouth rushing at him.

Frantically splashing, using every last ounce of strength he had, Tidal tried to swim clear of the advancing fangs. He felt something sharp rake across his chest, and then something heavy bashed into him. He spun around and around, screaming silently in pain and fear; and then, with no energy left, he gave up his fight to swim against the current and allowed himself to be dragged along with it.

As the frightening blackness of unconsciousness dimmed his vision, he just caught sight of what had hit him.

Scales glimmered on the creature's long body as it headed farther out to sea. Then it was gone, and Tidal remembered no more.

CHAPTER EIGHT

Leaf's house was a peculiar place; it smelled of ink and leather and ancient knowledge, and was as quiet as any graveyard. There were rumours that it was haunted, but Leaf always said the only things haunting her house were the memories of great minds recorded in the pages of the books she had spent a lifetime gathering.

Leaf had lived in Landmark for as long as most people could remember, and since her arrival she had done everything within her power to pass on knowledge to any children who cared to receive it and more than a few who didn't.

'Legends?' she asked, as Glass pointed to one of the books on her shelf. It was the book Nimbus had wanted to borrow; a very old and dusty volume that had an awful lot of words in it and not many pictures.

'They sound interesting,' Glass mumbled.

'I love reading about legends.' Leaf flicked through the pages of the book, nodding her head approvingly. Her friendly eyes glittered as they scanned the pages. 'I used to sit for hours and read about the dragons and unicorns.'

'I think it's sad.'

Leaf smiled, her usual friendly smile, and passed the book to Glass. 'It might seem sad,' she said. 'Most legends seem that way. But legends are full of hope, they live forever. Every time someone reads this book the legends live on.'

'But they're gone.'

'They may be gone from the world, but not from our hearts. And never from our dreams. Not even from the dreams of the people who claim they don't even believe in them.'

'I'd like to meet a legend.'

Leaf laughed, and it sounded unusually loud in the stillness of her house. 'Who knows, Glass? Maybe tonight, when you close your eyes and go to sleep, you will.'

'That would be nice.'

'What would you like to meet?'

'Gosh, I don't know. I think I would be frightened of a dragon. Mermaids are beautiful, but I can't really swim. It would be nice to ride a pegasus, or feed a unicorn.'

'Unicorns were always my favourite. They're the most magical of all the legends. They were some of the very last to disappear, and it's said there was even a unicorn in the great magical war, ridden by a fairie princess with the power of the sun in her eyes.'

'Is magic really bad?'

'It certainly became that way. The unicorn was defeated in battle, and after it was gone, there was no balance to the magical forces of the world. Magic became something evil and uncontrollable, something that could only hurt and kill.'

'So magic was banned.'

'That's right. And over time it faded out of all knowledge completely. With no legends, all magic slowly left the world, like a lake drying up in the sun. It is probably for the best.'

'And what happened to the fairie?'

'When the unicorn was slain, she crouched over its body and wept for it. She wept so hard the sunlight drained from her eyes, so instead her eyes were cold pools of blue moonlight. She changed her name to Moon, and she vanished into the West, beyond the borders of mankind, never to return.'

'Why did she leave?'

'Moon was a magic user, a great enchanter, and the unicorn was her familiar.'

'What's a familiar?'

'Whenever a magic user was born, a legend would also be born, a creature that would be forever connected with the magic user and bound to the same fate. When the unicorn died, Moon too, began to die. She left this world, perhaps to find a new familiar, or perhaps more likely, to fade away into the night.'

It was at that exact moment that Glass and Leaf heard the rumbling. At first it was a very distant sound, but it quickly got louder, until it seemed to be bearing right down on top of them.

Outside, several children who had lingered after Leaf's class were standing and staring with open mouths. Other children were running around excitedly, screaming and crying.

The ground shook violently, and several books fell down from the shelves.

'What's going on?' Glass asked.

'I'm not sure,' Leaf said, 'but let's go outside where nothing can fall on us.'

She quickly pushed Glass out of the house. The air was filled with a rushing, screeching noise, and a wave of water came crashing down the river.

Glass watched with wide–eyed terror as two men were sucked off the riverbank and into the foaming water, their arms waving hopelessly as they disappeared from sight. For a moment she thought she could see the arching, scaled back of a giant serpent in the middle of the wave, but it was gone before she could be certain. She held Leaf's hand tightly.

The tidal wave burst out of the river mouth, exploding into the ocean with a final roar and splash.

Moments later, two fishing boats, just visible on the horizon, were pulled under the water. After that, the sea was calm again, as if nothing had ever happened.

By the time Sky found Glass, the village was in chaos. People were screaming, and the twelve soldiers from the garrison had strapped on their swords and were running down to the seashore.

The tidal wave had left behind a terrible trail of destruction.

Fishermen's huts and boats were broken, and the pier was destroyed. Worst of all, there was no sign of the people who had been dragged into the water.

'Hey,' Sky said, standing beside Glass. 'Did you see that?'

Glass nodded.

'What do you think it was?'

'A wave.'

'I know that. What do you think caused it?'

'A snake.'

'Don't be silly, Glass. How could a snake cause that?'

'It was big. As big as the river.'

'You can't get snakes that big.'

'I saw it.'

'If it was a snake, where did it come from?'

'Maybe it came from underneath Sentinel Mountain.'

Sky thought of the dark cave where they had spent the night, of how they had laughed at Tidal when he emerged from the darkness, soaking wet and filthy.

It was possible that something had been down there, under the mountain. The Forbidden River was fed into by so many other streams, most of them with unknown sources. It was possible that something could have swum down, looking for a way out to sea. But a giant snake was ridiculous.

She put a hand on Glass's thin shoulder. 'Do you think you could have been mistaken?'

'I didn't get a good look.'

They both stood in silence, watching the soldiers on the beach running backwards and forwards among the shattered remains of houses and boats. Seagulls circled like white pieces of paper floating on the wind.

'What are they doing?' Glass asked.

The soldiers were lifting wooden boards and pillars, looking under everything that was washing back up on the dirty sand. Sky knew exactly what they were doing. They were looking for bodies.

An evil–spirited dread clutched at her heart. 'Where's Tidal?' she said.

Tidal's first indication he wasn't dead was the sound of seagulls cawing. To begin with, as confused as he was, he couldn't figure out how the seagulls were managing to make quite so much noise at the bottom of the ocean; but then he became aware of the heat from the sun, and distant voices, and it slowly dawned on him that his assumption that he had drowned was perhaps a little premature. When he finally opened his eyes to see threads of cloud drifting across the blue canvas of the sky, there was no room for doubt. Somehow, against all the odds, despite everything he understood about the sea, he was still alive.

His chest was burning, and it hurt when he breathed, but he was alive.

For a while he remained where he lay, unable to move. He could hear the lap of the sea, and feel the suck of gentle waves rolling over his feet; but he couldn't lift his head to see where he was.

He tried to remember what had happened. It was all hazy, but he could recall a wall of water rushing over him. Golden fish. Something else too. Something large, with scales and pointy teeth.

He sat up suddenly, despite the protests of almost every muscle in his body. He was on the beach, only a few feet from the crushed remains of the pier, surrounded by driftwood and seaweed. His feet were still in the water.

A terrified scream wedged in his throat as he dragged himself farther up the beach.

The sea looked calm and unthreatening, but there was something in it now. Something horrible.

'Hey, you!' a voice said from behind him.

One of the village soldiers was approaching through the mess of splintered wood.

'Captain Obsidian,' Tidal said. 'Glad you could make it.'

'What happened?' Captain Obsidian asked, as he slipped and slid over the hull of a smashed boat, sword in hand.

'Didn't you see? A huge wave came down the river and knocked me straight into the sea.'

'What happened to you? You're injured.'

Tidal looked down. There were three long cuts running diagonally across his chest. He had a momentary vision of teeth looming at him out of the murk of the turbulent water, and remembered his desperate attempt to get out of the way. He obviously hadn't been quick enough.

He touched the cuts cautiously.

'I don't know,' he said. 'I'm not sure what happened. I guess I got hit by some of this driftwood.'

'Can you stand?' The captain helped Tidal to his feet. 'Good lad. We should get the doctor to take a look at you. Do you think you can walk?'

'I'm fine.' Tidal paused, swallowed carefully. 'Did anybody see anything? I mean, did anyone see what caused the river to rise up like that?'

'Probably a dam burst. Must have been a pretty big one though.'

'There was nothing else?'

'Nothing that I saw.'

A second soldier was walking along by the sea, squinting at the horizon.

'What's he looking for?' Tidal asked.

'There were two boats out there earlier.'

'The fishing boats. I was watching them from the pier. Where have they gone?'

'That's what we'd like to know.'

'They can't have just disappeared. Is a search party being

organised?'

'We're getting together all of the boats that are still seaworthy, but not many survived.' Captain Obsidian removed his helmet. He had a sharp, angular face, black hair, and stern eyes beneath heavy eyebrows. He was named after a type of naturally occurring glass, which seemed perfectly fitting for such a hard and uncompromising man. 'I understand you have a boat?' he said.

'I did. I think it's gone the same way as the pier.'

'That's too bad, we could have used your help.'

Tidal glanced at the water, imagining what might be just below its innocent surface. 'I don't think I can help you,' he said. 'Sorry. I hope you find them.'

Obsidian put his helmet back on. 'Never mind. You should get your chest seen to anyway. You don't look too good.'

Tidal headed up the beach, as far away from the shore as he could get. Sky and Glass were walking down to meet him and he was more than slightly pleased to see Sky's look of concern. She had been worrying about him.

'Hello,' he said, when they were close enough to hear.

'What happened?' Sky asked. There was as much concern in her voice as there was in her face.

'I got blasted off the pier. Thought I was a goner for sure. Check this out.' He gestured towards the cuts in his chest proudly. 'I guess I managed to swim back to shore despite the pain.'

'Does it hurt much?' Sky asked.

'Sure does. But I'm pretty strong, I can take it.'

'Do you want me to clean the cuts? They look sore.'

'I...' Tidal flushed red, perhaps for the first time Sky could remember. 'I think... I mean, I don't...'

'You don't need to be the big hero all the time, Tide. Come on back to my house and I'll put a bandage on for you.'

'Your house?'

'Yeah, you know, the place where I live? Walls, roof, front door, all that stuff?'

'But, your dad...'

'He won't be there. He's probably at the tavern, discussing all this mess with the landlord. Come on, it'll be fine.'

'No, really. I'm okay. I've had worse injuries.'

'When?' Glass asked.

'Sorry?'

'When have you had worse?'

'Oh, it was a long time ago.' He kicked his heels. 'I forget when.'

Sky took his hand. 'Come on, you daft lump. I'm not taking no for an answer.'

They were just arriving back at the village when they met Cloud returning from the mill. He was wearing his usual serious expression.

'You three,' he said. 'Tell me what happened.'

'There was some kind of tidal wave,' Sky said.

'Was anybody hurt?'

'Some people are missing.'

Cloud looked at Tidal, and though nobody thought it was possible, his expression became even more serious. 'Come here,' he said. 'Let me see those cuts.'

'They're nothing,' Tidal protested, suddenly feeling very awkward and exposed.

'Let me see.' Cloud took a good look. 'What did this?'

'I don't know.'

'Was there something in the water?'

'I don't know. It was all a bit confusing once I got washed off the pier.'

Cloud turned to the girls. 'Did you see anything?'

'No,' Sky said.

Glass gulped. She looked at Sky, then Tidal. 'I saw something,' she said, quietly.

'What did you see?'

'I'm not sure.'

'What do you think you saw?'

'A snake. But big. A big snake.'

Cloud looked over his shoulder, at the calm expanse of the Everlasting Ocean, with his hands clenched. 'Where's Nimbus?' he asked.

CHAPTER NINE

At the foot of the southern slope of Sentinel Mountain, among a jumbled mess of boulders and rocks, there is a cave. The cave is very dark, very deep, and has never been explored.

Once upon a time, a great river flowed out of the mouth of the cave. The river twisted and turned through the trees of the Forbidden Woods (although they weren't called the Forbidden Woods in those days) before joining the Forbidden River (which was similarly not called the Forbidden River at that time).

Many years ago, that river dried up. The people of the nearby villages and towns believed this may have been due to a rock fall deep inside the mountain, but nobody was ever brave enough, or interested enough, to venture into the cave to see if this was true.

In fact, it was not a rock fall that caused the river to dry up, but something entirely different; and on the day Nimbus met Cumulo the dragon, he woke that entirely different something, and the river started to flow again.

That same day, a fox had his foxhole washed away by the reappearance of the river. Luckily, the fox was not at home; but he returned from hunting just in time to see Nimbus emerging from the cave with a huge dragon wriggling out close behind him.

The fox, who was wise even by fox standards, crept back into the undergrowth, deciding it was best not to get involved.

Nimbus, who was still carrying the Wing Warrior sword, looked at the sky, blinking. From the position of the sun, he guessed it couldn't be much later than one o'clock, which gave him plenty of time before he had to be home for dinner.

'What is that?' Cumulo asked, as he scrambled out of the cave, with his belly splashing in the river and his claws scratching and scrabbling on the rocks.

'What's what?' Nimbus asked.

'The yellow thing up there. I've seen it before. In my mind.'

Nimbus waded over to the riverbank. He had not forgotten how big the tooth he had found was, and he was not too keen to stay in the water any longer than he needed to. 'It's the sun,' he said. 'It shines through the day, then goes to sleep at night.'

'I like it,' Cumulo said. Having completely removed his massive bulk from the cave mouth, he let his gigantic wings unfurl with a thunderous crack. He flapped them, and the wind they generated was almost strong enough to blow Nimbus clean off his feet. 'Oh, that feels so much better. I like outside.'

'I thought you might,' Nimbus said. 'Now, follow me. We have to get you somewhere hidden before you get spotted.'

'Where are we going?'

'You'll see. And don't forget the armour.'

Cumulo put his head back inside the cave mouth and picked up a big sack between his teeth. The sack clanked metallically as it swung from his jaws. 'You should be wearing this, you know?' he said.

'You're kidding. It weighs a ton. How am I supposed to walk in it?'

'You've been chosen by the armour, you're supposed to wear it. And that means you aren't supposed to walk anywhere.'

'Oh, really? And how do you suggest I get home?'

'Wing Warriors fly. You're supposed to ride me.'

'You can forget that. I'm not keen on heights. I'll stick to walking.'

Cumulo rolled his eyes. In the gleaming sunlight his scales appeared to be purple, but sometimes Nimbus caught a glimpse of them in the corner of his eye and they looked red, or green, or sometimes even white. 'I've never heard of a Wing Warrior afraid of heights,' the dragon said.

'But I'm not a Wing Warrior.'

'The armour thinks otherwise.'

'The armour's wrong.'

'But it did pick you, and sooner or later you will have to wear it.'

'Why?' Nimbus headed off through the trees, dragging the dead weight of the sword behind him. Cumulo followed, examining everything with a childlike interest.

'Something made the armour call you. That means something magical has come back into the world.'

'That thing in the river?'

'No. Something else. The armour knew it was time to be found. I think we're going to war.'

Nimbus stopped. He was getting an awful feeling; a sense that events were spiralling totally out of his control and he was going to get dragged along with them if he wasn't careful. 'What war? Nobody mentioned a war to me. I can't fight in a war.'

'The armour –'

'Thinks otherwise, I know. But I'm just a kid, Cumulo. I can't fight, I can't even lift this sword. I can't fly around on your back. Maybe my dad could, but not me.'

'I don't think the armour gets it wrong, Nim.'

'I think it has.'

'I don't know if you have ever thought to look at it too closely, but there is an inscription on the sword you are carrying. Perhaps you should read it.'

Nimbus took a look at the sword. He had not noticed them before, but there were fine letters carved below the hilt. 'These letters are strange to me,' he said. 'I do not know what they say.'

'The inscription is in the language of the dragons. It says, "look to the clouds." Nimbus is a type of cloud, isn't it?'

Nimbus sighed heavily. He certainly didn't feel like a Wing Warrior. He knew he wasn't brave enough to go to war; he was barely brave enough to go out with Tidal in his fishing boat. He was so small, and the armour was so big.

'It's okay,' Cumulo said. 'I won't let you fall.'

Nimbus patted Cumulo on the side of the neck. The scales were as rough as the bark of a coconut tree. 'Let's not talk about war any more. Let's just worry about getting you hidden before people spot you and decide to chase you into the mountains with pitchforks.'

'Why would they do that?'

'People get scared of things that are different to them. And believe me, you are about as different as it gets.'

'What's wrong with being different?'

'Some people just don't like it. It's silly, but people can be like that sometimes. Come on. The Forbidden River is just through here.'

Cumulo wriggled between two trees, waking up some squirrels that had been sleeping in them and causing a small bird to dart into the sky with a screech. 'Tight fit,' he muttered, as he squeezed through and the trees twanged back into position behind him. 'I think I've put on some weight.'

'Too long sat in that cave,' Nimbus said. He was standing on the riverbank, watching the furious water bubble and spit as it accelerated out towards the ocean. 'This river is much faster now,' he added, thoughtfully.

'It's the extra water from the underground cave,' Cumulo said, dropping the sack of armour. 'It has made this river dangerous.'

Nimbus stared at his broken reflection in the water. 'It's probably ruined my fishing spot.'

'I think whatever has come out of that cave with us has probably ruined a lot of fishing spots, and much more besides.'

'I had the best fishing spot on the river. Maybe the best fishing spot in the world.' Nimbus put his hand into the river; the water rippled around his fingers. 'I don't see any fish here now.'

'There aren't any. The thing has scared them away.'

'What do you think it was?'

'I really don't know.'

'Did you see the size of the tooth I found?'

'I did.'

'It must be a monster as big as you are.'

'Bigger.'

'Aren't you afraid?'

'There are few things a dragon fears.'

Nimbus wiped his hands dry on his tunic. 'Is it wrong to be afraid?'

'I don't think so.'

Nimbus smiled hopefully.

Suddenly there was an evil laugh, as twisted as the surrounding trees, and the undergrowth was alive with a flurry of activity. A small, wiry creature, no bigger than a cat, darted out of the cover of some nearby brambles and stopped in the open. It was thin and crooked, like a brown twig that had come to life, and its beady eyes burned like coals in the heart of a fire as it looked straight at Nimbus.

Nimbus's breath caught in his throat. He had put the sword on the ground and was too scared to even pick it up.

Just as quickly as the creature had appeared, there was an explosion of motion from the opposite direction, and a gigantic stag burst into the clearing. The magnificent animal faced off against the small, ugly creature, and a deep and uncomfortable silence descended on the woods. It was as if everything was poised expectantly, even the trees, to see what would happen next.

Eventually, the stag snorted challengingly, and stamped the ground with its hooves. In retaliation, the tiny stick creature made peculiar barking, yelping noises, and beat its thin chest with its hands. The stag advanced a pace, lowering its antlers. The other thing threw back its head, laughed horribly, and then dashed off into the thicker undergrowth in a spray of leaves and branches.

The stag turned to Nimbus, and there was a look in its eyes that seemed to say, 'I don't fancy doing all the hard work by myself, so if you wouldn't mind helping out, that would be nice,' and then it ran off, disappearing in the dense foliage.

After a while, Nimbus managed to stop staring. 'I didn't dream that, did I?' he asked.

'Old rivers aren't the only things that have awoken today,' Cumulo said.

'What was it?'

'It was a stag.'

'No, not that. The other thing.'

'Oh, that. I'm not sure. But I think it was a goblin.'

CHAPTER TEN

'Goblins aren't real,' Nimbus said, as he splashed across the river. 'They're stories kids get told to stop them going into the woods.'

'Goblins are just as real as dragons and trolls.'

'Trolls!'

'Ugly things, live under bridges. You must have heard of them.'

'Trolls aren't real.'

'And what makes you so sure of that?'

'I've been coming to these woods all my life. I've explored every inch of them, in the day and night, and I've never seen a goblin or a troll before.'

'But you bumped into dragons every day?' Cumulo's grin was wide and sharp and a lot more intimidating than the dragon probably intended it to be. It was probably very difficult to grin in anything other than an intimidating way when you were a giant winged lizard with teeth that could bite through rocks.

'How would you know it was a goblin anyway? You've never seen one before.'

'You're right, but I told you before, I have a lot of memories knocking around inside my head, and I don't know how I got them.'

'If it was a goblin, why now? Why has it woken up now?'

'Magic is coming back into the world. Things that once were, will be again. And there is something more. A dark threat from the West. The armour sensed it, and knew war was coming, and the other magical folk sense it too. I would no longer suggest walking in these woods alone. Goblins are small, but they are evil. They will snatch you away if you give them the chance.'

'Isn't anywhere safe?'

'I think you're safe enough with me.'

Nimbus stroked Cumulo's long nose. 'I guess you're right there, but what about my friends, my family? They live close to the woods. Will they be hurt?'

'Goblins are wicked creatures. They play tricks on humans, and take careless children from their parents, but they are cowards too. They would never attack your village.'

'And the thing in the cave?'

'That, I'm not so sure about. Hopefully whatever it was has gone out into the ocean, and we'll never see it again.'

'What about other things? If the goblins have returned, will there be other legends?'

'There are other things coming alive all around us. I can feel it in the trees, in the ground, the river.' Cumulo's tongue flicked out. Ribbons of cloud moved in curious patterns, attempting to obscure the face of the sun. 'Something else too. Something much bigger. The thing that started this. I can feel it in the air. The world trembles around it.'

'Is it dangerous?'

'Deadly.'

A horrible feeling had taken root in Nimbus's stomach, and with each new revelation the feeling grew a little stronger, choking him with fear. 'Does it know about me?'

Cumulo nodded.

'What does it know?'

'It knows there is one last Wing Warrior in this land.'

'Stop calling me that. I'm not a Wing Warrior.'

'But you are. And the dark magic knows it.'

Nimbus gulped. The sword in his hand seemed heavy and uncontrollable.

'Is it coming for me?' he asked.

'It is.'

All the strength went out of Nimbus's legs, and he sat down

just in case he fell over. 'You might be wrong,' he said. 'You admit you don't know a lot of things. Your memories are all mixed up, and you've been living in that cave for years. You could be wrong about this. Who's to say you can't be wrong?'

'It's true, the memories I possess are only half–formed, but I'm not wrong about this.'

'How can you tell?'

'Some things you just know are true, in your heart. Like you know you are a Wing Warrior.'

Nimbus let his head sink until it was almost touching his knees. He hated to admit it, but the dragon was right. He could deny being a Wing Warrior with every bit of his common sense and reason, but it wouldn't make a single bit of difference. Eventually he would wear the armour.

'But I'm not ready for all this.'

'Whether you are ready or not, this thing is coming.'

Nimbus ran his hand over the surface of the Wing Warrior sword. The metal was cold and unforgiving, the edges sharp enough to cut through bone. It made him sick to think of using something so cruel against another living thing. 'Do you think I can beat it?' he asked, without looking up.

'I think you can do more than you have ever realised.'

'Do you think I can beat it?' Nimbus repeated.

'Yes.'

'You really believe that?'

'I'm a dragon. I have to believe in the unbelievable. And you have to believe it too. You have to be prepared when the time comes.'

'How do you expect me to be prepared when I don't know what it is I'm preparing for?'

Cumulo shrugged his massive shoulders. 'I don't have all the answers, Nim. Nobody does. We just have to do the best we can based on what we know.'

'That's my point, Cumulo. I don't know anything. I'm just a

stupid kid. Probably the most stupid kid in my village. My dad's forgotten more than I've ever known.'

Cumulo was silent.

Nimbus picked at his fingernails nervously. Between his feet a small, black spider was spinning a web in the grass.

'The sword is too heavy,' he went on. 'The armour is too big. I don't know what to do. I can't be what you want me to be.'

Cumulo suddenly glanced at the sky, his eyes narrowing with concentration. The sun was no longer visible behind the high banks of thickening cloud. 'Wherever you are taking me, I think you should take me there soon,' he growled.

'What is it? Can you hear something?'

'No. I can sense something. It's in the air, but I don't know where. It's looking for you.'

'An enemy?'

'I'm not sure, but I think it would be a good idea to take cover quickly. We aren't ready for a fight.'

Nimbus stood, his pulse quickening. 'I want to go home,' he said.

'You're supposed to be taking me to a new hiding place. You can't go home.'

'I need to see my mum. I want to make sure she's okay.'

'But, Nim...'

'Just through these trees there is a ruined castle. That's where I was taking you. It used to be a guard post, a watchtower protecting the eastern paths through the Grey Mountains. It's been empty for years now. Nobody ever goes there, they think it's haunted by evil spirits.'

'Is it?'

'Up until today, I would have said no. But you'll be safe there. Trust me. Just head through these trees and get inside the ruins. Stay hidden and I'll come back tomorrow, just as soon as I've made sure my family are okay.' He stuffed the sword into the sack with the armour. 'Hide this for me.'

Cumulo stretched out his wings as far as they would go. 'Be careful,' he warned, and then with one gigantic flap that blasted Nimbus off his feet he shot into the sky, punching a dragon–sized hole through the overhanging leaves.

'No,' Nimbus shouted, as branches and bits of wood rained down on him. 'No flying. You'll be seen.'

It was too late though. Cumulo was already nothing more than a tiny speck in the distance.

CHAPTER ELEVEN

Hawk was a soldier at Flint Lock Fort. Being a soldier was an incredibly important job, and involved doing lots of incredibly important things like polishing suits of armour, sharpening spears, and marching in the courtyard. Why these things were so incredibly important, Hawk wasn't sure; but they definitely were, otherwise why else would he have to do them?

Hawk was seventeen years old and had officially been a soldier for just over a month, having only recently finished his tuition at the Crystal Shine Academy of Archery and Swordplay. He had never really taken to sword fighting, it was tiring and very hard work; but archery was something he had really enjoyed, and he had graduated from the school with honours.

His skill with a bow was such that he was selected to perform a demonstration at the palace before Lord and Lady Citrine, the rulers of Crystal Shine and all the adjoining lands. The demonstration was received so well he was immediately appointed a position under the command of Captain Shard, whose responsibility it was to protect the Western Borders from invasion.

'This is a very important position,' Captain Shard had once said.

'Yes, Captain,' Hawk had said.

'If we are ever invaded, those of us here at the fort will be the first line of defence,' the captain went on. 'That means we are entirely responsible for looking after all of our people. You must remember that at all times.'

The Western Borders had never been invaded, as far as Hawk knew, but he was sure that didn't make his job any less important; and he had no reason to doubt that what the captain said was absolutely true. Thinking it through logically, the fact the Western Borders had never been invaded spoke volumes about what a good job the soldiers of Flint Lock did.

'But really, think about it. Who's going to invade us?' Clay, one of the other soldiers, had said.

'I don't know,' Hawk replied. 'But there must be someone, otherwise we wouldn't be here.'

And that, pretty much, summed Hawk up. He was a simple boy with a simple mind, and he tried his best not to concern himself with business he shouldn't be concerned with. He didn't know why he was positioned at the fort, and he didn't need to. He had been told being there was important, and that was good enough for him.

'Don't you ever feel like you're wasting your time here?' Clay had asked.

'Why should I?' Hawk said. 'How can you ever be wasting your time when you're doing something you love?'

And indeed, Hawk loved being a soldier.

He had started loving being a soldier the first day he had put on his suit of shiny new armour, and he had thought nothing in the world would ever make him stop loving it.

But on the day the Forbidden River rose up, and goblins returned to the realms of men, Hawk made an important discovery.

He discovered he was completely wrong.

It was late afternoon, and the shadows were lengthening as the tired sun dipped below the horizon, turning the sky a fiery orange. There were no birds, and the land as far as the eye could see was silent and sleepy.

Hawk was standing watch on the north turret of Flint Lock, which was the tallest and therefore most important turret. He was dressed in the armour of a Flint Lock guard, with a silver breastplate and a red–crested helmet. He was armed with his ceremonial spear, as was traditional for all guards at the fort, but he also had with him his bow and a full quiver of new arrows.

He had been on watch for almost six hours, and was beginning to get tired. Staring at an empty landscape where nothing ever moves can have that affect on a person. His mind, despite his best efforts not to let it, was beginning to wander; and the prospect of a hot supper was getting more and more appealing.

White flakes of cloud tangled around the distant tops of the Sanguine Mountains, rising like steam from the humped back of a monster. He watched, drumming his fingers on the wall of the turret, as the clouds peeled away and broke on invisible air currents.

There were rumours the mountains that loomed menacingly on the north–western edge of the borderlands were home to foul and evil creatures. Most people didn't believe such rumours, but Hawk did, and that was why he always watched the mountains so closely, especially when night was beginning to fall.

He yawned and let his gaze travel south to the calm, massive expanse of the Everlasting Ocean. There were no travellers on the main road linking Crystal Shine with the port city of High Tide. There were no boats out on the ocean. The world was as still and quiet as an undiscovered tomb.

Hawk's stomach was not so quiet. It was grumbling and complaining, and he was all too aware how long it had been since he last ate.

He turned his attention back to the empty borderlands. The last fingers of sunlight had turned everything a deep red. It was as though the ground itself had been caught on fire.

Spoon and Carp, the two chefs, would be in the kitchen right now. They would be boiling potatoes and carrots, and roasting chickens. They would be cooking parsnips and making huge vats of gravy, nice and thick the way Hawk liked it.

There would be fresh bread baking in the oven, filling the whole fort with a delicious smell; there would be churned butter on the table; there would be hot tea boiling on the stove.

He licked his lips and his eyelids drooped sleepily.

Suddenly a terrifying screech echoed across the landscape, and a black shape ripped through the clouds above the mountaintops. So deafening was the sound, Hawk lost his balance and fell flat on his back. By the time he was on his feet again the shape, whatever it might have been, was no longer in sight.

He leaned his spear against the turret and tied his quiver of arrows around his waist. He was no longer thinking about food.

Moments later the tower trapdoor opened and Clay climbed out. Clay was a huge man, and getting through the trapdoor took him a lot more scrabbling and squeezing, puffing and panting, then it did for other people.

'Did you hear that?' he asked.

'Hear it? I saw it,' Hawk said.

'What was it?'

Before Hawk could answer, the shape reappeared on the horizon, looping and weaving above the clouds before heading directly for the fort.

Startled shouts were already rising from other turrets, and an alarm bell started ringing in the courtyard. Soldiers were running backwards and forwards, putting on helmets and strapping on swords. From Hawk's viewpoint they looked like scurrying silver ants swarming over a termite hill.

Although Hawk had never seen a dragon before, he knew that was exactly what the thing swooping down over the jagged peaks of the Sanguine Mountains was. There really weren't that many things a huge flying lizard could be mistaken for.

The dragon's wings made a flat, slapping sound, and as it raced above the open wilderness any living thing its shadow touched, every blade of grass, withered and died.

Hawk watched, almost hypnotised, as the sunlight flickered on the dragon's sleek, black scales.

'Hawk,' Clay said, drawing his sword. 'Hawk, shoot it.'

Hawk continued to stare, mouth open.

The dragon bellowed furiously and soared above them, hanging momentarily like an ugly stain on the red sky.

'Hawk,' Clay repeated.

'What?'

'Shoot it. Use your bow.'

'Right.'

Hawk picked up his bow with shaking hands. The dragon came plummeting down from the sky, as fast as a shooting star, into a hail of arrows fired from soldiers all around the fort. Each arrow pinged and snapped uselessly on the dragon's armoured skin.

Hawk fired an arrow of his own, aiming for one of the dragon's wings, but at the last moment the dragon banked away and the arrow twanged on its scaly back instead.

'Try again,' Clay said.

The dragon roared over the fort. Soldiers ducked or ran screaming for cover. A black vapour was coming out of the dragon's mouth and nose: an acrid, thick smoke that billowed around the dragon protectively.

Hawk fired another arrow, watching in dismay as it bounced off.

'It's no use,' he said. 'Its armour is too strong.'

'We must be able to hurt it,' Clay said.

'We can't.'

The dragon wheeled and came back, trailing a black cloud behind it. This time it came lower, pulling up at the last minute to perch on the fort wall. Its claws clamped down and great chunks of stone broke away, crashing into the courtyard below.

'Shoot it now,' Clay shouted.

The dragon spread its leathery wings and the whole fort was

cast in its terrifying shadow. The hounds in the kennels began to wail pitifully, and men dropped to their knees, coughing and choking. Preserved meat in the kitchen immediately turned black and rotten, newly baked bread crumbled to dust, and freshly laid eggs cracked and oozed green puss.

'The beast is diseased,' the soldiers screamed. 'It brings death. We must escape.'

Another flurry of arrows filled the sky, before clattering harmlessly on the dragon's broad chest and shoulders. Soldiers threw spears that splintered into pieces.

Captain Shard emerged from his chamber with a sword in one hand and an axe in the other. He was bemused at first as to what could have thrown his well–managed fort into such chaos, but then he saw the towering horror of the dragon.

'What are you?' he gasped.

The dragon reared up, glaring at Shard with eyes that had seen years of misery and had enjoyed them all. 'I am Sorrow,' it hissed. 'I am the end of the world.'

Defiantly, Shard stood for a heartbeat longer; then he threw down his weapons and ran.

Up on the turret, Hawk drew aim, trying to stop his arm from shaking. The dragon swung its large head around to look directly at him, and he cried out, letting the bow slip from his grasp.

Soldiers in the courtyard were running to find somewhere to hide, tripping over each other in an attempt to escape. Nobody was fighting any more.

'We have to get out of here,' Hawk said.

'Right,' Clay said.

They ran to the trapdoor and Clay squeezed through. Hawk was about to follow, but risked looking back one last time at the terrible monster that had so quickly broken the defences of the fort.

The dragon narrowed its eyes to tiny slits, and then opened its mouth in a terrible scream. Jets of black fog poured out of its throat, spewing into the courtyard. The air filled with the rotten, earthy stench of a slow and lingering death.

After that, Hawk could only remember the horrified cries of the soldiers, and a suffocating darkness.

CHAPTER TWELVE

Back at the village a lot of people were gathered in the square for a meeting. The mayor was standing on a hastily constructed wooden platform, and everybody else was shouting and waving their fists angrily. It was all such a fuss that nobody noticed Nimbus arrive. He quietly sneaked into the crowd, pretending he had been there all along.

'There's no need to panic,' the mayor was saying, but he was obviously finding it very difficult not to panic himself. There were beads of sweat glistening on his forehead and in his moustache.

'Then tell us what's going on,' someone in the crowd shouted. 'We have a right to know.'

Nimbus pushed his way through elbows and shoulders until he was right in front of the platform. There was a soldier standing on either side of the mayor. They were in full armour and carrying swords. They looked ready for a fight. The mayor didn't look ready for a fight; he looked ready to crawl inside his coat and hide.

'We don't have a lot of information to go on at this time,' he said.

'What information do you have? Are we safe?'

'Of course we're safe.'

'Can you guarantee that?'

The soldiers shifted nervously and looked out at the mob of angry villagers from beneath their helmets. The crowd was restless, full of farmers carrying pitchforks and fishermen carrying harpoons.

'Listen,' the mayor said. 'Everybody just needs to calm down. Return to your homes, and let our soldiers do their job.'

'These fat oafs,' someone sneered. 'They've been posted here for years and never had to do so much as rescue a kitten out of a tree. They've been sat in that garrison playing cards and getting lazy. What do you think they're going to do?'

The soldiers looked at each other, perhaps wondering whether they should really stand for such insults.

'No need for unpleasantness,' the mayor said, hopefully. 'Our men may not have been tested in combat like their colleagues in the city, but they are still trained professionals.'

'Then maybe they can tell us what they intend to do.'

The soldiers cleared their throats and stared at their feet. Neither of them spoke.

'See,' one of the farmers in the crowd said. 'They don't know what to do. Nobody knows what to do. We need to call on Crystal Shine for assistance.'

'And say what, exactly?' the mayor said.

'We need to tell them what's happened here.'

'And what has happened? There was a tidal wave. That's all.'

'Seven people are missing.'

'It's a terrible thing. But we don't know what happened to those men yet. They may not be...' The mayor paused, taking a deep breath before he continued. 'They may yet come home.'

'And if they don't?'

The mayor looked out across the village square to the Everlasting Ocean. Soldiers on the beach were picking through bits and pieces of wood. The only two boats that had survived the wave were out on the water. Two men in each boat were casting nets, but they weren't trying to catch fish in them.

'Mayor?'

'Sorry? What?'

'What if we can't find our friends?'

'We can't think about that just yet. We've got boats out searching, and more men on the beach. Three soldiers have gone upriver to see if they can establish the source of the wave. Maybe we'll know more tomorrow. Maybe we'll find them all.'

'So we should just wait?'

'That's exactly what you should do. Wait, and pray for the safe return of our friends.'

'And what about the wounded?'

'They're being cared for in the village hall. We have a number of very capable volunteers.'

'Shouldn't we get surgeons from the city?' a woman asked. She looked more frightened than Nimbus had ever remembered a person looking before.

'That won't be necessary.'

'And what if there's another wave? What measures are you putting in place to stop something like this happening again?'

'Look, really, be reasonable.' The mayor mopped his forehead with a handkerchief. 'You've all lived here as long as I have. You know that this tidal wave was just a freak occurrence, a one off. Nothing like this has ever happened before.'

Nimbus didn't stick around to hear any more; it sounded like a debate that wasn't going to end any time soon and he wanted to get home. He wiggled his way back out of the crowd and dashed up the street towards his house.

A huge black shadow – bigger than any bird – passed directly over him, but by the time he looked it was gone.

He hoped Cumulo wasn't getting into trouble.

'Mum?' Nimbus shouted, as he burst through the front door of his house. 'Mum, are you here?'

'Nim?' His mother was standing at the stove with a bowl in one hand. Her face was white as a sheet, and her eyes were red raw with tears.

'Mum?'

For a second his mother was rooted to the spot, like she was frozen behind a sheet of glass. The bowl fell out of her hand and smashed, sending jagged shards of pottery skittering across the floor.

'Mum, what's wrong?'

'Nim.' Suddenly, as if a spell had been lifted, she was free to move. She catapulted herself towards him, throwing her arms around his neck and squeezing him so hard he thought his head might pop right off. 'Nim, you're okay.'

'I'm fine. What's wrong?'

'You stupid boy. You stupid, stupid boy.'

'Mum?'

She looked him straight in the eye, and he could see how frightened she was.

'You've been crying,' he said.

'Where have you been? And don't tell me you've been with your sister because I know you haven't.'

'I... I went to the woods again. I'm sorry.'

'Why?'

'I just...'

What could he say?

I just found a dragon in a cave under Sentinel Mountain. He told me I was a Wing Warrior. He gave me a suit of armour and a sword, and told me I had to get ready to fight for my life against a great evil that has come into the world.

Oh, and I think I woke up a sea monster too.

How could he tell his mother that?

'Nim?' she said.

'I don't know,' he said. 'I just wanted to get away from Glass for a while.'

'Why are you so selfish?' The relief in his mother's voice was gradually being replaced with a stony anger. His mother very rarely got angry. When she did, she was scary enough to make a dragon turn tail and run. 'How could you do this to me and your father? How could you do this to your friends? We've been worried sick. Glass hasn't stopped crying since your dad went out.'

'Went out where?'

'Looking for you.'

'Why was he looking for me?'

His mother took a deep, shuddering breath. 'Oh, Nim,' she said, and there was a painful sadness in her voice. 'You really are too young to understand these things.'

'What things?'

'All the big things that are facing you.' She wiped her eyes, and looked around at the mess of broken pottery. 'My goodness, this will never do. I'll have to clean this up before he gets home.'

She took a broom from the corner of the room.

'Why's Dad looking for me?' Nimbus asked, uncertain if he really wanted to know the answer.

'The world has changed, Nim. Very suddenly, and very unexpectedly. It isn't the safe place it once was. Didn't you see what's going on out there? There's been an accident. A bad one. We thought...' She began to frantically sweep the floor. Nimbus had seen her act like this before. When she was really upset she would always start cleaning. He wasn't sure why; he guessed it just made her feel like things were still normal. 'Your father thought you may have been involved in the accident.'

'I'm sorry. I didn't mean to worry you.'

'Tidal was injured.'

'Is he okay?'

'He'll be fine. He'll be sore for a few days, but he'll recover. Sky's a good nurse.'

'Sky?' Nimbus felt a glimmer of anger flare in his gut at the thought of Sky and Tidal being together while he wasn't around. 'Why was Sky looking after him?'

'They're friends, aren't they?'

Nimbus started chewing on his bottom lip. He certainly didn't like the sound of all this. 'Where's Dad now?'

'Probably in the woods. He knows you like it there.'

Nimbus's heart leapt into his mouth. 'Is he on his own?'

'Yes.'

'But the gob...' He drew a sharp breath. He couldn't tell his mother about goblins; he'd have to tell her everything else, and she was already worried enough. 'It could be dangerous,' he said.

'I'm sure your father will be fine. He's big and strong, and cleverer than a lot of people think.'

'He's just a mill worker. He doesn't know what the woods are like. He might get hurt.'

His mother stopped sweeping and looked at him carefully. There was a neat pile of pottery pieces by her feet. 'Nim, is there something you want to tell me?'

'You said yourself, the world has changed. I don't think the woods are safe any more.'

'You're probably right, and I don't want you going back there. You understand?'

Nimbus nodded. 'I understand.'

'Good.'

He looked out of the window. The crowd was still in the square, shouting and waving pitchforks.

'What happened today?'

'There was a tidal wave.'

Nimbus tried his best not to look as guilty as he felt. 'How many people got hurt?'

'Not many. But some others have gone missing. If I were you, I'd go and see your sister. She really thought something awful had happened to you.'

'Where is she?'

'At the village hall, with Sky.'

Nimbus hugged his mother. 'I'm sorry, Mum.'

She kissed his head. 'It's okay now.'

He smiled, but it was a thin smile, in danger of shattering at any moment. 'I'm not so sure,' he said.

***

The village hall was quite large, and hardly ever used, so it was the perfect place to set up a temporary hospital. Beds with clean blankets and comfortable pillows had been put up in neat rows and eleven of them were already occupied. Nine more waited expectantly.

Tidal was sitting on the bed closest to the door. His chest was tightly bandaged, and he looked uncomfortable as he talked to Sky.

Glass was curled up on the pillow, sobbing quietly.

Nimbus stood, unnoticed in the wide entrance to the hall, and felt his stomach twist with anger as he watched Sky touch Tidal's hand. He had obviously missed a lot while he had been away.

'Hello,' he said.

Sky looked up, startled. 'Nim.'

Glass lifted her head. Her bleary eyes shone out through tangled hair. 'Nim.'

'Guessed you'd be okay,' Tidal said. 'Never were one to put yourself in the thick of the trouble, were you?'

Glass hopped down off the bed and threw herself at Nimbus. He picked her up, ruffling her hair and trying his best to ignore the twinge of guilt he felt for having made her worry so much.

'Did you miss me?' he said.

'I thought you'd gone into the water like the others,' Glass said.

Sky touched Nimbus's arm gently. 'You okay?' she asked.

'Fine.' His eyes narrowed as he looked at Tidal. 'What happened to you?'

'It bit him,' Glass said.

'The girl's off her rocker,' Tidal said, getting more comfortable on the bed. 'She thinks there some kind of monster in the water.'

'Like a snake,' Glass said. 'Only bigger. Much, much bigger.'

'Are you sure?' Nimbus asked.

Tidal snorted a thoroughly unpleasant laugh. He sounded like a pig with mud stuck up his nose. 'Oh, come on, you don't believe all this, surely? She's obviously imagining things.'

'But something made the water rise up, and something took a chunk out of your chest,' Nimbus said.

'The pier was smashed to pieces. It's not surprising I got a few scratches.'

'So you didn't see anything in the water?'

'No. Nothing.'

Glass pressed her lips to Nimbus's ear. 'He's lying,' she whispered. 'He saw it too.'

There was a man lying on the next bed to Tidal's. His eyes were closed and his face was deathly pale. His chest rose and fell with his impossibly slow breathing.

Nimbus shivered.

'Your dad's out looking for you,' Tidal said.

'Where were you, anyway?' Sky asked.

Nimbus looked at the floor, in case something in his eyes gave away the truth. 'Nowhere, really.'

'You went back to the cave, didn't you?' Tidal said.

'Don't be ridiculous. That's the craziest thing I ever heard.'

'You did,' Tidal pressed. 'You went back. Why? What did you find down there?'

'Nothing.'

'There must have been something.'

'There was nothing. You went down there with me.'

'Not all the way.'

'I hate that place. Why would I want to go back?'

'You tell us.'

'I didn't go back.' Nimbus had started to raise his voice, and his words were loud enough to wake the sleeping man in the next bed. Other people in the hall were watching, tutting disapprovingly at all the commotion.

Nimbus took a slow breath before continuing in a calmer tone. 'There's no big secret about where I was today. I just didn't want to go to Leaf's class, so I went for a walk instead.'

Glass tugged on Nimbus's tunic to attract his attention. Her eyes were full of tears. 'You aren't allowed to do that again,' she said. 'You aren't allowed to go anywhere without me.'

'You can't always go where I go.'

'Yes I can. From now on, no matter where you are, I'll always be there. We have to stick together.'

He tried to smile, but couldn't quite manage it. He could feel an evil shadow looming over him like a hungry vulture, waiting to peck away at him until there was nothing left.

'We're a team,' Sky said.

'Yeah,' Glass said.

'And you know you're too much of a wimp to do anything by yourself,' Tidal added.

Nimbus appreciated what his friends were saying, but he knew in his heart that no matter what they said or did, there was only one suit of armour and there was only one sword.

There could only be one Wing Warrior.

CHAPTER THIRTEEN

The hour grew late, day turned to night, and millions of white stars peppered the black vastness of the sky.

Nimbus sat on his bed, huddled under a blanket, and watched a tentacle of moonlight worming its way through a crack in the shutters.

Time passed.

Shadows moved like slithering creatures in the corners of the room, sneaking out to watch him when he wasn't paying attention, then bobbing back out of sight when he turned to look. The night was alive with evil, and he no longer felt safe in his own bed.

His mind was full of dragons and goblins, giant snakes, horrors in the deeps of the ocean; all manner of monsters that the world had long forgotten. Monsters that, for some reason beyond his understanding, had come back.

What was one boy supposed to do in the face of such things?

He hugged his knees, and waited.

The cold moonlight continued creeping through the shutters.

His bedroom door creaked open.

'Who's there?' he hissed.

A small figure appeared in the doorway, framed by the glow from the hallway beyond. 'It's me. Glass. I can't sleep.'

'Me neither,' Nimbus said. 'Come in, and we'll sit up together.'

'Like the time we got sick?'

'Just like that.'

Glass sat on the edge of the bed, wiping her eyes sleepily. She had her favourite ragdoll with her, the one she always cuddled when she was upset about something. 'Daddy's not back yet,' she said. 'Mummy's still sitting by the stove.'

'I know.'

'I think she's crying, so I didn't go in.'

'I know.'

'Why can't you sleep?'

'I'm not really tired.'

'Are you worried about him?'

'Dad's the biggest, bravest man I know. He'll be safe. You wait and see.'

Glass looked at her doll. The doll looked right back with empty, glass eyes. 'Dolly's worried about him. I told her it would be okay, but I don't think she believes me.'

Nimbus touched Glass's hand. 'Do you think Dolly would believe me?'

Glass shrugged. 'Maybe.'

He took the doll, and carefully sat it on his knees. 'Right, Dolly,' he said, trying to sound as adult as possible. 'We'll have no more of this worrying. My dad is very brave, and I know he'll be just fine, and back in time for his breakfast.'

Glass watched him silently. The doll watched him too.

'Did she believe me?' he asked.

Glass giggled, and snatched the doll back, hugging it to her chest protectively. 'She believes you. Thanks.'

'Good.'

They sat in silence for a moment, watching the patterns the moonlight made on the wall. On any other night the patterns may have been pretty, but tonight they just looked like witches on broomsticks, horrible bats, and cave monsters.

'What about you?' Glass asked, stroking her doll's hair. 'Do you believe me?'

'About what?'

'About today. Did you believe me when I said about the snake and the river?'

'Yes.'

'Really?'

'Of course.'

They both fell silent again, listening to the crickets outside the window. Their chirruping was like the metallic grinding of scales on the back of an unknown menace.

'Why do you think Tide was lying?' Nimbus asked.

'I don't know. I don't understand boys.'

He brushed Glass's hair out of her face. 'Do you think he has something to hide?'

'Maybe he's just scared.'

'Maybe.'

In the distance a wolf howled at the moon. It was a lonely sound, full of terrible sadness.

'I'm scared,' Glass said.

'What of? The thing in the river?'

'Yes. But not just that.'

'What else is there?'

'The thing that's come back.'

'What thing?'

'I don't know, but it's everywhere. It's a bad thing, like a dream you can't wake up from. It sneaks up behind you, but when you turn around it's gone, and it makes you think it was never there at all. But it is there.'

Nimbus shuddered. 'I know what you mean,' he said.

'It came while we were sleeping. Softly. So quietly we didn't even see it happening. I think it wants to hurt us.' Glass snuggled up against him. 'But don't worry. I'll protect you.'

'Of course you will,' Nimbus said, but Glass never heard him; she was already fast asleep.

'Well, at least one of us will get some rest tonight,' he yawned. 'I'm not sure I'm ever going to be able to sleep again.'

**

He woke suddenly. It was dark and cold. Still night. Glass was pressed up against him, sleeping peacefully.

He yawned so wide he thought he might dislocate his jaw, and rubbed his eyes. There was whispering coming from the next room.

'Something's happened,' a very serious voice said. Nimbus nearly jumped out of bed with excitement. It was his father. He was back. 'Has Nimbus returned while I was away?'

'Yes,' his mother said. 'He missed his reading class to play in the woods, like we thought he had.'

'Was he hurt?'

'No, he didn't know anything about the tidal wave. What's this all about? You're scaring me.'

'Our worst fears are confirmed. The world is alive again. There are goblins in the woods.'

Nimbus gasped. His father already knew about the goblins. What else did he know?

'There haven't been goblins for hundreds of years, not since before Moon went into the West,' his mother said.

'There are goblins now, and they are fiercer and stronger than they once were. They have had much time to grow in the depths of the earth.'

'Were you attacked?'

'I'm fine, but there were three soldiers from the village. They have been taken.'

'Are they..?'

'Not yet. The goblins will no doubt want to cook them. I intend to free them tonight. I only returned for my sword and my spear.'

Nimbus couldn't believe what he was hearing. His father was a miller. The son of a miller. He had never been in a war, had never fought any great battles or done any heroic deeds. He didn't have a sword. He didn't have a spear.

'It will be dangerous,' his mother said.

'I remember danger, and I remember most of the tricks required to get out of it,' his father said.

'It has been a very long time, Cloud. You aren't used to this sort of work any more.'

'I am older than I was, that much is true. The whole world is older. But I am not useless yet, and I can't leave those men to be eaten by goblins.'

'Send others. Call on the officers of Crystal Shine.'

'They're no use here. This is a fight they have never prepared for. I can't risk their lives.'

'But you cannot go alone.'

'You don't understand. If the goblins are awake, then other things are awake, and the tidal wave that struck the village was more than just the river rising up. The ancient things that have lived for years only in our dreams will live again.'

Nimbus swallowed hard. Could his father know what it was that had slept beneath Sentinel Mountain? Could he know about Cumulo, and the other more sinister creatures?

That couldn't be possible. His father had always said he didn't believe in dragons.

His father would never have lied to him.

'I fear what is to become of us all,' his mother said.

There was a pause. When his father spoke again he was barely audible. 'It gets worse. As I was journeying home, I met a soldier from Flint Lock on the road. An archer by the name of Hawk. He was sick. Coughing violently. He could barely stand, and his eyes were wild, like he had been forced to endure every nightmare imaginable. I had to carry him to the village hall for medical assistance.'

'What had happened to him?'

'I don't know. He just kept saying the same thing over and over again. He just kept saying Flint Lock has fallen.'

Nimbus shook his head in disbelief. Flint Lock was a powerful fortress full of soldiers: A well–defended stronghold.

Its walls were high and impossible to climb. Its gates were indestructible. There was no enemy strong enough to destroy it.

'How has this happened?' his mother said.

'A great terror has destroyed it. The soldier could not tell me, but I feel in my heart that Sorrow has risen in the West and she is responsible.'

'That's not possible. She was destroyed.'

'Beaten. Not destroyed. We always knew there was a chance she could return. That was why I built the fortress in the first place.'

'Has she come back for you?'

'No. She doesn't even know I'm alive.'

'Why else would she attack the fort? She must have been looking for something.'

'I haven't been to Flint Lock in many years, not since I decided the armour should be moved.'

'That doesn't matter. She can sense you. She's always been able to sense you. After the dragon war, and all the hurt it brought, you put your life into that fort because it was all you had left. She will know your heart is always there.'

'My heart is always with you.'

'And if you did not carry the weight of so many years on your shoulders, I could believe that. But I have always known you could only love me as much as your destiny would allow.'

'Strata.'

'No, Cloud. Don't say it's otherwise. You love me, in your way, and you love the children. That's enough for me. But you can only disguise what you are, you can't change it.'

'Listen, Strata...'

'Do you think I don't know my own husband? Do you think I have never noticed how you stare at the moon? I have always known what the war cost you, and I have always known that the life you have here is not the one you would choose. If ever the chance came for you to make things different, if you ever had the chance to go where I could not follow, you would leave me behind. I know that, and I understand. We all have our burdens to bear.'

There was a moment of silence; the terrible silence before the worst of the storm.

Nimbus held his breath. His hands were tight fists.

'I'm sorry,' his father said.

'Don't be. And don't dwell on what can't be helped. Think about Sorrow now.'

'But she can't know I'm alive.' There was no conviction in Cloud's voice any more, only a sad realisation. 'There must be another reason for her attack.'

'Like what?'

'I built the fortress to protect our lands. To watch the West and repel invaders. Without the fortress, we are defenceless to an assault. An army could march right across us.'

'What are you saying?'

'I think a war is coming, and we must be ready for it.'

'There has been no war in this land since before my birth. How can everything change so quickly?'

'I don't know, but we must be ready.'

'What are you going to do?'

'I'm going to rescue those soldiers before the goblins eat them.'

'And what about Flint Lock?'

'I have already sent word to Crystal Shine. They will send troops to treat the wounded and reinforce the defences. After that... After that, we will see.'

Nimbus listened to his father leave, then carefully untangled himself from Glass's arms. He quietly put on his tunic and his walking boots, then tiptoed over to the door.

He stopped with his fingers resting on the door handle. He

knew what it was he had to do, he just wasn't sure he was brave enough to do it alone. The urge to run out after his father and tell him everything was overwhelming.

'Nim?' Glass murmured.

'Go back to sleep,' Nimbus said.

'Where are you going?'

'I'm not going anywhere. I just needed to stretch my legs a bit.'

'You're lying.'

Glass clambered down from the bed, wiping the sleep from her eyes and yawning. Her doll remained sprawled on the pillow, forgotten for the moment.

'You were going again,' she said. 'You were going off without me after I said you weren't supposed to any more.'

Nimbus grinned in the darkness. 'I wasn't. Dad came home. He's okay.'

'He came back?' There was a heartbreaking tremor in Glass's voice.

'I told you he would.'

'I didn't think... I mean, I knew he would. But Dolly didn't... She said...' Her bottom lip trembled as she tried not to cry. She hated crying in front of Nimbus.

'Everything's going to be okay,' he said, hugging her tightly. 'It's all okay now. I promise. Go back to sleep.'

'Sleep?'

'Yeah. Get back into bed before you catch cold.'

'No way. You're going somewhere. You have to take me with you.'

'I'm not going anywhere.'

She put her hands on her hips and tilted her head to one side. 'You're a fibber. You better take me, or I'm going to tell on you.'

He sighed, shaking his head. There was no denying it; he had been well and truly caught out. There was at least a small part of him that was actually grateful.

'Why do you want to come?' he said.

'Someone has to watch out for you.'

He opened the shutters to look at the pale moon. The deserted streets of the village were bathed in an eerie blue light, shrouded in a shadowy mystery. He could not even begin to imagine what things might be waiting for him out there.

'Please take me,' Glass said.

He ruffled her hair. It could be dangerous where he was going, but what other choice did he have?

'You're going to need some boots,' he said.

Glass's face lit up, and she clapped her hands enthusiastically until Nimbus motioned for her to be quiet.

'Where are we going, anyway?' she asked.

'Flint Lock Fort.'

'What's at Flint Lock?'

Nimbus stared out at the shadows of the night. 'Sorrow,' he said.

CHAPTER FOURTEEN

As soon as Glass had put on warm clothes and good boots, the two children crept out of the house into the night–bandaged streets of the village.

'Flint Lock is miles away,' Glass whispered, as they flitted through the gloom.

'I know,' Nimbus said.

'How are we going to get there?'

'By horse.'

'We don't have a horse.'

'No, but the mayor does.' His mischievous grin flashed momentarily.

'We can't take the mayor's horse.'

'We're not taking it, we're borrowing it. We'll bring it back.'

'But...'

'He won't miss it for one night.'

'It's wrong to take other people's things.'

'I know, but this is a special situation.'

'You'll be in trouble.'

'And you'll be sent back home if you aren't quiet.'

Glass bit her tongue. Her brother had used his stern voice, and that usually meant it was best to shut up and try not to get noticed.

An owl shrieked, and its cry seemed haunting and bleak in this colourless night–time world. The windows of several houses glowed with candlelight. They looked warm and inviting, and Nimbus was filled with the desire to go back to bed and pull the blankets up over his head until this was all over. It would be so easy to run, to hide away and pretend that everything was still okay; but he knew he couldn't. No matter how he felt, he had to be brave.

He took Glass's hand and darted down a street at the side of the mayor's house. Keeping to the shadows, they slipped over the back wall and then cautiously made their way towards the stable where the mayor housed his black stallion, Onyx.

Onyx was a huge animal with powerfully muscular shoulders and a look in his eye that suggested he knew a lot more than he was letting on. He was fast too. He had won the Landmark derby three years running, and was rumoured to rival Lord Citrine's finest stock for speed and stamina.

He was also a good–natured creature, and often allowed the children of the village to ride him under the mayor's supervision. As such, he knew Nimbus and Glass, and wasn't particularly surprised when they opened his stable door. As the children saddled him up, he did wonder why the mayor wasn't around; but he certainly had no intentions of saying no to the opportunity of having a bit of a night–time canter.

'This doesn't seem right,' Glass said, as Nimbus lifted her onto Onyx's back.

'It's fine,' Nimbus replied, hopping up behind her. 'I've watched them saddle this horse hundreds of times, and I've ridden her a bit.'

Onyx snorted disapprovingly.

'I think it's a him,' Glass said.

Onyx nodded and pawed the soft ground with one foot.

'Whatever. You worry too much.'

'I'm not worried about your riding. I'm worried about you getting arrested for stealing a horse.'

'I told you already. We're not stealing it.'

'And will you be given the chance to explain that if the soldiers catch you, or will they just shoot you right out of the saddle?'

Nimbus thought about it. She was probably right. He had broken into the stable in the middle of the night. Who would believe he wasn't intending to keep the horse?

He glanced at the mayor's bedroom window. There were no lights. What if the mayor was watching him? What if there were soldiers already waiting for him out in the lane, ready for an ambush? He would be arrested. Cumulo would be alone.

'I have to do this,' he said, as much to himself as to Glass.

'I know,' Glass said. 'But can you do it fast, please? Before anybody finds out what we've done.'

He wrapped his arms around her, then pressed his heels into Onyx's flanks. Onyx set off at a gentle trot, heading out of the gate and down the lane.

Nimbus held his breath and tried to stop his hands from shaking.

No guards ambushed them.

As they left the village, being as quiet as possible, the moon appeared from behind a bank of brooding clouds to light their road west. Night creatures snuffled in the undergrowth, snorting and growling and generally sounding unfriendly. Nimbus tried not to think about goblins.

'What's going on, Nim?' Glass asked.

'I'm not sure. Something happened out at the fort. I don't know what it was, but I think Dad's involved in some way.'

'Is Daddy at the fort?'

'Not yet. I wanted to go to take a look before he got there.'

'Why?'

'I don't know really. Just to see, I guess.'

'Is Daddy in trouble?'

Nimbus tightened his grip on the reins. He didn't answer.

'Nim?'

'Did you know Dad has a sword?'

Glass giggled. 'Daddy works at the mill. He doesn't have a sword.'

'That's what I always thought.'

He urged Onyx to trot a little faster. He didn't really want to reach the fort in any great hurry, but he didn't want the mayor to find out his horse was gone either.

After a little while Glass began to nod. Eventually she fell asleep against his arm.

The only sound was Onyx's hooves crunching on rocks as he weaved between hedges and trees.

Clouds continued to roll across the purple sky, occasionally obscuring the stars and making it look like they were blinking on and off like tired eyes.

Nimbus's own eyes started to feel very heavy. His head sagged onto his chest.

The clip–clop clip–clop of Onyx's hooves was almost hypnotic.

He closed his eyes.

It wouldn't hurt if he fell asleep.

'Wonder how far it is now?' he muttered, to nobody in particular.

As if in answer, Onyx suddenly stopped. Nimbus jerked fully awake in the saddle.

A peculiarly angled shape – the silhouette of a demon – was looming on the horizon. He blinked, rubbed his eyes. It was no demon; it was just a mess of broken towers and shattered walls, crumbling rubble and blocks of collapsed stone.

'Flint Lock,' he said.

The gates of the fortress, which had long been thought of as indestructible, were hanging on their hinges like splintered teeth. Black smoke drifted around the ruins.

A single flag whipped and snapped on the remnants of the only turret that had survived the destruction. It was a lonely symbol of a place that no longer existed.

'What happened here?' he whispered.

Onyx shook his head. He didn't have any answers, he was just a horse.

A wolf howled.

Glass stirred in Nimbus's arms. 'Are we there yet?' she asked.

'I guess so,' Nimbus said. 'I'm going to take a closer look.' He paused uncertainly. 'Yeah. That's what I'm going to do. That's what Dad would do. I'll take a closer look.'

He climbed down from the saddle, then lifted Glass down to walk with him. Onyx followed without being led. He may only have been a horse, but he wasn't stupid and he certainly wasn't going to stay on his own. This place gave him the creeps.

As they approached the sorry remains of the fort, they could see people in the murky darkness. Some were slumped against stones and cracked pillars, others were on their hands and knees, coughing and choking and struggling to breathe.

'Who are they?' Glass asked.

'I think they're the guards who were posted here,' Nimbus said.

'Are they all sick?'

'It looks like it.'

'I don't understand. What could have destroyed the buildings and made everyone ill at the same time?'

'I don't know. And I have a feeling we don't want to know.'

Onyx nodded in agreement. He had seen more than enough to know he'd rather have stayed back at the stable.

'I'm afraid,' Glass said.

Soldiers were staggering around among the chunks of broken fortifications, heroically calling out names in an effort to list the wounded despite being obviously sick themselves.

Grasping fingers of black smoke were settling over the fort, as if they were desperate to choke the life out of everything inside.

'Could we get sick too?' Glass asked.

'I don't really want to stay here to find out,' Nimbus said. 'We should leave.'

'Yes, please.'

Suddenly there was an ear–piercing scream – the scream of a

thousand wounded men – and something gigantic flew across the face of the moon.

Nimbus's breath caught in his throat. The soldiers of Flint Lock cowered, burying their faces under their hands and weeping as the thing passed overhead.

'Cumulo?' Nimbus whispered.

But this wasn't Cumulo.

'What is that?' Glass asked.

Nimbus's mouth moved, but no sounds came out. He should have brought the Wing Warrior sword with him. He was totally defenceless. If there was a fight, he couldn't hope to win.

'Nim?' Glass said.

He swallowed. His mouth was too dry to speak. He needed to be brave, to take control. Glass was in danger, and it was his fault. If something happened to her, how could he ever live with himself? He had to get her to safety.

'Nim?'

The thing in the sky threw its head back and roared, then tore off into the West.

For a while Nimbus couldn't move, he could only stare at the patch of sky where the thing had been. Glass tugged at his sleeve. 'Nim?' she said. 'Nim? What was that?'

'We have to go,' he said.

'Was it a dragon?'

'We really have to go. We have to find Cumulo.'

'Who's Cumulo?'

Nimbus chewed his bottom lip thoughtfully as he looked out at the broken ruin of Flint Lock and its equally broken soldiers. 'He's the only one who can help me now,' he said.

CHAPTER FIFTEEN

The mayor of Landmark had a set routine he followed most mornings. Generally he would wake up at six o'clock, get dressed, and have breakfast in his kitchen. Breakfast was usually something warm in the winter, like eggs and bacon, but when the weather was better he tended to have milk and some toast.

After breakfast he would put on his top coat, kiss his wife on the cheek, and then go out to the stable to feed Onyx. After that he would head out for a busy day of being the mayor.

Being the mayor meant he had to deal with all manner of problems: Land disputes between neighbours, complaints about the state of the village square, gathering taxes, and just recently, organising search parties for missing people. But on the day Onyx went missing, such problems became secondary.

The morning routine had gone entirely to plan. He had woken before first light, dressed, and enjoyed a good breakfast of scrambled eggs. He had put on his top coat, kissed his wife on the cheek, and then he had gone out to the stable.

The stable was empty.

The mayor stood in the open doorway and scratched his head. There were hoof prints in the soft mud leading from the stable down to the gate, and two sets of human footprints. One of his best saddles was missing.

'Stolen,' he muttered to himself. 'Someone has stolen my horse.'

And that was the exact moment Nimbus became a wanted criminal.

***

Cumulo woke with the sun streaming down on him through a large hole in the roof. This was an entirely new experience for him, as before that day he had only ever woken in a deep, dark cave.

It took him several minutes to gather his thoughts and realise where he was. This was the ruined castle Nimbus had spoken of: the shattered remnants of a once mighty stronghold that had long ago fallen into disrepair.

He rose, stretched each of his four limbs in turn, and then gave his wings a good flap.

After he had left Nimbus in the woods the previous day, he had taken the opportunity to give his wings a proper workout. He had been a little concerned he wouldn't know how to use them, as he had never been out of the cave before; but as soon as he was up in the sky it was if he had been flying his whole life, and any fears he may have had about crashing into the side of a mountain were quickly forgotten.

Soaring above the clouds was a real thrill. He had been able to see the surrounding land for miles, from the toothy outline of the Grey Mountains in the East, off to the vast oceans in the South, and the desolate plains in the West. To the North he could see a huge, sprawling city with tall, white towers, and beyond that, barren and inhospitable lands that seemed empty of human life entirely.

The sky was never–ending, filled with clouds and startled–looking birds that circled around him, tweeting and chirruping excitedly.

When his wings began to get tired, he landed on the beach where he let the lapping waves of the Everlasting Ocean bubble up over his claws. He watched seagulls as they dipped in and out of the water, and he even tried to talk to a crab that was scuttling over some nearby rocks, but it ran away.

If he could have, Cumulo would have stayed on the beach for the rest of the day, but he knew he had to get into hiding soon.

Being spotted would just cause problems, and he didn't really fancy the idea of being chased with pitchforks, even if he wasn't entirely sure what pitchforks were.

The ruined castle was situated east of the Forbidden Woods, on an abandoned and overgrown track that disappeared into the darkest and most foreboding shadows of the Grey Mountains.

This place had once been an outpost for defending against intruders from beyond the mountains, but it had stopped being used many years ago. Now, only part of the watchtower and a storehouse with part of the roof missing remained standing among huge piles of cracked and sun–scorched rubble.

Cumulo had stashed the armour of the Wing Warrior in the back of the storehouse, and then curled up in the doorway to get some sleep. He had drifted into dream watching the tiny pinpoints of starlight twinkling in the darkening heavens.

He quite often had dreams he didn't really understand, and he was quite certain they usually weren't dreams at all but actually memories. That night, sleeping in the grim remains of a dead fortress, he dreamed of desperate battles fought between men and beasts; knights fleeing in terror before the onslaught of a giant, winged monster.

He woke feeling as though he had borne witness to the sorrow of an entire nation, and in his heart it felt as though he had lost something he never realised he had before.

Once he had wriggled out of the storehouse and stretched every part of his body, he sprawled out on a grassy hillock and enjoyed the feeling of the sun beating down on him. He wondered when Nimbus would come back.

The day wore on slowly, and the sun got higher. Birds fluttered down to perch on nearby stones and rocks. Cumulo drifted in and out of sleep.

He was actually just dozing off when he heard a voice call out. At first he thought he must have imagined it, but when he lifted his head to look around he clearly heard the voice again.

'I say, hello there.'

His gaze was drawn, for no apparent reason, to the broken tower. The door was open, revealing only darkness inside. Black clouds appeared from nowhere, rolling over the face of the sun and casting the world in temporary shades of grey.

Inside the tower, something moved.

'Hello?' Cumulo said.

'Well, look at that. You speak. And I thought I'd seen just about everything,' the voice said.

'Who's there?' Cumulo asked, straining his eyes to peer into the darkness. It was strange. His eyesight was good enough to see in even the blackest places, but no matter how hard he looked he could not see anybody inside the tower.

'My name is Captain Spectre of the seventy–third archers regiment, master of the watchtower.'

'Are you in the tower?'

'I am.'

'Come into the light, I cannot see you.'

'You don't need light to see me, Mr Dragon, you need belief.'

Cumulo padded towards the doorway. Nearby birds scattered. 'Belief?' he said.

'What is it a dragon believes in?'

Cumulo shrugged. 'I believe in everything.'

The air just inside the mouth of the tower doorway shimmered, and suddenly a man was standing there. He was dressed in full chainmail armour with a silver helmet. His visor was pulled down over his face so all that could be seen was his mouth and jaw. He gleamed with a magical light, and although he was now perfectly visible, there was something about him that made him look like he wasn't actually there. At first Cumulo thought this might have been because the man didn't appear to have any shadow; but the more Cumulo looked, the more he got the impression that it was the shadow he could see and it was the body that was missing.

'Do you see me, Mr Dragon?' the man asked.

'I do.'

'Excellent, you wouldn't believe how many people can't see me.' He paused, then laughed. His voice sounded distant and timeless. 'Actually, you probably would.'

'Who are you?'

'I told you, I'm Captain Spectre of the seventy–third archers regiment, master of the watchtower. Who are you?'

'I'm Cumulo. The dragon.'

'A talking dragon. That's smashing. So, Mr Cumulo, what are you doing in my tower?'

'I needed a place to stay.'

'On the run, are you?'

'Something like that.'

'Indeed. Can't imagine you can just go walking around the place. Might cause a bit of a fright.'

'You aren't afraid of me.'

'True. But ghosts don't have anything to fear from the living.'

'You're a ghost?'

Spectre leaned against the doorframe. 'Afraid so. I'm dead as a doornail, have been for years. Me and all my men.'

'That's terrible.'

'Oh, it's not so bad. Things haven't really changed that much from when we were alive. The tower's a little draughtier now half of it's fallen down, but that's it.'

'How long have you been dead?'

'Not really sure. Quite a while, I should think. But you tend to stop counting the days after the first two or three hundred.'

'What happened?' Cumulo asked, sitting down. 'Do you remember how you got this way?'

'I've often thought about that. As far as I can figure it, I went to sleep as normal, and woke up... well, didn't wake up... dead. It's the same for everyone else too.'

'How horrible. Didn't anybody come to find out what had

happened to you all?'

'Oh yes, lots of people came. But...' Spectre shook his head. 'Somehow our bodies were moved.'

'So they thought you'd vanished?'

'That's right. I tried to get a few people to notice me, threw some plates and things, but that just scared them away. Nobody comes here now, they all think it's haunted.'

'It is.'

'I suppose so.'

'Is there anything I can do to help?'

'Kind of you to ask, Old Boy, but I don't think so. Not unless you happen to know where our bodies are. If we knew where they were, maybe we could...' He gestured with one hand. 'You know, shuffle off. Go into the light. Whatever it is people are supposed to do once they're dead.'

Cumulo scratched his nose with one claw. 'I'll certainly keep an eye out for them.'

'Excellent. You're a true gentleman.'

'Do you mind me using your tower for a few days?'

'Not at all. It's nice to have someone new about the place. Especially someone who can see us. The men will be delighted.'

'I only see you.'

'Oh, the others are around here somewhere. Now, tell me more about you. Have you always been able to talk?'

Cumulo thought hard, trying to see if the answer to the question existed somewhere in one of his memories. 'We can all talk,' he said, eventually. 'The Wing Warriors taught us how, but most dragons choose not to.'

'Really, that is a revelation. The last of the dragons disappeared from the world when I was still a child, before the great magical battles destroyed much of our lands. I never got to see one, and I never really thought I would. It's such a thrill.'

'You were alive when the dragons were still alive?'

'Oh yes. Although I never saw one, I would often listen to

the stories of people who had.'

'What were they like?'

Spectre's thin mouth twitched into a shape that was similar to, but not quite, a smile. It could most accurately be described, for obvious reasons, as a ghost of a smile. 'From what I can gather, they were a lot like you.'

'Really?' Cumulo grinned toothily.

'Of course, after they were gone, war broke out. Those were terrible times. It felt like the whole world was being torn apart. Every village and every city was looking out for itself. Nobody knew who to trust. Wizards and sorcerers from all the corners of the land were drawn together, and the results were terrifying.' He chuckled. 'You never knew if one day you might wake up as a frog.'

'Did you fight?'

'There was little room in that war for those of us with no magical power. Whole armies could march on a single wizard and be reduced to terrified children before a sword was drawn. We used to sit in our homes and watch as the magic set fire to the sky. It never would have happened if the dragons had been alive.'

'I would never have allowed it to happen,' Cumulo said.

'I was only eleven at the time. I lived with my mother and father in a small village just north of Crystal Shine. We avoided much of the conflict, but there was this one day...' Spectre wrapped his fingers around the hilt of the sword in his sheath. 'It was early, still morning. My father had risked the journey to Crystal Shine in the hope of finding work. A man, a dark force of evil, came into our house. He was a magic user of the worst kind, a thing they called the necromancer. He had a pale face and deep burning eyes filled with hatred for all mankind.'

'What happened?'

'I don't know why he had chosen to come into our home. He was all in black, and he seemed twenty feet tall. He crackled with magical energy powerful enough to bring the mountains crashing down, and all his anger was directed at my mother. He didn't see me until it was too late. I rose up with my father's hunting knife and stabbed him between the shoulder blades.'

'Did you..?'

'Kill him? No. He was too powerful to be killed with a knife, but the attack took him by surprise and hurt him badly. He staggered out into the street, screaming horribly, and the other villagers threw stones at him until he ran away. It was a victory long talked about, and earned me a place in Crystal Shine's Military Academy where I learned the ways of combat and became the captain you see before you now.' Spectre looked down at his feet. His mouth was serious. 'But I will never forget the look in the necromancer's eyes as he fled the village.'

'Why?'

'He looked directly at me, and his eyes were pure fury, the kind of fury that can destroy the strongest of men. At that moment I knew, one day he would come back to get me.'

'Did he?'

'I don't know.'

A crack appeared in the clouds, and a tiny sliver of golden sunlight filtered through.

'You must tell me more of the time of dragons,' Cumulo said.

'I will,' Spectre said, 'but not now.'

'Why not?'

'I don't wish to alarm you, but soldiers are approaching. And they don't look friendly.'

Cumulo looked behind him. Six horsemen were charging down into the ruins with their swords drawn. 'I have to go,' he said, stretching his wings. 'I have to find Nim.'

'Aren't you going to fight them?'

'I can't risk any confrontation. Not yet. Not until I've seen Nim.'

'But I've always wanted to see a dragon... you know?' Spectre gestured aimlessly with one hand. 'Do what dragons do.'

'Perhaps another time.'

Cumulo took one last look at the approaching soldiers. The leading rider had someone else sitting in the saddle with him: A young boy with his hands bound together. As the horse galloped, the boy bobbed up and down and his head slumped forwards. Even though Cumulo could not see the boy's face, he instantly recognised him.

'Nimbus?'

Cumulo drew himself up to his full height. The clouds broke apart. Sunlight glittered on his blood red scales and sharp claws.

'Right,' he growled menacingly. 'If it's a fight they want, it's a fight they'll get.'

CHAPTER SIXTEEN

Nimbus's capture, and the subsequent attack on Cumulo, was down to a series of unfortunate misunderstandings that started several hours earlier when the mayor of Landmark realised Onyx was missing from his stable. Such misunderstandings are frequent among humans and can usually be quickly resolved with the minimum of fuss. However, in some circumstances fuss is unavoidable, especially in circumstances involving people who actually quite like a bit of fuss.

The first misunderstanding was on the part of the mayor, who made the very reasonable assumption Onyx had been stolen rather than borrowed.

After assuming he had been robbed, the mayor immediately raised the alarm. He ran to the garrison and frantically bashed on the door until it was opened by a bleary–eyed soldier. 'Get up,' the mayor demanded, barging inside. 'Get up, all of you. My horse is missing.'

The soldier scratched his neck and wrinkled his nose. He may have managed to get out of bed, but he certainly wasn't awake enough to fully understand the orders being barked at him. 'Ugh?' he asked, which was about the closest thing he could manage to a real word.

'No time to explain,' the mayor said, flapping his arms.

The other soldiers were filing out of the bunk room, rubbing their faces and yawning. None of them were fully dressed and not one of them had his sword. Captain Obsidian, the garrison's senior officer, was the last to come in. He looked more tired than the others, but not tired in a way that suggested he had just woken. He looked tired in a way that suggested he had never slept.

'What's going on?' he asked.

'My horse,' the mayor snapped. 'My horse, my horse, my horse.' He stamped his feet to make his point.

'Is there a problem with your horse?' Obsidian asked, sarcastically.

'Aren't you listening to me?' the mayor screamed. 'Am I speaking in a foreign language?' He grabbed the soldier who had opened the door, shaking him vigorously. 'Can you see my lips moving? Can you hear the words coming out of my mouth?'

The soldier looked at Obsidian. Obsidian shrugged.

'My horse is missing,' the mayor said, releasing the soldier and stomping around the room like a caged tiger. He kicked a wall, just for good measure, and then had to pretend he hadn't hurt his toe.

'Right,' Obsidian said. His voice was calm, but hard–edged. 'Why don't you sit down, Mr Mayor? Private Silver, get the men ready. Light arms only.'

The recently shaken soldier, who was now looking a little more awake, saluted smartly and led the other men back into the bunk room. Obsidian took a seat by the window and motioned for the mayor to sit next to him.

The mayor sat.

The morning sunlight was creeping through the grey streets, turning the world every shade of yellow. It was light without warmth.

'Right then.' Obsidian put his fingers together in a steeple. His expression was grim. 'Mr Mayor. Let's have a little chat about priorities, shall we?'

'Priorities?'

'Yes. To be more specific, let's chat about my priorities.'

'Priorities?'

Obsidian sighed heavily. 'Is it the word or the concept you're having difficulty with?'

'Now look here, Soldier...' The mayor wagged his finger.

'No, Mr Mayor. You look here. Yesterday a tidal wave struck this village. People went missing. Good people. People I know. People we all know.'

'It was terrible,' the mayor said.

'Yes, it was terrible. It's the greatest tragedy this village has known in years, perhaps the greatest ever.'

'It was terrible,' the mayor repeated.

'On your orders, I then sent three of my men into the woods. They never came back.' Obsidian clenched his fists. His mouth remained straight and serious as a knife edge. 'My men have been searching the beaches, dredging the ocean for bodies. They're tired. I'm tired. And now your horse has gone.'

'He was stolen.'

The captain drew a deep breath. 'And now, only now, you decide to come down here and scream and stamp your feet.'

'It's a good horse.'

'And they were good people.'

'What are you suggesting?'

'If I didn't know better, I might think you cared more about your horse than those missing villagers and my missing men.'

'Nonsense.'

'Whether it's true or not, finding your horse is not my priority. I am very busy right now.'

The mayor stood, clearing his throat carefully. 'Soldier, I don't like your tone,' he said.

'And I don't like yours.'

'Do I have to remind you who is mayor in this village?'

'Oh no, Mr Mayor. We're all well aware of that.'

The mayor paused, trying to decide if he had just been insulted. 'Right,' he said, undecidedly. 'That's good. Just make sure you remember it. Now, what are we going to do about my horse?'

'I thought I'd made myself clear. Your horse is not my priority. My missing men are.'

'Your priorities are whatever I tell you they are, Captain.'

'I work for the village. Not for you.'

'I am the village,' the mayor screamed, stamping his foot as his face went bright red. 'You will do what I say, or I can assure you I will be filing a report of your conduct at Crystal Shine, and I will make sure you can't even get a job cleaning stables on this side of the Grey Mountains. Understood?'

Captain Obsidian sighed, glancing out of the window at the quiet village. When he finally spoke, he did his very best to sound civil. 'If you put it like that, I'm sure I can spare a few men to hunt down your horse. Why don't you start by telling me exactly what happened?'

The mayor returned to his seat, and cleared his throat again. 'He went missing during the night. He was there last thing before I went to bed. I took him in to the stable and shut the gate.'

'Did you lock it?'

'Don't be ridiculous. This is Landmark. We don't have to lock our doors here.'

'Recent events would suggest otherwise.'

'Are you making fun?'

'No.' Obsidian shook his head. 'I lost my sense of humour right about the time you knocked on my door.'

'Good.' The mayor puffed out his chest with self–importance. 'I'm sure you have more sense than to make fun of an elected official.'

'I normally have more sense than to talk to one too.'

'Are you attempting to insult me?'

'I was actually hoping I'd succeeded.'

The remaining soldiers came back in from the bunk room. This time they were in light leather armour with chain link vests.

Private Silver saluted. 'First company await your orders, Captain,' he said.

'Excellent,' Obsidian said. 'Ready the horses immediately. I need five men to come with me. The rest are to resume yesterday's unfinished business along the beaches.'

The soldiers exited the garrison in an orderly manner, leaving Obsidian with the mayor.

'Who do you think has taken your horse?' Obsidian asked.

'How would I know?'

'You must have some idea? Have there been any suspicious people hanging around lately? Or have you made any enemies who might want to teach you a lesson?'

The mayor removed a handkerchief from his coat pocket and wiped his forehead. 'I'm a good man, Captain. I don't have enemies.'

'Everybody has enemies.'

'Not me. But there were two sets of footprints in the stable. Like the footprints of children.'

'You do let children ride the horse.'

'Not at night, and never unsupervised.'

Obsidian nodded understandingly. There were sounds of hooves and voices outside; the general noise of a war party readying itself for a fight. 'The men are prepared,' he said. 'Which way did the horse's tracks lead?'

'Into the West, towards Flint Lock Fort.'

Obsidian pulled a pair of riding gloves out of his belt and wriggled his fingers into them. 'Don't worry, Mr Mayor,' he said, heading for the door. 'We'll find your precious horse.'

'What about the thieves?'

'What about them?'

'What will you do with them?'

Obsidian stopped with his hand on the door latch. 'Capture them. Or failing that, kill them.'

Obsidian's search party picked up Nimbus's trail just outside of the village.

'So what are we looking for?' Private Silver asked.

'Two horse thieves,' Obsidian replied. 'They took the horse some time during the night, so they could have a good few hours head start on us by now.'

'Two riders on one horse won't be travelling at speed. There's a good chance we can catch them before they hit the Western Borders.'

'I wouldn't be so sure. Onyx is the fastest horse I've ever seen.' Obsidian pulled on the reins to bring his horse to a sudden stop. He dismounted, sucking his teeth thoughtfully. 'And there's something else too.'

'What?'

He knelt by one of Onyx's hoof prints, examining it carefully. 'The prints here are faint, considering they're only a few hours old.'

'What does that mean?'

'It means the two riders are light. They probably weigh less than one of us. And that's going to be a big advantage to them.'

'Why would they weigh less?'

'Because they're children.' He turned his gaze to the horizon, watching for any signs of the horse thieves. 'They could be in the Sanguine Mountains by now. If that's the case, we'll never find them. You could hide an army of men up there.'

He shielded his eyes from the sun with one hand as he squinted into the distance. Two soldiers on horseback came into view, galloping over the plains.

'Riders,' Silver said. 'Could be trouble.'

Obsidian jumped up on his horse. 'Follow me,' he said, riding off. Silver gestured for the rest of the party to wait where they were and then set off after his captain.

As the riders drew nearer, Obsidian could see they were wearing the black and gold armour and insignias of the Crystal Shine palace guards: Lord Citrine's personal bodyguard. Obsidian himself had trained for a position in this elite unit, but even with all his skill and cunning he had been unable to prove himself worthy, and had ended up at Landmark instead.

He stopped his horse and removed his helmet, wiping the hair and sweat out of his face. He sat straight in his saddle and attempted to look as significant as possible. 'Good day to you,' he shouted, as the palace guards reined in their snorting horses with a clatter of hooves on the stony ground.

'Good day it is not,' one of the guards said, lifting his helmet's visor and looking at the sky dubiously. 'I must ask you to turn back.'

'Why? There has always been passage this way to the fort.'

'No longer. My name is Claw, and this is my colleague and brother, Tooth. It is our duty to inform you that all ways into the West are under the guardianship of Lord Citrine's military elite. None may pass.'

'We are soldiers from the village of Landmark,' Obsidian explained. 'I am Captain Obsidian. My companion is Private Silver, my most loyal friend and bravest of all my garrison. We are tracking two criminals who came this way by horse. We must have passage.'

'And I repeat to you that none may pass.'

'You are obstructing official business.' Obsidian's voice was as hard and unforgiving as the mountainside. 'It is my duty to bring these criminals to justice.'

'And we are honour–bound to allow you no farther.'

'It would appear our orders conflict.'

'But our orders come from Lord Citrine himself. Our orders are the law of the land.'

Obsidian nodded. 'Then we must abide by your orders and turn back. But perhaps we can be allowed to know why. What has happened that makes the West so dangerous?'

Claw looked at his brother. He spoke reluctantly. 'The fort has fallen.'

'Impossible.' Obsidian could not keep the disbelief from his tone.

'It's true. An evil creature came out of the night and reduced it to nothing more than broken rock,' Tooth said, excitedly. 'A black cloud hangs over the ruin and all of the soldiers are sick, too weak to be moved. They have a disease that has sapped their strength and filled their brains with nightmares.'

'What kind of creature could cause such destruction?' Obsidian asked.

'We don't know,' Claw said. 'Not yet. We have attempted to question the survivors, but all we get is nonsense about dragons. Stupid children's fairie stories.'

'They all say the same thing?'

'The entire fort seems to have suffered from some kind of mass hallucination, seeing something that just couldn't possibly be real, yet believing it is.'

'You don't believe the story then?'

'No,' Claw said. 'I cannot believe a dragon has returned into the world. The soldiers have gone mad.' There seemed to be little conviction behind his words.

'Then how do you explain it?'

'I don't know. That's why we're out here. We're looking for someone who can tell us what really happened.'

'Is there such a person?'

'One of the victims we questioned says there were two other witnesses, two people who were not under the influence of the disease. They were seen at the fort during the night. They headed east. We are tracking them.'

Obsidian looked at Silver. 'What do you think?' he asked.

Silver shrugged. 'Could be them.'

'Could be who?' Claw asked.

'These people you are tracking. They are two, on just one horse?'

'Yes.'

'A great black horse? Very powerful? Very fast?'

'So we have heard. And also...'

Obsidian smiled knowingly. 'And they are children?'

'Yes. A boy and a girl.'

'It seems our orders may not be as conflicting as we first thought.'

'Are you trying to tell me the two villains you have been sent here to capture are these same two children?' Tooth laughed. 'They must truly be fearsome bandits.'

'You may laugh,' Obsidian said, 'yet these two children committed a crime punishable by death. Then they came to your fort this very morning, and now your fort lies in ruins.'

Tooth stopped laughing. 'You mean to say these children could have been responsible for what happened at Flint Lock?'

'I don't know. But they must have wanted to come here very urgently if they were prepared to steal a horse to do it. They would have known that to be caught would mean their deaths.'

'That would make sense if not for one thing. We received word of the destruction late last night, before the arrival of the children at the fort. They couldn't have been involved.'

'But they did come here. They must have had a reason for that.'

'Perhaps they knew what was going to happen and came to make sure it had,' Tooth said.

'Of course,' Claw said. 'Perhaps these two children may appear innocent, but are actually the ones who plotted the fall of the keep. They are conspirators, planning the ruin of our country.'

'We must capture them immediately and question them before anything else happens,' Silver said.

'I agree,' Obsidian said. His horse snorted and stamped one hoof, shaking its mane agitatedly. A small rabbit emerged from a patch of briers, twitching its nose and watching the soldiers interestedly.

'Will you join us?' Claw asked. 'We could use the extra manpower if these children are as dangerous as they appear to be.'

'It is our duty to bring them to Landmark to stand trial for their crime,' Obsidian said. 'We will travel with you as long as you allow us to do our duty.'

'That seems fair, Captain. But you will not be allowed to execute the children... I mean, thieves... until the palace guards have spoken with them and established if they are in some way responsible for all this madness at the keep.'

'I understand. Do you know where they were heading?'

'We thought at first they may have been heading to your village of Landmark, but their tracks have skirted around the borders of the farmlands. We believe they are going to the Forbidden Woods.'

'Those are dangerous woods these days. We have recently lost three men to their dark depths. We would be searching for them now if it were not for these young villains.'

'Then we must catch them before they get that far.'

Obsidian turned his horse around. 'Let's waste no more time,' he said.

The rabbit, who went by the rather unfortunate name of Bunnykins, sniffed the air carefully. He scratched his nose with one paw, and watched until all of the soldiers and horses were nothing more than dust on the horizon.

'Silly humans,' he said to himself.

If they had only thought to ask him, he would have told them about the evil dragon; about its huge black wings and its terrible appetite for death and destruction.

But humans never thought to ask rabbits anything. Most humans didn't even know rabbits could talk.

CHAPTER SEVENTEEN

Of course, Nimbus had absolutely no idea the mayor had sent a search party after him, and he had no idea he had become the prime suspect in a conspiracy.

All Nimbus knew was there was a dragon on the loose, and not the nice Cumulo type of dragon. This was the type that was massive and evil and terrifying: A monstrous winged demon with the strength to uproot mountains and smash castles to dust. A wicked and cruel beast with a thirst for misery.

There was no doubt, the dragon was the dark power Cumulo had spoken of, the black magic that knew of Nimbus's existence and had only one aim in life: to hunt him down and kill him.

His only possible chance to survive was to get back to Cumulo, to seek his protection. Without Cumulo, Nimbus was totally defenceless.

After riding for three or four hours, Onyx was beginning to look tired and was breathing heavily. Nimbus, despite his desperate urge to reach the safety of Cumulo's lair, stopped by one of the many streams that fed into the Forbidden River. By his reckoning, they were only a few miles north of Landmark.

He dismounted, helped Glass out of the saddle, and then went and washed his face and hair. The sun was hot, and he could feel the dirt in the creases of his neck.

'What was that thing at the fort?' Glass asked, sitting on the bank of the stream and dipping her toes in the water.

Nimbus scooped water up in his hands to drink. He was hungry, and wished he had thought to bring some food. 'It was a dragon,' he said.

'A real dragon?'

'Yes, a real dragon.'

Onyx lowered his head and chewed some grass, glad to take a break from galloping.

'I didn't think there were any real dragons any more,' Glass said.

'Well, it would appear there are.' Nimbus stood, examining the sky carefully. There was no sign of it yet, but who knew when it would decide to attack?

'Was the thing in the river a dragon?'

Nimbus sat next to Glass. She continued to splash her feet in the water, wiggling her toes like worm bait for the silvery fish darting around them. 'I don't think so,' he said. 'I don't know what that was, but I don't think dragons live in the water.'

'Where do they live?'

'Maybe on mountaintops, maybe in caves. Anywhere where there are no people, I suppose.'

'Are they scared of people?'

'People can be dangerous.'

Glass picked up a stone. It had been polished from being in the river for a long time, and its dark surface shimmered in the sunlight. Reflections in the stone were like black graveyard spirits. 'Has the world gone bad?' she asked.

'I don't know if bad is the right word. It's changed. A lot of people think change is bad, but who really knows?'

'What do you think?'

'I think the world has always been a dangerous place, we just didn't always see it.'

Glass nodded, still holding the black stone like it was an ancient treasure, and stared into the flowing waters of the stream. The water was very shallow and full of tiny fish. The more she looked, the more fish she could see. 'Did the dragons ever really go away? Or did we just forget how to see them?'

Onyx lifted his head for a moment, looking to the West.

Nimbus followed the horse's gaze, but the uneven ground made it hard to see very far. A cold chill ran down his spine, but he ignored it, turning his attention back to Glass.

'Are you ready to meet Cumulo?' he asked.

Glass dropped her stone into the stream. The fish scattered in an explosion of silver, making beautiful flickering patterns. 'Who's Cumulo?' she said.

'Cumulo is a friend of mine.'

'What sort of friend?'

'The... the dragon kind.'

'You're friends with a dragon?'

'Sort of. I found him.'

'When?'

'Yesterday. In the cave. He was guarding a suit of armour.'

'But you said...'

'I know. I'm sorry. I told you there was nothing down there, but I lied. I didn't mean to, I just didn't want anyone else to know until I'd had a chance to figure out what to do.'

'What about Tide? Tide said there was nothing in the cave. Was he lying too?'

'Tide doesn't know anything. I haven't told him.'

Glass's brow wrinkled. She scratched her head thoughtfully. 'You've never lied to me before.'

'I know.' Nimbus stood, brushing dust from his clothes. 'I didn't want to, but I had to protect Cumulo. If people know about him they might hurt him.'

'But I won't.'

Nimbus ruffled Glass's hair. 'I know you won't. You're a good girl.'

'Then why didn't you tell me?'

'It's complicated.'

'No it's not, you're just saying that.'

'I guess, I wasn't thinking straight.'

'That's not true either.'

She stared up at him, and he could see the hurt in her eyes. She was right. He was still lying. When did lying get so easy?

Taking a deep breath, he tried one last time to explain himself.

'I messed up, Glass. I made a fool of myself trying to catch that stupid fish, and then Tide made me look like a wimp. I got us completely lost. Then I went down in that cave and I found something that nobody else knew about. It was just for me. I guess I was trying to prove something.'

'Prove what?'

'That I'm not completely useless. That there was something that I could do that Tidal couldn't. I don't know. I was stupid.'

'You got that right.'

He crouched down, resting a hand on her shoulder. 'So, do you forgive me?'

She grinned. 'I suppose so. But you owe me, big time.'

He returned her smile. 'Come on then, let's get out of here.'

'You're taking me to see a dragon?' Her eyes grew wider and brighter. 'I'm going to see a real dragon?'

'That's right. But we have to go now.' He took her hand and led her back to Onyx, who was standing stock–still and watching the West expectantly. Nimbus suddenly became aware of the sound of hooves.

'What's that?' Glass asked.

Eight horsemen had appeared on the horizon, moving at speed. Nimbus quickly lifted Glass up into the saddle.

'What is it?' Glass asked.

'Landmark soldiers,' Nimbus replied, climbing up into the saddle and pulling Onyx around. 'And two other soldiers carrying the symbol of Lord Citrine on their chests.'

'Do you think they'll help us?'

Nimbus clenched his fingers on the reins. 'I don't think so. We're horse thieves, remember?'

'But you said we were only borrowing Onyx!'

'I said there was nothing in that cave too.'

He dug his heels into Onyx's flanks and the horse jumped forwards, leaping the bubbling stream.

'Hold on tight,' Nimbus said, getting lower in the saddle. His voice was almost lost in the tearing wind as he urged Onyx to greater speeds. 'I'm going to have to go really fast.'

Glass clutched him tightly, and buried her face against his arm. He looked back at the soldiers. They were much closer than he had first thought, and they were gaining ground.

'I hope this horse is as fast as the mayor says it is,' he said, through gritted teeth.

Onyx snorted angrily. Of course he wasn't as fast as the mayor said he was.

He was faster.

The ground flew by underneath; rocks, grass, branches, shrubs, leaves, all speeding by in a blur. Nimbus pressed his knees into Onyx's sides, got as low as he could behind the horse's neck, and tightened his grip on the reins. Glass whimpered.

Everything was going so fast, Nimbus could barely see. His eyes were watering, and his teeth were clenched so hard he thought they might break. His knuckles were white, his back arched, his legs locked in position. He wasn't sure he would be able to stop Onyx from galloping now, even if he wanted to.

Branches slapped against his shoulders and face, leaving stinging red marks on his skin. Onyx brayed and snorted, clattering over stones and down rutted embankments.

Nimbus risked another look over his shoulder. The soldiers were beginning to drop back. Their horses weren't good enough to keep up with Onyx. Nimbus would have thrown his arms in the air triumphantly if he hadn't been so afraid of falling.

The Forbidden Woods loomed ahead. If Nimbus could make it that far he could lose the soldiers in the undergrowth. He would be safe.

Glass would be safe.

Suddenly a fallen tree appeared in the path. With no time to go around, Onyx bounded into the air, missing the rotting trunk by mere inches and slamming down hard on the other side. His hooves skidded in the mud and his front legs buckled. 'Hold on to me,' Nimbus shouted, as the world spun crazily.

Glass screamed.

And after that everything became too jumbled and muddled to remember.

When Nimbus opened his eyes, he was lying on his back in the dirt with his arms wrapped around Glass protectively. Tall trees, full of birds, towered over him. There was no sunlight here, just the cool, dark mystery of the Forbidden Woods.

'We made it,' he whispered. 'We made it.'

'Not quite,' a voice said.

Nimbus sat up, shaking his head. It felt like the world was still spinning beneath him. He wanted to be sick. Glass groaned and clung to him even more tightly.

Onyx was standing under a tree looking sheepish. Seven men in armour were standing around him with their swords drawn. An eighth soldier, the one who had spoken, was sitting on a tree stump watching Nimbus closely.

'I know you,' Nimbus said, rubbing the back of his head. 'You're Captain Obsidian.'

'That's right,' the soldier said. 'And I know you. You're the miller's son.'

'Nimbus.'

'The troublesome one.' Obsidian removed his helmet and wiped sweat off his forehead. A very sharp–looking sword was resting on the tree stump beside him. 'You're the one who went missing a few days ago.'

'That's me,' Nimbus said. 'Glass, are you okay?'

There were tears streaming down her face. 'I'm okay,' she said.

'No thanks to you,' Obsidian said. 'You could have killed her. You're too young to be handling a horse like Onyx. What were you thinking?'

Nimbus stood. Glass stayed close beside him, holding his hand.

Very slowly, Obsidian took his sword and placed it across his knees. The blade glistened sickeningly. 'You are aware, are you not, that the horse standing over there is the property of the mayor and has been reported as stolen?'

'Oh, we didn't steal it,' Glass said. 'We borrowed it.'

'Of course. And I suppose when you were done with it, you were just going to take it right on back to the mayor and say thanks.'

'That's right,' Nimbus said. He thought for a moment. 'Actually we probably wouldn't have said thanks. We probably would have just sneaked it back when nobody was looking.'

Obsidian ran his finger up and down the hilt of his sword. 'Are you aware that stealing the property of an elected official is punishable by death?'

Nimbus gulped. A hard granite ball of fear was wedged in his throat, and no amount of swallowing would shift it. 'I... Actually... I just want you to know my sister had nothing to do with this.'

Obsidian's gaze flickered from Nimbus to Glass. She was such a small girl, so fragile, so frightened. 'Are you saying you acted entirely alone in this venture?' he asked.

'I am.'

'And the girl is here because..?'

'She...' Nimbus licked his lips. It was uncomfortably quiet under the canopy of woodland leaves, and it seemed to be getting quieter by the second. 'She followed me,' he said.

'So you stole this horse by yourself?'

Nimbus nodded.

'He didn't,' Glass said.

'I did,' Nimbus confirmed.

'He didn't.'

Nimbus squeezed Glass's hand hard enough to make her realise she should keep quiet. 'I worked alone,' he growled. 'My sister is innocent.'

Obsidian motioned to soldiers standing by Onyx. 'Private Fish, Private Cage. Take the girl and the horse back to the village.'

'Yes, Captain.'

'Return the horse to the mayor, and the girl to her family.'

'Yes, Captain.'

The two soldiers approached.

'Nim?' Glass said, clinging on to his arm. 'Nim, what's going on?'

'It's okay,' he said. 'You have to let go now. No–one's going to hurt you.'

She released his arm. 'What about you? Is anybody going to hurt you?'

Nimbus shrugged, the sad gesture of a boy resigned to whatever fate awaited him. 'I don't know,' he said.

'Can your dragon friend help?'

In a second Obsidian was on his feet, sword in hand. 'What dragon?' he snapped.

Nimbus lowered his head. 'She's talking rubbish. You know what girls are like. Everything's a fairie tale to them. She believes in Prince Charming too.'

Obsidian took a step nearer. 'I think I'd like to hear more about this dragon.'

'It's a stupid child's fantasy.'

'Well, maybe your sister isn't the only person who believes in fairie tales.'

'She's making it up,' Nimbus said, agitatedly. 'There are no dragons any more.'

'Well,' Obsidian smiled a wide, open smile that didn't quite fit the look in his black eyes. 'Why don't we just see what the girl has to say about that, shall we?'

Private Fish scooped up Glass in his huge arms. At the same time, Cage and Obsidian pounced at Nimbus. Nimbus was quicker than they had expected, and he ducked out of the way, throwing a punch that hit Cage in the side of the head so hard his helmet span right around.

As Cage stumbled blindly, Nimbus darted behind him and snatched his sword. The weapon was no way near as heavy as the Wing Warrior sword, and Nimbus found he was able to use it quite comfortably, swinging it at any of the soldiers who got too close.

'Keep back,' he screamed. 'Keep back, and put down my sister.'

'You're only making this harder on yourself,' Obsidian said.

'Stay away from me.'

'You're outnumbered. You're surrounded. You can't win this fight. Give up.'

'Never.'

'Put down the sword, or I'll take it from you.'

'Just try it.'

Obsidian moved fast, knocking the sword out of Nimbus's hand as he barrelled into him. Nimbus cried out as he was lifted clean off his feet and then smashed down on his back in the dirt.

He coughed and wheezed as he struggled for breath, but made no effort to get up.

'Right,' Obsidian said, sheathing his own sword. 'Get the girl out of here, and return the horse to the mayor.'

Cage took a moment to straighten his helmet and retrieve his sword. 'Yes, Captain,' he muttered, before mounting his horse and leading Onyx out of the woods. Fish, with Glass in the saddle with him, followed close behind.

Nimbus watched them leave, his face red with anger. 'You better not hurt her,' he said.

'We wouldn't dream of it,' Obsidian said, returning to his seat on the tree stump. 'You, on the other hand, have the small matter of a death sentence to deal with.'

Nimbus sat with his knees pulled up to his chest. The other five soldiers, three of the Landmark garrison and two dressed in the armour of the Crystal Shine palace guard, were watching him intently, as though they expected him to do something special. 'You're really going to kill me for taking the mayor's stupid horse?' he asked.

'Maybe. Maybe not. First, why don't you tell us why you took it?'

'I needed it.'

'Why?'

'I had to see something with my own eyes.'

'You mean the fort?'

'Have you seen it too? Are you helping the people?'

One of the palace soldiers shrugged. 'We're doing what we can for them, but it's hard when we don't know what happened.'

'Did you see a dragon at the fort?' Obsidian asked.

'There are no dragons.'

'Did you know a dragon was going to be there?'

'Of course not.'

'Ah. So there was a dragon there?'

'No... I mean... There was...'

'Why did you go to the fort, Nimbus?'

'Because...' Nimbus ran through several possible answers in his head before deciding that there was nothing he could say that wouldn't make him sound like a villain or a lunatic. He decided lunatic was the lesser of two evils. 'I had a dream. I dreamed something terrible had happened, and I had to see it with my own eyes to believe it.'

'Be honest, Nimbus. You knew about the dragon, didn't you?'

'Strange things have been happening recently. There are...'

'There are what?'

'Nothing. It doesn't matter. But everything seems different at the moment. The tidal wave hitting the village, people going missing. They're bad omens. They're signalling the coming of something even worse.'

Obsidian started drumming his fingers on one knee. 'This all seems very strange to me,' he said. 'Why did your sister say you were friends with the dragon?'

'She didn't.'

'We all heard her.'

'She said I was friends with a dragon. She didn't say I was friends with that dragon.'

'There's more than one?'

'Please, just to let me go. If you don't, more terrible things will happen.'

'Is that a threat?'

'No. I'm not threatening anyone. I'm one of the good guys.'

'If that's true, then take us to the dragon.'

Nimbus felt as though the weight of the whole world was bearing down on him. If he didn't help the soldiers, they were going to execute him as a horse thief; but if he did help them, Cumulo might get hurt.

'I can't,' he whispered. 'Cumulo is my friend. I can't say where he is.'

'But don't you want to prove he's a good guy, like you say he is?'

Tears sprang up in Nimbus's eyes. He wiped his nose on the back of his sleeve. 'Of course I do.'

Obsidian leaned closer. When he spoke again his voice was almost friendly, but there was something in his eyes that let Nimbus know it was all just an act. It was obvious Obsidian didn't trust Nimbus, and it was very unlikely he was going to trust a dragon. 'This is your chance to prove your friend is innocent. Just tell us where he is. I promise he'll be safe.'

'But he's already safe.'

'Not really. If you don't tell us, we'll take you back to Landmark for sentencing, and then we'll hunt the dragon down ourselves. Sooner or later, we'll find him, and if you aren't there to speak in his defence, we may have no other choice but to kill him.'

Nimbus's insides cramped up, and a painful convulsion went through his chest at the thought of Cumulo being hacked up by these men with their cruel swords.

He wanted to be sick. He wanted to scream and cry.

He wanted to go home.

'Okay,' he said. 'I'll do it.'

'Good choice,' Obsidian said, with a note of triumph in his voice.

'But Cumulo hasn't done anything wrong. You have to promise not to hurt him.'

'Of course.'

Obsidian smiled. But his eyes didn't smile. His eyes remained as stern as always.

CHAPTER EIGHTEEN

Obsidian and the other soldiers watched the dragon from a nearby hill.

At first the dragon was lying in the sun, apparently without a care in the world; but then it got up and started to pad around its ruined lair. For a while it looked as though it might have been talking to somebody in the old watchtower, but no matter how hard Obsidian looked, he couldn't see anybody there.

'Is that a real dragon?' one of the soldiers asked.

'Either that, or the lizards get really big around these parts,' Obsidian said.

'Why is he here? This place is supposed to be haunted.'

'I'm not sure dragons care much for the dead.' Obsidian watched carefully, examining the movements of the dragon, and the way in which the light glinted on its thick armour of scales. 'I doubt they care much for the living either.'

The wind whipped through the leaves, causing branches to rattle together. The shadows of the trees danced and swayed, casting groping patterns over the assembled soldiers. They could hear the dragon's claws scraping on stone even from this distance.

Nimbus, sat in Obsidian's saddle and quickly realising how difficult it was to scratch an itch with your hands tied together, watched the way the sunlight shimmered on the soldiers' drawn swords. 'What are you going to do now?' he asked.

'Is that thing your friend?' Obsidian said.

'His name is Cumulo.'

'He doesn't look dangerous,' one of the soldiers said.

'Neither does a sleeping lion,' Obsidian snapped. 'That thing is a monster.'

'He's harmless,' Nimbus objected. 'He could have eaten me a long time ago if he wanted to.'

Obsidian's eyes narrowed. 'That's true. But he didn't. Why do you think that is?'

Nimbus shrugged. 'Why don't you ask him?'

'Let's do that.' Obsidian leapt into the saddle behind Nimbus. 'On my word, we attack.'

'Attack?' Nimbus yelped. 'Why are you attacking him? He hasn't done anything.'

'There are plenty of soldiers at Flint Lock Fort who would contest that.'

'No, wait. I already told you. Cumulo wasn't there.'

'I'm afraid we don't take the word of horse thieves.'

'No, please.'

Obsidian kicked his heels, and his horse bolted down the hill. The other soldiers followed close behind, screaming a battle cry loud enough to wake the dead.

For one hope–filled second it looked to Nimbus as if Cumulo was going to fly away to safety, but then he rose to his full height and spread his mighty wings as far as they would go.

Nimbus hung his head in despair. He had betrayed Cumulo, even if he hadn't meant to, and now there would be fighting. People would get hurt.

And it was all his fault.

When Sky found him, Tidal was sitting on the beach. He was staring hard at the water, like he was trying to count the fish in the foaming waves.

'Are you okay?' she asked, sitting beside him on the overturned remains of a fishing boat.

Tidal scratched his bandaged chest absentmindedly. 'I guess so. It itches a bit.'

'That means the wounds are healing. Don't scratch them.' She touched his hand gently. He stopped scratching. 'What is it you're looking for?'

Tidal frowned. 'Sorry?'

Sky pointed to the choppy ocean waters. 'Out there. What were you looking for?'

'Nothing really.'

'Were you thinking about the tidal wave?'

'Among other things.' He wiggled his bare toes in the sand. A crab scurried away, following a peculiar zigzag path to whatever rock pool it chose to call home. 'They still haven't found any of the missing villagers. I guess I was probably keeping an eye out for the boats.'

'Or perhaps you were looking for the thing that sunk the boats?'

'What thing?'

'The snake Glass was talking about. She wasn't imagining it, was she?'

Tidal snuffed a laugh through his nose. 'Don't be silly, Sky. There's no such thing as a giant snake.'

'I think you believe Glass saw something.'

'That's the stupidest thing I ever heard. Giant snakes. How silly. Just the kind of thing a stupid girl would believe.'

'Okay then, go for a swim.'

Tidal gulped. 'I... I don't want to just now.'

'Okay, I'll go for a swim.'

'No.' Tidal grabbed Sky's arm before she could move. She watched him closely. He grinned, and let go of her arm. 'I mean, no, don't do that. There are lots of bits of wood from the boats and the pier in the water. It's not safe. Look what happened to me.'

Sky dug a shell out of the sand with her long fingers. 'You are such a boy sometimes,' she said.

'What's that supposed to mean?'

'It means I'm quite capable of looking after myself without

you playing my knight in shining armour.'

'Girls are weaker than boys. Boy's have a responsibility to look after them. To protect them.'

'Who told you that?'

'No–one. It's just the way it is.'

'And what if we don't want to be protected?'

'Then you'll just have to grin and bear it, because you get protected anyway.'

Sky sighed and shook her head. 'You boys are all the same. You're as pigheaded as Nim is.'

'Yeah, but I'm better–looking.' He smiled cheekily, and then glanced up and down the beach. There were other people standing on the shore, doing the same as him, staring out at the ocean as though they expected something to happen but weren't sure what that something might be. 'Where is Nim, anyway?'

'I don't know. I haven't seen him since he was at the village hall. He's been strange recently.'

'He's always been strange.'

'But he's stranger now. More secretive.'

'Do you think he's hiding something from us?'

Sky threw her shell into the sea. It made a satisfying plop as it hit the water. 'I don't know. Sometimes he can be as mysterious as the ocean.'

Tidal returned to his study of the waves. 'He didn't seem surprised about the snake,' he said.

'You mean the snake that doesn't exist?'

'Yeah, that one. When Glass told him, he didn't seem surprised. Why do you think that would be?'

'Who knows? I gave up trying to understand Nim years ago. He's infuriating.'

'What if there was a snake?'

'I thought you didn't believe in that?'

'No, but if I did believe. What then?'

'Then I guess your job of protecting all the girls just got a little bit tougher, didn't it?'

'I guess so.'

'It also means you may not want to sit so close to the edge of the water in future.' Sky stood, wiping the sand off her skirt. 'I'm heading back to the village.'

'Why?'

'I'm going to see if I can find Nim. I think I'd feel more comfortable if I knew where he was.'

Tidal stared at the bobbing ocean horizon. For a moment he thought he could just see the arch of a long, silvery body on the surface of the water, but it was gone in the blink of an eye. 'I think I'd like to know where Nim is too,' he said.

At the bottom of the hill, Nimbus decided to take matters into his own hands. Swallowing his fear and doubt, he came up with a plan to escape from Obsidian and his war party before they could use him as a means of getting the upper hand against Cumulo. He knew it was dangerous, and he knew he could be seriously hurt, but he couldn't think of anything else to do.

He held his breath, closed his eyes, and threw himself off the horse.

As he hit the ground he closed his eyes and tried not to think about how messy it would be if he got stepped on. The earth shook violently as the horses continued their charge. The smell of mulched earth was overpowering.

Eventually the thunderous pounding of hooves began to fade. Only then did he risk raising his head to look around.

He was on a grassy embankment, not too far from the ruins. From here, he could clearly see the soldiers bearing down on Cumulo. Their swords glittered in the cold sunlight, and their armour shone silver–white. At any other time, Nimbus would have thought they looked magnificent.

But not this time.

He shook his head to clear it. His ears were ringing from the deafening noise of the galloping horses, and his eyesight was fuzzy. The rope his arms were tied with was biting into his wrists, and his arms and legs were stiff with bumps and bruises. He could feel the sting of a new cut just above his left eye.

Carefully, he got to his feet, stumbling around on wobbling legs as he blinked his vision clear. A trickle of blood went into his eye. 'Something sharp,' he said to himself. 'Must find something sharp.'

Near to where he had thrown himself, a hideously twisted oak grew out of the embankment. The tree was scarred and cracked, full of wriggling bugs and unpleasant crawling things, and its massive roots burrowed through the earth, occasionally breaking up through the ground in brown coils. Caught among those roots, as though the tree was holding it for Nimbus, was a broken fragment of a sword: a rusting shard of metal from a weapon that had been shattered many years ago.

Nimbus staggered over to the tree and cut his bonds on the metal fragment excitedly.

'Thank you,' he shouted to the great oak, before heading off to the ruins.

As he approached, he could see the soldiers were circling Cumulo, hacking at him with their swords. The blades were clashing against the dragon's scales, and each ringing blow sent a shiver of revulsion trembling through Nimbus's body.

'Cumulo,' he shouted. 'Cumulo, are you okay?'

Cumulo, who appeared to be a deep shade of red in the lazy light of the early afternoon, bellowed furiously. His roar caused one of the horses to rear up, throwing its rider. The rider fell with a clatter of armour and his helmet bounced off across the rocks. He crawled away as quickly as he could.

Cumulo swung his tail around, knocking a second soldier out of his saddle.

'Oh no,' Nimbus winced. 'No, Cumulo. Don't hurt them. If

you hurt them, they'll have no choice but to kill you.'

The other soldiers, led by Captain Obsidian, were still darting around Cumulo, stinging him with their swords every chance they had.

Cumulo screamed, lashing out with his claws and snapping with his teeth. The colour of his scales changed from red to dark purple to green to white. Smoke began to pour from his nostrils.

Nimbus stumbled against a massive piece of masonry. 'Cumulo,' he panted. 'Cumulo, please don't fight them.'

'Why are they hurting me?' Cumulo snarled.

'They think you've done something bad,' Nimbus said, and at that moment he couldn't remember a time when he had ever felt so guilty and useless.

'But I haven't done anything.'

The two dismounted soldiers had found their horses and were preparing for a second attack.

'I'm sorry Cumulo,' Nimbus said. 'This is all may fault.'

'It doesn't matter whose fault it is.' Cumulo snapped at Obsidian, who had got just a bit too close to his toothy end. 'All that matters is getting you out of here. I'll keep them busy.'

Nimbus shook his head. 'No. You don't understand. I've seen it. I've seen the bad magic. It's another dragon. I can't fight it without you.'

Cumulo laughed. White smoke came out of his nose. 'I am just a dragon, Nim. But you are a Wing Warrior. You are the one who will face the magic. You are the hero.'

Nimbus wiped the tears from his eyes. 'I can't leave you here with these men.'

'If you are captured, we are all lost. I cannot fight the magic without you.'

'But...'

'Run, Nim. Please.'

Obsidian turned, waving his sword in the air. 'Get the boy,' he shouted.

One of the soldiers dragged on his reins, turning his horse to run Nimbus down.

Smoke continued to belch from Cumulo's nostrils. His scales turned blood red. 'Go,' he roared, so loud that even Nimbus was afraid. 'Go now, or they will kill us both.'

Nimbus didn't stop around after that; he turned and ran, feeling more like a coward with every step that took him farther from the battle.

He did not look back when he heard Captain Obsidian scream at his men to charge. He did not even look back when the air started to crackle, and a searing blast of heat roared out from the ruins.

He put his head down and kept running.

CHAPTER NINETEEN

When the sun had finally set, and the sky had turned from gold, to red, to purple, and finally to black, Nimbus emerged from his hiding place among the roots of the old oak tree under the embankment.

The world was full of shadows, but none so dark as the one that was cast over his heart as he headed back to the ruins.

He was aching and bruised, but those little physical hurts paled into insignificance compared to the hurt he felt when he closed his eyes and imagined heaps of injured soldiers, or one dead dragon with Obsidian's sword stuck in its belly.

He held his breath as he moved among the stones, expecting the worst.

The ruins were deadly quiet, glistening in the starlight.

Empty.

He stopped on the spot where he had last seen Cumulo. The ground was blackened and scorched, as if from a terrible burst of fire. The surrounding stones and bricks were similarly charred. The unpleasant smell of burning was everywhere.

'Oh no,' Nimbus said, as he walked around the remains of the battle ground. 'Oh, Cumulo. What have you done?'

There were broken bits of sword and armour on the ground. The swords were no longer shining; the armour was no longer silver–white. Everything was covered in a fine layer of ash. There was no sign of the soldiers anywhere, and no sign of Cumulo. It was almost as if everyone had been burned away completely.

Nimbus put his head in his hands. He was too tired and cold and scared to stop himself from crying, and within moments the tears were streaming down his face. Giant sobs shook through his chest uncontrollably.

He had ruined everything. He should have tried harder to convince Obsidian that Cumulo was innocent. He should have stuck around rather than running away like a coward. He should have done so many things differently to the way he had.

Cumulo had believed Nimbus was a hero, and Nimbus had let him down.

'Is there really time for that, Soldier?' a voice asked, from somewhere over by the shattered remains of the watchtower.

Nimbus looked up. There was nobody there. 'Hello?' he said.

'They took him, you know?'

Nimbus couldn't see anybody, but there could have been any number of people hiding in the darkness beyond the tower doorway. 'Who are you?' he said.

Laughter echoed around the ruins. 'I think you really mean where am I, don't you?'

'Okay, where are you?'

'I'm right here.'

'I can't see you.'

'I get that a lot.'

'Why can't I see you?'

'Because you're not looking hard enough.'

Nimbus stuck his head through the tower doorway. There was nothing inside except the first three steps of a broken spiral staircase that led nowhere. 'Hello?' he said.

'Hello.'

The voice was so close to his ear, Nimbus nearly jumped clean out of his skin. His heart raced as he backed away from the door. He still couldn't see anyone.

'Are you invisible?' he asked.

The bodiless voice chuckled. 'I guess I am to you.'

'Why?'

'Because you don't believe enough. Now your friend... he could see me just fine.'

'My friend?'

'The dragon. I would have thought, with a friend like that, you would have been able to see me too.'

Nimbus peered back inside the tower, squinting hard. There was definitely nobody in there, but the air seemed a little bit thicker just by the stairs, like it wasn't quite as see–through as air really should be. 'Are you sat on the stairs?' he asked.

'Actually, I am.'

'Why can't I see you?'

'I told you, you don't believe enough.'

'I don't believe enough in what?'

'Gosh, I don't know. Life, I suppose. You don't believe enough in magic. And you certainly don't believe enough in yourself. I bet you don't even believe in ghosts, do you?'

'Of course not.'

'And yet, here you are talking to one.'

'You're not a ghost.'

'And that's my point.'

'If you were really a ghost, I'd be more afraid of you.'

'What makes you think that?'

'Because ghosts are supposed to be scary.'

'That's a pretty broad generalisation, especially from someone who doesn't even believe in ghosts.'

Nimbus sat on a rock and kicked his heels in the dirt. 'It's not easy to believe,' he said. 'Especially not when you have to believe the kinds of things I'm being asked to believe.'

'And what is it, exactly, you are being asked to believe?'

Nimbus wiped his nose with the back of his hand. 'I'm being asked to believe I'm a hero.'

'Oh, well no–one believes they're a hero. But that doesn't mean they're not heroic, does it?'

'Some hero I turned out to be. I let the dark magic destroy Flint Lock. I got arrested for stealing the mayor's horse. My sister was taken away by soldiers. Cumulo's gone. And now there's all this... I don't know what happened to the people here, but it looks like they got all burned up, and if that's true, then Cumulo's as bad as the other dragon.'

'Well, that's something, isn't it? You're not prepared to believe in me, or you, but you're prepared to believe your dragon friend did something as terrible as burning up those soldiers. If you ask me, you believe in all the wrong things.'

Nimbus sniffed. 'Do you know Cumulo?'

'We were having a nice chat before all the fighting started. I suppose I won't see him again. Not now they've taken him away.'

'Who?'

'The soldiers.'

'But, I thought...'

'I know very well what you thought, and you should be ashamed for thinking it.'

'But...'

'But, nothing. That dragon kept those knights busy just long enough for you to escape, then he surrendered.'

Nimbus felt fresh tears welling up in his eyes. 'Poor Cumulo.'

'Indeed, poor Cumulo. He was in a real situation, and no doubt about it. He was so angry he accidentally went and breathed fire all over the place.'

'Did he hurt anyone?'

'No. But that was when he realised he might, so he let them win. He's very brave.'

'He is.'

'And he believes in you. From what I can see, that would be the bravest thing of all.'

'You don't understand. I'm lost without him. I don't know what to do.'

'You're going to do exactly what you need to do, exactly what he would do in your situation.'

'And what's that?'

'Do I really need to tell you?'

Nimbus drew a deep breath. The air was still hot and smelled of baked earth. 'I'm going to rescue him,' he said. 'I don't know how, but I'm going to rescue him.'

'Spoken like a true hero.'

Nimbus lowered his head and closed his eyes. He could feel the blood thumping in his ears. The shadow of his destiny loomed over him: a tragic curse he couldn't outrun no matter how much he wished to. 'I don't think I can do this on my own.'

'But you aren't on your own, are you?'

'I'm the only one here.'

'Not strictly true. Your dragon friend hid the armour here.'

For just the briefest moment Nimbus thought he could see the shimmering silhouette of a man sitting on the stairs. 'The armour?' he said, in a barely audible voice.

'It's enchanted armour, isn't it? Blessed with the knowledge of the Wing Warriors. If you wear that armour, then you are no longer one small boy, you are an army. When you fight in that armour, the ancient spirits of those who came before will fight with you.'

'The armour is too big for me.'

'Then grow into it.'

Nimbus thought for a moment. He was just a boy, not particularly brave or clever or strong. Certainly nothing at all like his father, and not even anything like Tidal. How was he supposed to wear the armour of a Wing Warrior? How was he supposed to find and rescue Cumulo?

Eventually, he stood. 'What's your name?' he asked.

'Captain Spectre of the seventy–third archers regiment, master of the watchtower,' the voice said, proudly.

'Well, Captain Spectre. I'm out of time and options. I have to rescue my friend, and that means I need to be prepared. Where did he hide the armour?'

'In the storehouse, with the sword.'

Nimbus smiled wearily and trudged over to the wrecked remains of the storehouse with his shoulders hunched up around his ears.

'Good luck,' Captain Spectre shouted, and then Nimbus was perfectly alone.

It was darker in the storehouse than it was outside, but Nimbus had no trouble finding the Wing Warrior sword; the blade shone in the gloom as though the light of a flickering candle had been trapped inside. The armour was piled up in the corner, looking very heavy and not at all like something comfortable to wear.

Nimbus sat down.

The light from the sword reflected on the armour, making the shapes of stern faces in its polished surfaces.

Blessed with the knowledge of the Wing Warriors, Spectre had said. Ancient spirits.

The sword shone brighter.

Nimbus picked it up.

Suddenly there was a brilliant flash: A painful explosion inside his head. The world around him stuttered, swam out of focus, and then melted away into blackness completely.

For a moment he was blind and deaf, and he was seized by panic at the thought of being trapped in silent darkness for the rest of his life; but the fear lasted for only a second, and then he was overcome with a sense of unearthly calm and weightlessness. He was floating in a vast ocean far from everything and everyone he knew. Nothing could touch him here.

Nothing could hurt him.

Slowly, as if he was learning to use his eyes for the first time, images began to form out of the darkness. He realised he wasn't blind at all. He could actually see farther than he had ever been able to see before.

He could see across oceans, deserts, forests, and mountains. He could see across the whole land, down inside caves, and up to the tip of the tallest towers. He could even see across time.

For just a second he was everywhere and nowhere, part of the past, the present, the future, and he felt the urge to throw up. He closed his eyes, clenched his fists, and held his breath. The sensation of needing to vomit passed, and when he opened his eyes again, he could see his father.

'Dad?'

His father was moving silently through a dark cavern, with a sword in one hand and a spear in the other. He looked powerful and heroic, and not at all like the miller Nimbus had always thought him to be. The stale air was full of the terrible high–pitched giggling of goblins, and the nasty scuttling of their little feet.

'Dad?'

His father did not look up.

'Dad, there are goblins here. We have to get out.'

'Wait there,' Cloud said.

'Why?' Nimbus asked, before realising his father was not speaking to him at all, but was actually talking to three soldiers who were cowering a short distance behind him.

'They've realised we're not in the dungeon any more,' one of the soldiers whispered. 'They know we've been rescued.'

'They won't rest until they've hunted us down,' Cloud said. 'You're all too weak and hungry to fight. Go on ahead, and I'll hold them off for as long as I can.'

'There are hundreds of them.'

'I know.'

'You'll be eaten.'

'I appreciate the vote of confidence. Now go. Quickly.'

The soldiers scampered off. The creepy, echoing shrieks of the goblins were getting louder.

'Dad?' Nimbus said, his chest tightening with panic at the thought of an untidy horde of goblin warriors seething through the tunnels towards them. 'Dad, I'm scared.'

Still his father would not respond to his calls. Instead, a huge shape lumbered out of the darkness; a massive bulk of glimmering scales and claws. Nimbus was caught off guard by the sudden appearance of the menacing form, and screamed, raising his sword defensively.

'It's good to see you too,' the gigantic thing said.

'Cumulo!' Nimbus cried. 'Cumulo, you're okay!'

'I see you found the sword.'

'What happened? I picked it up, and now I'm here. And why are you here?' He looked at his father, who was pressed with his back to the cavern wall, waiting for the approaching goblins. 'And why is my dad here? What's going on?'

Cumulo grinned, and licked his nostrils with a flick of his lizard–like tongue. 'Actually, I'm not here, and neither are you. Your father isn't here either, although he is there.'

'That doesn't make any sense.'

'It is the power of the sword. When it needs to show you something, it will.'

'So where am I?'

'I should imagine you are still sitting in the storehouse where I hid the armour.'

'And where are you?'

'I'm in a dungeon in Crystal Shine. I've been locked up.'

'And my dad?'

'He's in the goblin stronghold. He went to rescue those soldiers you just saw.'

'But...'

'I know it's all a bit confusing. I don't really understand it myself. I only know what my memories tell me, and you know what they're like. But I know the sword you carry is more than just a weapon. The Wing Warriors were guardians, protectors of this whole land, and it was important for them to know of any danger. They created magical swords that would, on occasion, grant those who carried them infinite vision. The power to see all that has happened, all that is happening, and sometimes even the things yet to happen.'

'So, the reason Dad can't hear me is because we aren't in the same place?'

'You're sitting in a ruined storehouse, and he's miles away under the ground. You can see this stronghold, as clearly as if you were standing in it, but you aren't really here.'

'But you aren't here either, and you can hear me.'

'Oh, that's different. I'm a dragon.'

'Oh right.' Nimbus scratched his head. 'You know, that isn't really an explanation.'

'I know.'

The chattering of goblins was suddenly deafening, and the tiny stick creatures swelled out of the gloom, an ocean wave of pointy arms and legs. Nimbus's father sprang at them, swinging his sword, and the goblins swarmed all over him. There was a terrible screaming, and a gnashing of teeth.

'Can't I help him?' Nimbus asked.

'I'm afraid not. The power of infinite vision is a blessing and a curse. While you can see and hear that which is far away, you have no power to intervene.'

'So why am I being shown this, if I can't do anything?'

'Because vision is also a riddle. I do not believe the sword intends for you to help your father.'

'Then what does it intend?'

'Think about it, Nim. How many great warriors are there in your village?'

'Our garrison is twelve strong.'

'But how many of those men are great?'

'I don't know. Obsidian was brave enough to fight you, and I always used to think he was a good person before he broke his promise to me and hurt you. I don't know if that makes him great, though.'

'Assume he is.'

'Okay then. Captain Obsidian is a great warrior.'

'And where is he?'

'With you.'

'Correct. With a party of his men. Men who should be protecting your village.'

'And my dad... I didn't know it, but my dad is a soldier too.' He could still hear the clanging of his father's sword, even though he could no longer see him beneath the filthy mass of goblin bodies. 'And he's trying to rescue three more of our soldiers.'

'So there's your riddle, Nim.'

'Is the sword telling me my village is in danger?'

'That would be my guess.'

'Is the other dragon coming to Landmark?'

'It's looking for you. It seems a logical place to start.'

'Right.' Nimbus took one last look at his father struggling through the tightly–packed crowd of goblins. 'I'm coming to rescue you, Cumulo. My dad is going to have to look after himself.' A spindly goblin body went hurtling through the air, slamming into the cavern wall with a wet thud. 'I think he'll be okay.'

'There's no time to come for me,' Cumulo said.

'But I need your help.'

'There's no time, Nim. Get to your village. Hurry.'

Cumulo swam out of focus, fading back into the darkness like a reflection breaking apart on the surface of a disturbed lake. Then the cavern, Cloud, and all of the goblins, shimmered and vanished.

Nimbus was sitting in the storehouse.

Alone.

He looked at the Wing Warrior sword. The flickering candlelight inside the blade had died, and now all he could see was his terrified eyes reflected there.

The black dragon, the evil magic, had destroyed Flint Lock in a single night. What chance did his little village have?

CHAPTER TWENTY

The morning after she was returned to her mother by soldiers from the village garrison, Glass woke early and sat on the front porch of her house. Only the first few flickers of sunlight could be seen on the horizon, and the quiet street was cold and gloomy.

There was nobody else around; no birds in the sky. There was just her, alone in a sleepy world.

In truth, she had hardly slept. She had sat up through most of the night waiting for her mother to stop crying, and waiting for her father and Nimbus to come home.

She had waited, and waited.

But Nimbus didn't come home, and neither did her father.

Her mother only stopped crying when she finally drifted off to sleep in a rocking chair by the stove.

Glass folded her arms around her knees. Her head sank. She was really tired, but every time she closed her eyes she remembered all those soldiers chasing her, and then she started shaking so badly there was no way she could sleep.

Her heart beat fast every time she thought of how afraid she had been, and how brave Nimbus had been.

The mayor had been happy to get Onyx back, but he had been angry too. He had shouted at Glass, and he had said Nimbus should be locked away for the rest of his natural life. Glass said she was sorry, but the mayor said that wasn't good enough.

She sucked her teeth, and blinked tears from her eyes. Why wasn't saying sorry good enough?

What was good enough?

She rested her head on her arm, and watched the sky getting

lighter as the sun got higher. Slowly, people began to come out of other houses in the street. Night became day, and the village woke up.

Sky and Tidal appeared at the end of the street. They were walking side by side, and Glass wasn't sure why but she thought Nimbus might not like it if he saw the two of them so close together. She waved, but they were deep in conversation and didn't notice her until they were only a short distance away.

'Hello,' Sky said, sitting next to her. 'We stopped by yesterday, looking for you and Nim. Your mum said you were out. She looked concerned. I think she may have been crying.'

'She's been doing that a lot recently.'

'Where were you?'

'Different places at different times.'

Tidal shielded his eyes from the sun with one hand. 'You two weren't off having an adventure without us, were you?'

'Nimbus wanted to go to Flint Lock.'

'Why?'

Glass shrugged. 'Something happened, and Nimbus wanted to see what it was. People were hurt and sick. It was frightening.'

'We haven't heard any news from Flint Lock,' Tidal laughed. 'You're making it up.'

'No. It's true. Bad things happened. A sick soldier was taken in at the village hall. That's why we took the horse.'

'Horse?' Tidal asked.

'Soldier?' Sky added.

'Yeah. Daddy found a soldier from the fort.'

'Horse?' Tidal repeated.

'What happened to this soldier?' Sky asked.

'I don't know,' Glass said. 'He was really ill. I thought everybody in the village would have heard about it.'

'We haven't heard a thing. With all the panic after the tidal wave the other day, maybe the mayor is trying to keep it quiet,' Sky said.

'Excuse me,' Tidal said, impatiently. 'What horse?'

Glass looked at him. Her eyes were wet with the tears she was trying so hard not to cry. 'We took the mayor's horse.'

'You did what?' he said.

'We took the mayor's horse. We needed to get to the fort, to find out what had happened to this soldier.'

'So you stole a horse?'

'No, we borrowed it.'

'And of all the horses, you chose to steal the mayor's?'

'We borrowed it.'

'What were you thinking?'

'We needed a horse, and Onyx is the fastest horse in the village. It made sense.'

'Sense? None of this makes a jot of sense. Where's Nim now?'

'He's...' Glass's tiny hands started shaking, and her shoulders trembled. 'He was arrested by the village soldiers. They're going to lock him up.'

Sky gasped. 'No. They wouldn't. He's just a boy. He can't be locked up.'

'The mayor wants to lock him up forever.'

'He can't do that.'

'He's the mayor,' Tidal said. 'He can do whatever he wants.'

'Be quiet,' Sky hissed, putting her arm around Glass and hugging her tightly. 'I'm sure they'll let Nim go just as soon as he explains what you were doing.' She looked closely at Glass, who was staring at the ground and chewing her bottom lip. 'What were you doing?'

'Somebody had to go to the fort to see what had happened. Daddy couldn't because he was in the Forbidden Woods rescuing the soldiers from the goblins.'

'Goblins?' Tidal snorted. 'Goblins? There aren't any goblins, Glass. Have you cracked?'

'Nim said there were goblins. In the woods.'

'Rubbish.'

'They captured the soldiers and they were going to eat them. Daddy went to save them all.'

'Your dad works in a mill.'

'I know that.'

'You're not making any sense,' Sky said, stroking Glass's hair. 'Why don't you start at the very beginning?'

Glass sniffed, and wiped her nose. 'I don't know where the beginning is. But Flint Lock has been destroyed. Everyone in it is sick. And there was a monster in the sky. Nim seemed to know what it was, and... Nim has a dragon.'

'A what?'

'A dragon. He found it in the cave in the woods.'

Tidal folded his arms. 'Well I find that very hard to believe.'

Suddenly a shadow passed across the sun, and a cold wind whistled up the street. The sickly smell of poison filled the air. 'Look,' Glass screamed, pointing. 'Look!'

There was a terrible sound, like a clap of thunder, and a massive, black creature fell out of the sky, landing with an echoing boom at the end of the street in a cloud of smoke and dust. For a second the whole world seemed to be in the shadow of the monster and its outstretched wings, then the wings snapped closed on the monster's spiky back.

'Is that a dragon?' Tidal whimpered.

'I think so,' Sky said.

'And Nim has a dragon like that?'

'No,' Glass said. 'From what he told me, it's nothing at all like that.'

The dragon sat where it had landed, its large head swaying backwards and forwards. It was looking for something, or someone. Smog billowed from the nostrils of its cruel snout, almost completely obscuring its terrifying red eyes. Anything the smog touched went black and died.

'Can we go now?' Glass asked, tugging on Sky's sleeve.

As she spoke, the dragon swung around to look straight at her. Its eyes narrowed, and a purple tongue flicked out of its sharp mouth.

'I think it sees us,' Sky said, getting to her feet. 'Let's go inside the house.'

'I would,' Tidal said. 'But I can't feel my legs any more.'

'You aren't scared, are you?' Sky asked.

'Me? No. I'm absolutely terrified.' He grinned in an attempt to appear braver, but the colour had drained from his face, and it was obvious that "terrified" didn't even begin to describe the utter dread he felt at facing this monstrous creature.

The dragon heaved its huge body forward with muscular forearms. Claws as sharp as steel dug into the ground with each footstep, and the air seemed to tremble with fear.

The smoke belching out of the dragon's mouth and nose began to seep through the whole village, shrivelling gardens and farmland. Even the stone walls of houses were stained black.

Sky shook Tidal's arm. 'Come on,' she insisted. 'We really have to get inside the house.'

'I don't think Glass's house is big enough to stop that thing from getting in if it wants to,' Tidal said, unable to tear his gaze away from the approaching menace.

'He's right,' Glass said. 'That's the thing from the fort. That's the thing that made everyone sick.'

The dragon drew closer. Its tongue flickered, tasting the children's terror. 'You,' it hissed. 'You three.'

Tidal nearly fell over out of shock. His heart was beating so fast it hurt. 'Us?'

'Where is he? Where is the Wing Warrior?'

The three children backed away, pressing themselves against the front door of the house. The dragon's head was only a few feet away. Plants in the garden choked and crumbled to dust.

'We don't know any Wing Warriors,' Tidal said.

'Oh,' the dragon hissed. 'If that's so, then tell me, what use is there in me letting you live?'

Tidal's legs were lead blocks, anchoring him to the ground. He wanted to run, wanted to scream; but he couldn't. He knew he had to do something to save the girls, but what could he do? He was just a boy, and this was a monster. 'Well... Actually...' he stuttered. 'That is, I mean to say...'

The dragon opened its mouth wide. Its serrated teeth glistened wetly.

'Wait,' Glass shouted.

The dragon looked at her. 'Yes?'

'I know where the Wing Warrior is.'

'Where?'

Glass pointed to the end of the street. There, shrouded in the black dragon fog, was a knight in a suit of brilliant red armour. The sword the knight was clenching awkwardly in both hands looked much too big to be easily usable, and the way the plates of armour hung on him suggested he was not quite as big on the inside as he was on the outside.

The dragon turned around. 'Well, well, well. It is true. The dragon knights live on.'

'Certainly looks that way,' the knight said, his voice muffled from inside his helmet as he walked down the street.

'Aren't you missing something?'

'You mean a dragon? I don't need a dragon to deal with an overgrown lizard like you.'

The dragon rose up to its tree–toppling height. 'I am no overgrown lizard. I am Sorrow.'

'Nice name. It suits you.'

The dragon bellowed and stretched out its wings. Thick clouds of poisonous breath swirled out and around them. 'You dare mock me? I am Sorrow!'

'So you said.'

'I am Madam Sorrow. I am the destruction of all dragons, and the bloody death of all Wing Warriors. I am the shadow of

Kevin Outlaw

disease and famine and misery. I am the cold grip of despair.'

The knight took a tighter grip on his sword. 'I'm going to go out on a limb and suggest you don't have many friends. Am I right?'

Sorrow lowered herself down, and stuck out her neck so her head was level with the knight's. 'Aren't you afraid of me, Little Man?'

'Aren't you afraid of me?'

'I think you are terrified. Too terrified to even move. I see through you, Little Man. You may wear the armour, but it doesn't suit you. You're no Wing Warrior.'

'I am a Wing Warrior,' the knight said, defiantly. 'I'm the... uh... I'm the best Wing Warrior that ever lived.'

Sorrow tilted her head. She could not see the knight's face through the grilled visor of his helmet, but as she drew nearer she could just make out the frightened glimmer of young eyes. A child's eyes. 'You are not even a man,' she chuckled. 'You are just a boy. A foolish boy. Trying to be a hero.'

The knight lashed out suddenly, unexpectedly, and the Wing Warrior sword clanged against the hard, horny part of Sorrow's snout. She reeled, momentarily stunned by the attack. The sword blade vibrated so violently in the knight's hand he lost all sensation in his arms. His fingers went numb, and the sword fell to the ground.

'He's done for now,' Tidal said.

'We have to do something,' Glass said. 'He'll be eaten all up if we don't help.'

'And how do you suggest we fight that thing? Call it names? Throw stones?'

'Why not?' Glass said.

Sorrow looked at the knight as he scrabbled to pick up his sword. 'You little brat,' she growled, rubbing her nose. 'That nearly hurt. Nobody has hurt me for hundreds of years.'

The knight grabbed the handle of the sword, and looked up

to see one of Sorrow's great claws swinging towards him. He had just enough time to brace himself for the impact, and then he was flying through the air with his arms flailing wildly. He landed on his back in the dirt with all his senses jumbled.

'Not even a challenge,' Sorrow wheezed, as she loomed over him menacingly. 'Barely worth the breath it will take to kill you.'

The knight blinked, tried to get to his feet, but Sorrow had already opened her mouth wide. Stinking smoke gushed out all over him.

Being hit by the smoke was like being hit by the sudden, violent urge to be sick. The knight's head started spinning, his arms and legs turned to stone; and within just a few seconds he had fallen off the edge of the universe, down through the glimmering white–hot light of consciousness, into the black waves of oblivion below.

'And now,' Sorrow said, 'a little snack, I think.'

She craned her head forwards, but before she had a chance to take her first bite out of the unconscious Wing Warrior, a sharp stone bounced off the side of her head. She looked around as another three stones bounced and clacked on her scaly chest and legs.

'I think we got its attention,' Tidal said.

'Shut up,' Sky said. 'Just keep throwing stones.'

'And what, exactly, are we hoping to achieve?' Tidal asked.

'I'll let you know when I figure it out.'

'What's this?' Sorrow hissed, ignoring the stones as they ricocheted off her body. 'More stupidity?'

'Leave him alone,' Glass said, bravely. 'You get on out of here.'

Sorrow sighed, a deep and troubled sigh. 'Do you really want to get eaten as well, Little Girl?'

'If anyone is going to get eaten, it's you,' Tidal shouted. Sorrow frowned in puzzlement. Tidal glanced at Sky. 'That didn't make any sense, did it?'

Sky shook her head.

'So, it is stupidity then,' Sorrow said. 'What were you thinking you were going to do? Defeat me by throwing stones? Don't you understand anything? Whole armies have fired ten thousand arrows at me, and I barely even noticed. Eleven of the great dragons breathed their foul breath on me, and yet I did not fall. I cannot be defeated, and I cannot die. But you... You can be squashed like bugs.'

Sorrow paced nearer, and each footstep shook tiles from the roofs of nearby houses. Her thick tail flicked, crashing into the side of a house and knocking it completely flat.

'Actually,' Sky said, trying to keep her voice level despite the fact she was screaming on the inside. 'We weren't trying to defeat you.'

'That's right,' Tidal added. 'We were just trying to distract you.'

'Distract me from what?' Sorrow said.

'From him,' Sky said.

Sorrow looked behind her. The Wing Warrior sword was no longer on the ground. Instead, it was in the hands of a wide–shouldered man with a serious gleam in his serious eyes.

'You,' Sorrow said.

'Cloud,' Tidal gasped.

'Daddy,' Glass squealed.

'Daddy?' Sorrow glanced from the man to the girl. 'How very interesting.'

'Get inside the house, kids,' Cloud said, as he began to circle around the unbelievably large bulk of the dragon. 'There's nothing more you can do here.'

The children didn't need any encouragement, and they dashed off. Glass's mother met them on the porch, hurrying them inside and bolting the door.

Cloud took the sword in both hands. 'You got away from me once, Sorrow. It won't happen again.'

'Things were different last time,' Sorrow said. There was laughter in her evil, rattlesnake tone. 'Last time there were eleven dragons, and twelve Wing Warriors. Now, there is just you. And you are old. Much older than you were.'

Without another word, the dragon rushed forwards, a speeding flurry of snapping teeth and rending claws, all wrapped in thickening curls of black mist.

Cloud dropped to one knee, closed his eyes tight, and plunged the blade of the Wing Warrior sword into the earth. There was an explosion of brilliant white light that completely enveloped him, and he heard the scream of Sorrow as she was caught in the blast.

He rose, dragging the sword out of the ground. Sorrow had backed away, and her cloud of black smoke had all but vanished, burned away by the magic of the sword.

'You never learn, do you?' Cloud said.

'You remember how to use the sword, Old Man. Perhaps you should have taught the boy before he came here pretending to be of the order of the Wing Warriors.'

Cloud licked his lips. 'You have one chance to leave, Sorrow. One chance, or I swear I will cut you down where you stand.'

'What is this? Are you giving me a chance to redeem myself... My Lord?' The words were spat as though they were a curse. 'Do you think there is any redemption for me?'

'Leave this village,' Cloud said, sternly.

Sorrow nodded. 'I will leave, for now. But I will be back, and I will be coming back for you.'

'I know.'

'You can't stop it. A war is coming. Your defences are destroyed. It is inevitable.'

Sorrow soared into the sky. Cloud watched her until she was just a speck in the western skyline, then he ran to the side of the fallen knight.

He knelt, removing the knight's helmet with trembling hands.

As he did so, his breath caught in his throat. It was just as he had feared.

'Nimbus?' he said, clutching the body to him. 'My boy. What have you done?'

Nimbus's eyes opened. 'Dad?' he whispered.

'I tried to protect you, Son. I pretended I didn't know about the dragons, or anything else. I didn't want to lie, but it was too dangerous. I never wanted you to find out the truth.'

'Dad, I'm sorry. The writing on the sword said "look to the clouds." I thought that meant it was me. I thought I was the last Wing Warrior, but I'm not.' Nimbus coughed painfully. His vision began to fade again until his father was just a faceless silhouette in a sombre grey world. 'It's you, Dad. You did what I couldn't. You defeated the dragon. You are the last of the Wing Warriors.'

Nimbus's eyes rolled back into his head, and he slumped against his father's chest.

'No,' Cloud said, stroking his son's hair. 'Not the last.'

CHAPTER TWENTY-ONE

The sun was hanging low in the white and blue patchwork sky, gleaming brightly but without heat, as Cloud carried his son into the house.

For a moment it was as if the whole world was breathless, silently waiting for the return of the dragon.

Strata and the children watched as Cloud removed Nimbus from the Wing Warrior armour, and then laid him out on his bed with the Wing Warrior sword close to his right hand. Nimbus's face was deathly white except for black and blue marks around his mouth and eyes. His breathing was shallow, almost not breathing at all.

'Fetch water,' Cloud said, and Strata disappeared into the kitchen. 'Blankets.' Sky dashed off. 'And another pillow.'

Glass didn't move. She was staring quietly at her big brother as if she barely knew who he was.

'A pillow, Glass,' Cloud said.

'He's a Wing Warrior,' she said.

'Glass, we have to make him comfortable. We need a pillow.'

She nodded slowly and left the room.

'I don't understand this,' Tidal said. 'What was he doing? Why was he in that armour?'

'I don't know,' Cloud said.

'Did you know he had that sword?'

Cloud touched Nimbus's frozen hand. Said nothing.

'Cloud?' Tidal said. 'Sir?'

'He looks like he's sleeping. I don't think I will ever sleep again.'

'Sir?'

'We need more air in here,' Cloud muttered, opening the

window shutters. 'Good, clean air.'

'Sir?'

'What?'

'Did you know he had that sword?'

'No.'

'This is ridiculous. Nimbus isn't a knight. Nimbus isn't a hero. Nimbus is just a dumb kid.'

Cloud nodded. 'Yes. My son is a dumb kid.'

'Where did he get a sword from?'

'A secret place, under the ground. Somewhere he shouldn't have been.'

'The cave in the woods?'

'I had always thought the stories about goblins would be enough to protect the sword. I didn't reckon on you children being so determined to break the rules.'

'You knew about this sword?'

'I did.'

'And the armour?'

'Yes.'

'And Nim? Did you know he was going to play act being the big hero today?'

Cloud shot Tidal a glance that was so angry it would have made Sorrow herself cower in fear. 'Of course I didn't know he was going to do this.'

'Of course. I didn't mean to... It's just... What made him think he could stand up to that creature?'

'He must have had his reasons.'

'Nim's scared of his own shadow.'

'Maybe that's why he did it.'

'You should be glad,' Sky said, returning with an armful of blankets. 'We'd all be dead if it wasn't for Nim turning up like that.'

'Glad?' Tidal said. 'Glad? This is possibly the dumbest thing he's ever done, and I'm supposed to be glad?'

'Yes.'

'This is so stupid.' Tidal barged past her, heading outside.

'What's wrong with him?' Sky asked, handing the blankets to Cloud.

'He's angry,' Cloud said.

'About what?'

'About everything.'

Strata and Glass returned with pillows and bowls of water. They were both looking drawn and thin; their eyes were red with tears.

Strata knelt by the bed and began to dab Nimbus's forehead with a cloth. Her hands were shaking and her bottom lip trembled.

Glass sat by Nimbus's feet, looking intently at his quiet face. Although she was perfectly still, somehow she gave the impression she was incredibly busy.

'What are you doing?' Sky asked her.

'I'm trying to make him open his eyes,' Glass whispered.

Nimbus was scared.

His mind was full of memories: Terrible, gnashing, biting, snarling, spitting, fuming memories. Memories so evil and powerful they burned like fire and destroyed all his thoughts of anything good.

The memories were of the black dragon looming over him, its wings spread wide to block out all light from the sun. Nimbus was sprawled on the ground with one arm raised to defend himself as clouds of smoky poison gushed into him, filling his body with stinging pain.

He coughed and gagged and told himself it was only a memory. But still he choked, and still his blocked lungs struggled for air, and still the panic inside him rose as he suffocated.

This was death.

Kevin Outlaw

'Open your eyes, Nim,' a small voice said.

Nimbus tried to scream, but no sound would come out of his mouth. The dragon bellowed furiously and flapped its mighty wings. It smelled of disease and death and dark earth. It smelled of the grave.

'Open your eyes, Nim,' the voice said. 'You have to open your eyes or something bad is going to happen.'

'Glass?' he wheezed. 'Is that you?'

'Yes, it's me.'

'Where are you? I can't see you.'

'There's no time to explain. You have to open your eyes.'

'They're open.'

'No, they're not. You just think they are. You're sleeping now.'

'I'm afraid.'

'It's the poison in you. Do you remember the soldiers at the fort? Do you remember how sick they all were?'

'The poison...' Nimbus tried to get to his feet, slipped, tried again. There was nowhere he could go that was not within the cold shadow of the dragon. 'The cloud makes everything sick. That's what happened at the fort. All the soldiers breathed in the dragon's smoke. I breathed it too.'

'You can't give up, Nim.'

'I don't know where I am. Show me how to get out of here.'

'Open your eyes. See for yourself.'

The dragon lunged at him with snapping teeth, but Nimbus felt that those teeth would not bite into his flesh and bone, they would bite deeper, into his spirit. He was afraid now, not for his life, but for whatever came after.

'Nimbus!' Glass screamed. 'The dragon didn't eat you. You're not dead!'

With all the will he could muster, Nimbus rolled to one side, and the black dragon's snout ploughed into the earth close to his right arm. A moment later, and he was on his feet.

'Please be strong,' Glass said, and with each of her words Nimbus felt new energy flooding into his shaking limbs. As long as Glass was with him, as long as he could hear her voice, he had nothing to fear.

He looked the dragon dead in the eye. 'You're going to have to do better than that,' he said.

The dragon recoiled slightly, but only slightly, and its nostrils flared.

Black smoke billowed around Nimbus, choking the light of the world, and leaving everything in perpetual night.

'As you wish,' the dragon said.

For a second, Nimbus's eyes flickered, and almost opened. Then they were still again.

'I can see the shadows,' Glass said, staring at him. 'He's almost invisible now.'

Sky touched Glass's hair. 'Is he going to be okay?' she asked Cloud.

'I can't say. I don't know how long he was exposed to the dragon's breath.' Cloud's voice was soft, and not at all like the voice of a man who had just fought a dragon.

'So it was a dragon then?'

'Not just a dragon. That was Madam Sorrow, disease and suffering made into flesh and scales.'

'It seems like she knows you.'

'She does. We met before, a very long time ago. I had hoped never to meet her again.'

'Why did she come here? What was she looking for?'

'I thought, perhaps, she might have been looking for me, but I was wrong.'

'She was here for Nimbus,' Glass said, quietly. 'He is a Wing Warrior now.'

'But there haven't been Wing Warriors for hundreds of years,'

Sky said.

Cloud looked out of the window. The street was busy with people, gossiping and crying, or rummaging through the rubble of the houses in search of their most prized possessions. 'There haven't been dragons for hundreds of years either,' he said. 'And I had always hoped I had done enough to make sure there would never be a time when they returned. It seems I have failed.'

'But you're just a miller, aren't you?' Sky asked.

Cloud glanced knowingly at Strata. 'You can disguise what you are, but you can't change it. I realise that now.'

'Now may be too late,' Strata muttered.

'I don't understand,' Sky said. 'Are you a miller or not?'

Cloud turned back to the window, his hard features concealed from everyone in the room. 'What I am, Sky, is very old. Very old and very foolish.'

'I'm going to get the doctor,' Strata said. Her words were perfectly calculated, not showing a single drop of the crippling emotions surging like crushing waves inside her.

'It won't do any good,' Cloud said.

Strata made fists with her hands. 'I'm going to do whatever I can to help my son. One of us has to.' At the doorway she stopped. 'You know, if you had told him...'

Cloud tensed. Strata walked out, her sentence unfinished. Glass watched her mother leaving, and then turned to her father, clearly expecting him to run out after her.

He didn't.

Sky touched Nimbus's cheek. His skin was ice cold.

'She's right,' Cloud said, gruffly. 'I always thought to protect him from all this. I told him the dragons weren't real, that there were no Wing Warriors. I had seen so many things, so many terrible wars, and I never wanted him to be a part of that. I thought, perhaps, he could live his life as a normal person. I was wrong. The Wing Warrior is in his blood, and it called to him just the same.'

'I don't understand any of this,' Sky said. 'Nimbus is a Wing Warrior? A dragon rider?'

Cloud bowed his head. 'Yes. He is a dragon rider, just like his father before him.'

'You? But that can't be possible. That would make you hundreds of years old.'

'I told you. I am very, very old.'

Sky stared at Cloud in disbelief for a long time. Glass stared too, battling with mixed up emotions that she couldn't even name. Her dad was a Wing Warrior. He was a hero, and her brother was too. That was exciting. That was incredible.

It was also terrifying.

The room was quiet.

'Must be something of a shock for you,' Cloud said, eventually. 'But all of the Wing Warriors were blessed with the same gift. The finest honour the dragons could bestow on us. The power to live forever.'

Sky pushed the hair back from Nimbus's face. 'Does this mean..?'

'No. Strata is a mortal, and that means Nimbus is mortal too. If he could spend years in the presence of dragons, like I did, then it would be different. But there are no good dragons left in the world. There is only Sorrow.'

'So Nimbus, Glass, Strata... They will grow old. But you won't.'

'That's right.'

'And Nimbus doesn't know about this?'

'Nimbus believes I am a miller, and nothing more. As does everybody else in this village. I thought it was for the best. Now I cannot believe that anything I have done since Sorrow was defeated has been for the best. The keep I built has fallen, and now my son...'

'He is still very strong,' Glass interrupted. 'I think he wants to open his eyes. That's a good thing, right? Wanting to open your eyes? And his breathing is better. I'm sure he's going to be okay.'

'I'm sure he is too,' Cloud said.

Glass climbed down from the bed, and took her father's hand. 'I don't think we can help Nim any more,' she said. 'We should go to find the dragon now.'

'No,' Cloud said, dismissively. 'That's not a good idea. We aren't ready to face Sorrow. I need more time.'

'No. Not her. The other dragon.'

Cloud crouched beside her. 'What other dragon?'

'Nim's dragon.'

'Nimbus has a dragon?'

'He found it in the woods.'

Cloud grabbed Glass's shoulders and gripped her in the same way that excitement now gripped him. 'You mean the dragon has hatched? It's grown?'

'I guess so.'

'Have you seen it?'

'No, but Nim told me about it. We were going to see it when we were arrested by soldiers.'

'You were arrested?'

'I think a lot has happened you need to catch up on,' Sky said.

'I think you're right.' Cloud looked at the sword lying by Nimbus's side. 'Would you kids go find Tidal, and bring him back here for me? I need a few minutes alone.'

The children filed out of the room, leaving Cloud with the motionless body of his son.

The blade of the Wing Warrior sword began to glow faintly.

It had been many years since Cloud had last used the power of infinite vision. The last time, he had seen a vision of the future. A terrible vision of dungeons and misery that he had no wish to see again.

But he had no other choice.

He took the sword, and immediately the world faded away to darkness. Then slowly, piece by piece, fragments of that which had happened, and that which would happen, or might happen, began to build around him like a giant jigsaw puzzle.

He could see valleys and woods, plains and mountains, castles and caves. Nations at war, cities crumbling, people crying, black shadows filling the skies.

And dungeons.

His stomach knotted. No, not this. He didn't want to see this. Not dungeons.

He tried to turn away, but he knew better than anyone that it was impossible not to see what the sword wished to show; and he could only watch as he drifted down endless corridors of prison cells.

Finally he stopped in front of a barred prison entrance.

He looked through the bars into the dungeon beyond. It was dank, cold, and almost completely filled by the massive bulk of a sleeping dragon.

Cloud's breath caught in his throat.

The dragon stirred and opened one lazy eye. 'Who are you?' he said.

'I am Cloud. Who are you?'

'I am Cumulo.'

'That's a fine name.'

The dragon blinked and yawned. 'You're a Wing Warrior,' he said, stretching as much as the cramped dungeon cell would allow.

'And you're a dragon.'

'I guess that means we have things to discuss.'

'I guess you're right.'

CHAPTER TWENTY-TWO

Tidal was sitting on the front porch, watching the people across the street as they picked through the remains of their house. Occasionally they would pull out a blanket or pot from the wreckage, and the simple delight of finding something that had not been completely ruined turned their tears of grief to tears of joy.

'What are you doing?' Sky asked, sitting beside him with Glass.

'Look at those people,' Tidal said. 'Just look at them. Their home has been destroyed, knocked down like a house of cards. The dragon did that without even realising. How can there be a creature in the world so evil it can ruin something without even noticing? Without even caring?'

'Are you okay?' Sky asked.

Tidal shook his head. 'I just didn't want to be in there any more. It was all a bit too much for me.'

'Then how do you think Nim feels? You should be there for him.'

'Why?'

'He's your friend.'

'He's a jerk.'

'Hey, that's my brother,' Glass said.

Tidal paused thoughtfully. They were right. Nimbus was his friend, and Nimbus was Glass's brother. Nimbus was part of their group. 'I'm sorry,' he said. 'I didn't mean that.'

But he did mean it. Nimbus was part of their group, but he had done this alone. He had snuck into the cave in the woods and found the armour and the sword. He had lied to them all when he said there was nothing down there.

He had wanted to do this by himself. Not as part of the group. He had wanted to pretend to be some kind of hero.

And that meant Nimbus was a jerk.

'What's wrong?' Sky pressed, putting her arm around him. 'Why so angry?'

Tidal shrugged. 'Nimbus turning up like that, dressed as a knight with a magic sword. He put his life on the line for us. He stood up to that monster.' He pressed his hands together to stop them shaking. 'He did that, and I didn't.'

'What are you talking about?' Sky said.

He smiled wistfully and shook his head. He couldn't explain to Sky how he was feeling. Not really. 'I'm older than he is,' he said, hopelessly.

'What's that got to do with it?'

'Nothing... Everything. I don't know.' He rested his chin on his hands. He had never felt like this before. He was bigger than Nim was; he was stronger and braver and faster. He was the one who was supposed to do all the impressive things. Nimbus was the stupid kid who got scared and needed to be rescued. It had always been that way.

It was always supposed to be that way.

'Nobody thinks anything less of you, Tide,' Sky said.

'Did I say I thought they did?' Tidal snapped.

'No. Of course. I just mean, if that's what you're mad about. You don't need to worry. You were really brave. You did what you could, and you threw stones the same as we did.'

'I don't care about that. What I care about is Nim lying to us. He went into the Forbidden Woods and found that armour, and he told us there was nothing there.'

'He must have had his reasons.'

'He's always known that he's weak and stupid, and he wanted to keep this all to himself.'

'Stop talking like that,' Glass said, angrily. 'You can't talk about my brother like that.'

'Your brother is a liar.'

'Shut up.'

'I won't shut up.' Tidal jumped to his feet. 'And I won't stay around here pampering him just because he's gone and got himself hurt. He's only got himself to blame.'

'Tidal?' Sky said. There was a pained look in her eyes. 'Why are you being like this?'

Inside, he was seething with anger and embarrassment. He had gone to the cave with Nim. He could have found the armour. He could have been the Wing Warrior and fought the dragon. Maybe that would have meant that he was the one lying in that bed with a serious injury, but even that would be better than standing here as a useless coward.

'Tidal?'

'I just...' Words failed him, and he choked back a sob before trying again. 'I just wanted to save you, Sky. That's all.'

For a second longer he stood there, wide–eyed and awkward, then he turned and ran off down the street, heading towards the beach and the crushed remains of the pier.

'I don't understand boys,' Glass said.

Sky shook her head helplessly. 'I don't understand boys either, but I'm beginning to think I understand Tidal a little better. Better than I understand your brother, anyway.'

'Nim isn't as complicated as you think he is.'

'After all this, I don't agree.' She watched Tidal until he disappeared from view at the end of the street.

'Are you going to go after him?' Glass asked.

'No. I'll let him cool off for a bit.'

'I didn't mean Tidal.' A strange look, like a black storm cloud, passed momentarily across Glass's features. Then it was gone, and she smiled her widest smile. 'Come on,' she said. 'Let's go and tell my daddy Tidal has run off.'

***

Cloud was sitting on the bed, staring at his reflection in the Wing Warrior sword. He did not look up when the girls came back in, and though he tried to mask them, his gloomy thoughts were clearly evident.

'Where's Tidal?' he asked.

'He's gone,' Sky said, walking over to the bed and touching Nimbus's hand. 'He's pretty mad.'

'People react to these things in different ways. He'll come around in time. I'm sure of it.'

'It's difficult for all of us,' Sky said, stroking Nimbus's stone–cold fingers. 'Everything changed too quickly. I can't keep up. And there were so many things I wanted to say.'

'You and me both,' Cloud said.

'Stop that,' Glass shouted, stamping her foot. 'Stop talking like he's not there any more.'

'It's okay, Glass,' Cloud said.

'No. It's not okay. He's not... gone. Not yet.'

'No, of course. You're right. And we don't have time for this sort of talk. What we need to do is make sure we're ready for the next time Sorrow attacks.'

'She's coming back?' Sky said.

'Without a doubt, and we don't have much time to make preparations. Nimbus has a dragon. A very powerful one. I've seen him, spoken with him. He is being held captive in the dungeons of Crystal Shine and we need to free him.'

'We? Meaning us?'

'You have to come too. You've taunted Sorrow, thrown stones at her. She won't forget that in a hurry. I can't protect you if you aren't with me.'

'But, I can't. I mean, my dad. Things are all messed up, and he needs me.'

'He'll understand.'

'No, he won't. He...' Sky's breath was quickening, and there was a look in her eyes that reminded Cloud of the look in a rabbit's eyes just as the hunter's trap springs shut.

'Do you need me to talk to him?'

'No! No. Definitely not. This is all so crazy. He needs me. Since Mum went, he needs me. I can't just leave.'

'It's not forever.'

'Then why does it feel that way?'

'Your father will be fine. Believe me. He's got friends here.'

Sky looked at Nimbus. He was totally still, more like a statue than a boy. 'I want to help Nimbus,' she said. 'But I can't go without seeing my dad first.'

'Then run on and do that now while I make the preparations for our journey.'

'What about Tide?'

'If Tidal has run off, then he will have to fend for himself.' Cloud stood. It was a decisive action, indicating the time for talking was well and truly over. 'I need to go to the garrison and get a new sword. I lost mine fighting goblins.'

'Aren't you going to take the Wing Warrior sword?'

'No. This sword stays with Nimbus.'

'But he doesn't need it.'

Cloud smiled proudly. 'A hero always needs his sword.'

CHAPTER TWENTY-THREE

Back home, Sky pushed open the front door, and poked her head inside. The house was quiet and cold. The hallway was shrouded in gloom.

'Dad?' she said, her voice hardly more than a whisper. 'Are you home?'

There was no answer.

She listened carefully. No snoring. No singing. No sobbing. Perhaps he was already at the tavern, too drunk to care where she was, or even if she had been hurt in the attack.

'Dad?' She moved inside, closing the door behind her. As the latch clicked, there was a smash from the kitchen.

Her heart immediately started to pound, and she was almost overcome by the urge to run back out into the street.

Smashing was normally bad. Smashing normally meant he was angry.

'Dad, are you okay?'

There was no answer, so she started through the hallway, her fists clenched tightly. There was another sound from the kitchen; maybe bowls being rattled together. Was her father trying to cook something?

She reached the kitchen door and stopped for a moment, one hand on the door handle, one hand clenched on the doorframe.

There was still time to turn around and leave. She was only going to be gone for a few hours. Her father might not even notice she wasn't there. If she left him some porridge, or some bread and cheese, he might not even think to look for her.

She didn't have to tell him what she was up to.

Why should she?

She sighed, shaking her head. She knew the answer to that

question well enough. She had made him a promise. For all his faults, he was her dad, and she wasn't about to break that promise.

The hinges creaked as she went in.

She could not hold back a yelp of surprise when she was confronted by something very different to what she had expected.

There was a creature sitting on the kitchen table. It was a fat thing, with many characteristics that were common to man; but it was small, perhaps no bigger than a cat. Its tummy was hanging out over the top of breeches that had been fashioned out of leaves, and its pudgy cheeks wobbled as it nattered away to itself in an unusual, squeaky voice. It was wearing a wooden bowl on its head, and was in the process of sticking its long tongue down the neck of an empty bottle. There were knives and forks and mixing bowls scattered over the floor, and there was flour everywhere, in which the creature had left its little footprints.

Sky stopped in the doorway. The creature turned to look at her with big eyes that spoke of a hidden and almost human intelligence. Its chubby fingers tightened around the neck of the bottle, and it made its mouth into something that was almost a smile, but which revealed too many sharp–looking teeth to be considered friendly.

'What are you?' Sky asked.

In response, the thing stood up, and with an unearthly giggle, hopped the gap between the table and the windowsill. Despite its portly physique, the creature moved with surprising agility, and it had disappeared into the bushes outside long before Sky crossed the distance to the window. The leaves rustled, and she heard the thing giggling and scrabbling for a little while as clods of mud flew up into the air. Then it was gone.

Sky realised she had been holding her breath, and she slowly exhaled before pulling the shutters closed and turning away from the window.

Knowing it would cause trouble if her father returned to see the kitchen in such a mess, she began to pick up all the discarded cutlery and bowls.

As she worked, she laughed quietly. She had just seen a legend in her kitchen. She didn't know what it was, maybe a gnome or a goblin, but there was one thing she did know. She had been far less scared of it than she was of her father.

After the gnome had fled through the kitchen window, he headed back into the woods, excited to show off his new wooden hat to the rest of his family.

On his way home, he had to pass a clearing where a goblin hunting party was in the process of chasing down a badger.

The gnome hated goblins; they were stinky, untrustworthy little monsters who always cheated at cards. However, this particular gnome had already lost two brothers, one cousin, and a third aunt twice removed to badgers, so wasn't fond of them either.

Finding a good spot halfway up a tree, the gnome settled down to watch the fight. The badger was of a good size and wasn't shy about getting stuck in; and he was making the hunt into a fascinating spectator sport. Three goblins were already wounded and were staggering off into the undergrowth, but the badger was heavily outnumbered, and he couldn't hope to last much longer.

Suddenly, there was a howl, and two wolves sprang into the clearing. The goblins scattered, screeching and waving their little arms in the air as they realised the fight had turned in the badger's favour. The wolves ran among them, snatching up the slowest hunters and shaking them savagely.

The whole scene was incredibly gruesome, and the gnome applauded every time a goblin got mauled. He clapped so hard that he actually lost his balance and fell out of his tree. As he got to his feet, shaking his head groggily, he became aware of something waiting in the shadows: a giant stag that was silently surveying the carnage the wolves were causing.

The gnome had heard terrified whispers of this stag. He was called Sage, and by all accounts, he was the boss around these parts.

As the gnome was edging away, Sage turned to look at him; and even though the stag didn't say anything, the gnome knew that it was time to leave. He scurried off, leaving the sounds of snarling wolves and yelping goblins far behind.

CHAPTER TWENTY-FOUR

Gradually, the black smoke cleared, revealing a desolate and uninhabited landscape: A huge, seemingly endless wilderness of sharp, jagged stones and deep crevasses. There were no trees here, no plants, no animals, no people, and no dragon.

Nimbus was totally alone.

He blinked stupidly, looking around in complete bewilderment at this strange, alien environment. He felt like he had just woken from a dream, but had somehow managed to wake into a world that was less real than the dream had been.

Instinctively, he reached for the Wing Warrior sword, expecting it to be hanging from his waist.

But there was no sword. No sheath.

No armour.

He was dressed in some worn breeches and a leather tunic.

A moment of panic, a second of sheer terror at the prospect of being unarmed and unarmoured should the black dragon return, was almost immediately replaced with a sense of pure release.

In the armour, people would have expected him to be a hero; but in these clothes, he could just be plain old Nimbus again.

The sword was lying in the dirt, discarded like a piece of rubbish. He made no effort to pick it up. He wasn't a Wing Warrior – he never had been – and the sword wasn't for him. Better to leave it there for some real hero to find.

'Glass?' he called. The purple sky was entirely empty. As empty as he felt. 'Glass?'

There was no response, only the mournful wail of the wind as it swooped across rocks and stones, and down into deep scar–like ravines.

Nimbus wrapped his arms around his chest and squinted into the horizon. There were no landmarks in this place. No distinguishing hills or trees or buildings. Everything looked the same. He could walk for a hundred miles and still feel like he hadn't taken a step.

'Well, I don't know what you did, Glass, but you helped me get away from that dragon. I guess I owe you one.' He took another look around the bleak landscape. 'I just wish you could have told me where I'm supposed to go now.'

He sat on an angular finger of stone. Being as he didn't know where he was, or where he should go, he figured that sitting down would be just as useful as anything else.

The wind continued to whoop and howl. He kicked his feet in the dirt, and tried his best not to listen to the moaning in the air.

Some hero he had turned out to be. He'd had the armour and the sword, but when it came down to it, he just wasn't strong or brave enough. The dragon had pounded him without hardly needing to try.

'I almost believed it was me,' he whispered. 'I almost convinced myself I could be the Wing Warrior.'

He shook his head in disbelief. How could he have been so stupid? He had put Glass's life at risk by taking her out to the fort, and poor Cumulo had allowed himself to be captured because he believed Nimbus was going to save everyone. If it wasn't so sad, he would have laughed. He couldn't even save himself, let alone save his friends. And now he didn't even know where he was.

The Wing Warrior sword glimmered faintly. It wanted to be picked up. But not again. Never again. He was finished with trying to be a hero. From now on, he was going to be a regular kid.

He looked around at the empty scenery.

As soon as he figured out a way home, he was going to be a

regular kid.

The sky seemed to darken, and a figure appeared on the horizon. Another person? Perhaps someone who knew where the nearest town was?

'More likely a hungry wolf looking for its next meal,' Nimbus said, resting his chin in his hands. 'Well, if he wants to eat me, he can do all the running. I'm not moving from this spot.'

The Wing Warrior sword continued to glow.

Black clouds gathered, piling up one behind the other to build a dark wall before eventually spilling over to spread across the sky like ink in a wishing well.

Nimbus was tired. He closed his eyes. Almost immediately he had the sense he was no longer alone, and when he opened his eyes again there was a man standing just a short distance away. The man was leaning against a gnarly wooden staff, and his face was almost completely obscured by the wide hood of his travelling cloak.

'Sleeping?' the man asked, in a voice that sounded young, but felt old.

Nimbus wiped his eyes and yawned. 'No, not sleeping. I saw you on the horizon.'

'Really?'

'That was you, wasn't it?'

'It's possible. Some people see me coming.' The man approached; the end of his staff clicked on the stones. 'Do you mind if I sit beside you?' Without waiting for an answer, he sat. 'I have been travelling for a long time. It's good to sit down every once in a while. Good to catch your breath.'

Nimbus rubbed his chest. His lungs still burned with the memory of the dragon's smoke. 'I suppose so.'

'Tell me, do you have a name?'

'Nimbus.'

'Like the cloud?'

'I was named after my dad, but I'm nothing like him.'

'Sometimes it's hard to live up to the expectations of our parents.'

'I don't think my dad had any expectations of me. I think that's probably the worst thing of all. I think he hid a lot of things from me, told me a lot of lies. He knew I wouldn't be strong enough or brave enough to handle the truth.'

'Sometimes parents can be cruel, can't they?' Nimbus caught a glimpse of the man's mouth curling into a wicked smile. The rest of his face remained hidden by his hood. 'But life can be cruel. I'm sure I don't need to tell you that, considering where we are.'

'And where, exactly, are we?'

'A limbo. A place between the world of the living and the world of the dead. This is the place where spirits wander if they are lost. A very sad place. Something terrible must have happened for you to be here.'

'There was a dragon. I tried to...' Nimbus almost laughed. 'I tried to do something very silly.'

'I'm sorry to hear that. It's a terrible, tragic waste of life.'

'What do you mean?'

There was another flicker of a smile, partially masked by the folds of the hood. 'You don't understand, do you? You're dead, Nimbus. Or so close to it there's barely any difference. The dragon killed you.'

Nimbus jumped up, although he felt more like he had been yanked up against his will by an icy hand that was firmly gripping his lower intestines. 'It's not possible,' he gasped.

'I'm afraid it is. You're a wandering spirit now, trapped between your world and the other world, where the dead people are.'

'No.'

'Don't worry. Denial is just the first step on your journey.'

'No. I won't believe this.'

'Believe it, don't believe it. It makes no difference in the end.'

'It's too soon.'

'It's always too soon. Just relax.'

'How am I supposed to relax? You've just told me I'm dead.'

'Or almost dead.'

'How do you expect me to be calm? And who are you anyway? Why are you here?'

'I'm a guide.'

'What sort of guide?' Suddenly Nimbus was wary of this man, and he had the urge to be anywhere other than where he was.

'I'm here to help you, to guide you into the next world.'

'But I'm not ready to go to the next world. I have to go back. There's a dragon, and it's going to hurt my friends.'

'Your friends aren't your concern any more.'

'Yes they are. They're always my concern. You have to help me, take me back.'

'I can't.' The man got to his feet. 'I'm afraid I don't know the way. I can only guide you to the world of the dead. I have no knowledge of the living.'

'This is crazy.'

'It's always a shock to find out you've been eaten by a dragon, but these things happen.'

'You don't understand. The dragon didn't eat me.'

'What makes you so sure?'

'I don't know. My sister, I think. I heard her voice. Somehow she was able to communicate with me.'

'Only magic users, very powerful ones, have the power to talk to the spirits here. Is your sister a magic user?'

'She... I...' Nimbus chewed on his lip. 'No.'

'Then it was not your sister you heard. Sometimes the lost spirits here like to make fun of the newcomers, and give them hope where there is none. I'm sorry. It's over for you. Please let me do my job.'

The man put a hand on Nimbus's shoulder. His touch was as cold as a mountain stream. His face remained a mystery.

'I can't be dead,' Nimbus whispered. 'I need to be alive. Just for a little bit longer.'

'Come with me. It will be okay. Once you are in your rightful place you will be able to look over your friends, as all of the dead can. It will be like you are still with them.'

Nimbus backed away from the man's touch. 'If there is a path to the dead, there must be a path to the living. And if you guide those who want to die, there must be another guide who can take me back to my friends. Isn't that true?'

'I know of no such guide.'

'But that doesn't mean he doesn't exist.'

The man planted his staff in the ground and leaned on it. 'Naturally, this is your choice. You don't have to come with me. But as far as you are concerned there are two options. You can come with me to the world of the dead, where you will be safe and happy, and where you can watch your family and friends, and where, eventually, they will all join you when they die.'

'And my second choice?'

'You stay here in the wilderness, and you never see anyone you love ever again.'

Nimbus stared at the horizon; it was gloomy and threatening. 'But I'm sure I heard my sister's voice. She helped me. Somehow. I'm sure it was her.'

The man leaned in close, whispering in Nimbus's ear. 'Do you really want to be here on your own for the rest of eternity?'

'I won't be alone, if my sister can talk to me.'

'And what if you're wrong? What if you never hear her or see her again?'

Nimbus's head sank. Tears trickled down his cheeks. He had learned what it was like to be defeated when the black dragon had poisoned him, but only now did he understand what it felt like to be completely and utterly destroyed.

'I've been crying a lot recently,' he said. 'I don't want to cry any more. I don't want to keep hurting. I'm not strong enough.'

'Then you'll come with me?'

'I don't suppose I would be much use even if I could go back.'

'Is that a yes?'

Nimbus nodded reluctantly.

'Good. That's good. Let's get started right now. We have a very long journey ahead of us.'

Nimbus looked over at the Wing Warrior sword. It was still glowing. 'Shall I bring the sword?' he asked.

'No. You won't need it.'

'I think I would feel better if I took it along.'

'Why? You have nothing left to fight for.'

'It's glowing. It glows when it wants to show you something.'

'Remember, Nimbus. This is a limbo, a world between worlds. Nothing here is real. That sword is just your memory of the sword you once had.'

'But...'

'You're confused. But death is confusing. Better not to try to understand it. Better just to come with me.'

Once again, Nimbus thought he could see a cruel expression beneath the man's hood. No eyes, no nose, just an unpleasant mouth. 'Do you have a name?' he asked, nervously.

'You may call me Guide.'

Nimbus wrapped his arms across his chest, and hunched his shoulders against the wind. 'Okay, Guide,' he said. 'Lead the way. I will follow you.'

CHAPTER TWENTY-FIVE

Glass and Sky were stood on the outskirts of the village, staring off into the West where the distant sharp points of the Sanguine Mountains cut the horizon into shards of light and dark. At any second the dragon might appear, swooping across the wilderness in a poisonous smoke cloud. What would happen if she came back? How could the village hope to survive?

Sky touched Glass's hand. Around them, villagers rushed frantically. Most of them, despite the mayor's protests, were packing up, looking to move farther east in hope of outrunning the dragon. But in the East there were the Forbidden Woods and the Grey Mountains, places that were now no safer than anywhere else.

Sky knew there was nowhere to run. In the end, somebody would have to fight the dragon.

'There's big trouble ahead for us, isn't there?' Glass said, quietly.

'I guess so,' Sky replied. 'But maybe if we can get Nimbus's dragon to help us...' She didn't bother to finish her sentence. She wasn't even convincing herself.

'You kids leaving too?' an old man asked, as he staggered beneath the weight of a heavy travel chest overflowing with clothes. 'You should. Take a leaf out of everybody else's book. Get out while you still can. Look what that dragon did to the street, and these houses. Destroyed it all. We'll have nothing left at all if she comes back.'

'What do you have you are so worried about losing?' Sky asked.

The old man frowned. 'Everybody has something they don't want to lose,' he said, staggering away.

Sky smiled faintly, and squeezed Glass's hand.

'I think he'll be okay,' Glass said.

'Who?'

'Nim. I think he'll be okay. He's been poisoned quite badly, but he's strong and brave. I think he'll be strong enough to fight it. He's got a lot to fight for. He's got us.' Glass's eyes glowed. 'He's got you, hasn't he?'

'Me?'

'You're as silly as the boys are sometimes.'

Sky shook her head. 'And you're as mysterious as your dad sometimes. Speaking of which, he's been a long time.'

'He's probably making sure the soldiers are ready for if the dragon comes back.'

'I wish we could just hide somewhere until this is all over.'

'No you don't. Not really. You want to help Nim as much as he wanted to help us.'

The hot fingers of the sun stretched across the sky, burning away every last trace of cloud. Birds darted and weaved together, chirping and twittering playfully. If it was not for the destroyed houses and withered trees, nobody would ever think that the dragon attack had been anything more than a terrible dream.

'Do you still wish you were a bird?' Glass asked.

'Now, more than ever. But I guess we don't always get to be what we want to be.' Sky glanced behind her, towards her house; but slowly her gaze drifted off farther down the road, finally coming to rest on the open doors of the tavern and the men who were stood around it in quiet conversation. 'It would be nice to have the choice though.'

There was the sound of horse hooves and the trundle of wheels as Cloud appeared at the end of the street. He was riding in a rickety old cart, pulled by a magnificent black horse.

'That's Onyx,' Glass squealed, clapping her hands together excitedly.

'I convinced the mayor that selling me his horse was the best thing to do for the people of Landmark,' Cloud said, pulling the cart to a halt and climbing down. The look on his face suggested that his method for convincing the mayor hadn't involved much talking.

Glass ran up to Onyx, stroking his snout. Onyx snorted approvingly.

'I'm sorry the cart isn't better,' Cloud said. 'It was the best I could find at short notice. You're going to roll around in there like a couple of cabbages.'

'Better than walking,' Sky said, hopping into the back of the cart and finding a seat.

'And if we make good time, we'll be at Crystal Shine before nightfall,' Cloud said, helping Glass up.

'And then what?' Glass asked.

'And then we get Cumulo out of that dungeon.'

'Will Lord Citrine let us do that?' Sky asked.

Cloud positioned himself at the front of the cart, taking up the reins. 'I very much doubt it. But we're not exactly going to ask for his permission.'

'So this is a jail break?'

'And you were thinking of going without me?' Tidal said, popping up beside the cart. 'Shame on you.'

'We thought you'd gone,' Sky said.

Tidal climbed into the cart. 'I figured you might need my help.'

'More likely you were scared of that dragon coming back for you,' Glass muttered, under her breath.

'I'm not scared of that dragon,' Tidal snorted. 'You just wait and see.'

Cloud snapped the reins and Onyx set off at a canter. The cart bounced and rocked as they passed the village border, heading out on the potholed road to Crystal Shine. 'Let's hope we don't have to prove who is and isn't afraid of Sorrow,' he said.

'Are you afraid?' Tidal asked.

'Of course. Sorrow destroyed every one of the old dragons, and every Wing Warrior.'

'Except you,' Sky said. 'You're a Wing Warrior.'

A look of sadness came into Cloud's eyes. 'I gave up that title a very long time ago.'

'But why?'

'It's a long story.'

'Good for a long journey then.'

'And I'm not sure it has a happy ending.'

'Please, Dad?' Glass said. 'You have to tell us now. Why is Sorrow so mean? Why does she want to hurt Nim?'

'Sorrow wants to hurt everyone. Everything. She is evil in the most simple and purest form.'

'You fought her once before, didn't you?'

'All of the Wing Warriors did. Twelve of us.' His expression turned thoughtful. 'Only I survived. I thought, or at least hoped, we had destroyed her, that the death of my friends had meant something.'

'I think you just made her mad,' Tidal said, taking a bite out of an apple he had found rolling around in the back of the cart. 'Which means we have one very mad dragon with a nasty reputation for killing other dragons and Wing Warriors. How are we supposed to fight something like that?'

'I honestly don't know. But Cumulo has hatched, and he may have the answers we need.'

Tidal sat forward. 'Cumulo is Nim's dragon, right?'

'That's right.'

'You had something to do with that, didn't you? It's no coincidence Nim found him.'

'Nobody was supposed to find him. I hid the dragon, and the armour. I encased the sword in a mystic diamond that could only be broken by the hand of a Wing Warrior. Nobody knew where it was, and nobody was ever supposed to know.'

Tidal laughed through his nose and tossed his apple core out of the cart. 'Smells funny to me.'

'You smell funny to me,' Glass said.

'Shut up, Stink Witch.'

'You shut up, Bog Breath.'

'Both of you shut up,' Cloud said. 'I thought you wanted to hear about Sorrow?'

'We do,' Sky said. 'Where does she come from?'

'Nobody knows. But she is ancient, maybe as old as evil itself. Hold on.' The cart bumped over a particularly deep pothole and rocked so badly Glass nearly fell out. 'Sorry about that. And there are some trees coming up here. Watch out for low branches.'

The children ducked, and clung to the edges of the cart as leaves and branches crackled and snapped around them.

'So, what has Leaf taught you about dragons?' Cloud asked.

'Just the basics,' Sky said.

'So you know there were twelve dragons?'

'Why only twelve?' Tidal asked.

Glass giggled. 'Tide doesn't go to Leaf's classes, Dad. You might need to start at the beginning.'

Tidal gave Glass a shove. She shoved him back.

'Twelve dragons,' Cloud said. 'Flame, Fang, Smoke, Smog, Earth, Mayhem, Chaos, Wrath, Time, Hurricane, Snake, and Mother. The oldest of all the old things.'

'Who gave them their names?' Sky asked.

'Mother, the golden dragon. She gave birth to each of them, and named them on their first birthdays based on the unique abilities each one possessed.

'Flame and Fang, the twins, breathed fire so hot it could dry up the oceans and melt the snowy mountaintops, and they both had particularly nasty bites, but their brothers and sisters all had different talents. Smoke, it is believed, was supposed to be a fire breather, but he never learned how, and could only produce clouds of smoke that were impossible to see through.'

'What good is that to anybody?' Tidal scoffed.

'Perhaps one day you will learn the strength of being unseen, although I'm sure that goes against your nature.'

Tidal hunkered down in the cart, folding his arms and scowling angrily.

'The next dragon was Smog, who could breathe great gouts of acrid black smoke. Smoke so black it hurt your eyes and made you cough and wheeze.

'Then there was Earth, the first of Mother's daughters. She was the most magnificent jade dragon. Her scales were dark green, and light green, and every shade in between. Unlike her brothers, her breath was not a destructive force. Instead, she had the ability to breathe life into that which was dead. It was the most incredible of all the dragon gifts, but unfortunately it was also the most limited, and extended only to the rebirth of plants and trees. We had always hoped that perhaps one day...' His voice trailed off to a surprisingly small whisper. 'But some things are not meant to be.'

'What were Mother's other daughters like?' Sky asked.

'Mayhem, the next dragon to be hatched, was very different to her sister. She had the destructive fury of her brothers, and she could scream so loud that rocks would shatter, towers would crumble, and animals would run wild in the woods. She was sweet once you got to know her, but few people ever did.

'After Mayhem, there were no new dragons for many years. Mother couldn't stand the children bickering and fighting among themselves. They gave her a headache, and never allowed her a minute's peace. However, eventually her children were old enough to look after themselves and went out to make their own nests in various parts of the world. Mother started to get lonely, and in no time at all, there was another egg.'

'Another girl?' Glass asked.

'No. Chaos came next, and he had the power to breathe

lightning and summon rain clouds. He was very unusual, and had little time for his brothers and sisters.'

'Didn't he love them?' Glass asked.

'He loved them well enough. He just wasn't always sure how to show it. He was possibly the saddest of all the dragons, and certainly one of the ones I regret not spending more time with now he is gone. Another pothole coming up, hold on.'

The children laughed as they were jolted around inside the cart, bashing into each other.

'I wish they'd fix this road up,' Cloud muttered, enjoying the bumps far less than the children did. 'Now, where was I? Oh yes. The next dragon was Wrath, who could breathe a terrible wind that caused anything caught in its blast to age instantly. Trees withered and died, and sailing ships rotted to dust.'

'How horrible,' Sky said.

'It was horrible. So horrible a gift that Wrath only ever used it once, and even then she didn't want to.'

'Was that when you were fighting with Sorrow?'

'That's right.'

'What happened?' Tidal asked, interestedly.

'Hey, wait,' Glass said. 'There were more dragons. I want to hear about the other dragons first.'

'Well,' Cloud said, deftly manoeuvring Onyx around a log in the road, 'Time was the next to be born. He could breathe a cold vapour that froze anything it touched. And then there was Hurricane, who could breathe gale force winds, strong enough to rip trees out by the roots or knock down castles.

'The last dragon was Snake, who was killed before she was old enough to grow her wings. Had she lived, she would have learned to bring the dead back to life just as Earth could, but as it was, she could only heal that which was injured. A great power in its own right, but one stunted before it could fully develop.' Cloud blinked a rogue tear from his eye. 'I have always believed that if she had survived, she would have learned to do that which

Earth could not.'

'Bring back dead people?' Tidal said.

'We will never know now. The evil of Sorrow has seen to that.'

Glass counted on her fingers, her brow creased with concentration. 'Eleven,' she said. 'That's eleven children, and Mother makes twelve dragons in total.'

'Correct.'

'So what power did Mother have?'

'Can't you guess? She had the ability to create new life. New dragons.'

'So they all came from Mother?'

'All of them except Sorrow. Sorrow wasn't hatched in any of the known lands, she just appeared one day, and the world was never the same again. She destroyed everything.'

Glass leaned against Sky and closed her eyes. 'I think it's sad,' she said. 'All those dragons, and then they're just gone, like they were never there at all.'

'But where did the Wing Warriors come from?' Tidal said. 'The dragons were wild, right? Not pets?'

'Yes, in the beginning the dragons, all except Mother, were wild and unruly, like spoiled children. They fought among themselves, much like Nimbus and Glass have done in the past, and just like all brothers and sisters do. They raged across the sky in multicoloured flurries of wings and teeth and claws. They destroyed crops as they waged petty wars against each other over trivial matters. They boiled rivers dry and brought mighty forts crashing down. So angry and uncontrollable were the dragons that most mortal men and women lived in fear of them, hiding whenever the shadow of giant wings darkened the day.'

'And the Wing Warriors changed all that?'

'We were not known as Wing Warriors then. We were just soldiers who wanted an end to our people living in fear of the dragons. We knew we could not fight and kill them, so we sought to befriend them.'

'You were lucky not to get eaten,' Sky said.

'Not really. Turns out dragons don't eat humans, the bones get stuck in their teeth. Of course, it wasn't easy. Most of the dragons were still very young and not very easy to get on with, but in time we were accepted, and became known as Wing Warriors. There were twelve of us in total, one knight for each dragon. We forged special armour, and in time we even learned to ride our new friends.'

'Riding a dragon must be great,' Tidal said.

'It is. There is no better feeling than the one you get when you are carried above the clouds.'

'I can imagine,' Sky said.

'And the dragons made you immortal too?' Glass asked.

'That's right. I'm not really sure how, but by spending so much time with the dragons we somehow developed some of their powers, and became ageless as they were.'

'If I'd known history lessons were this interesting, I would have gone to Leaf's classes,' Tidal said.

'Well,' Cloud said, 'perhaps when this is all over you might consider that.'

'I'd rather be out in my boat.'

Cloud smiled kindly. 'I see a lot of my son in you.'

'What? That sissy?' Tidal said, but he grinned and puffed out his chest proudly anyway.

After that they rode in silence for a long time. Glass fell asleep against Sky's arm, and eventually Sky too nodded off. Tidal put his hands behind his head and stared at the clouds for a while, but soon even he had drifted off into a fitful sleep full of dreams about being dragged below the surface of the raging ocean by a scaly monster with sharp fangs and glittering eyes.

The sun reached the highest point in the sky, and then began to dip back down again. The world got darker. Slowly the night–time came, and with it the fearful shadows.

The cart hit a rough patch of road. Tidal jolted awake, clutching at his bandaged chest as though whatever had caused his injuries was attacking him again. He breathed a deep sigh of relief when he realised where he was, and carefully clambered past the sleeping girls to sit next to Cloud.

'You're awake just in time,' Cloud said. 'We're almost there.'

Tidal looked around, there was no sign of Cystal Shine, with its brightly lit towers and streets. They were still in the black wilderness, surrounded by grim leafless trees with grasping limbs. 'Almost where?' he asked, confused.

'At the secret entrance. You weren't expecting us to ride up to the gates were you?'

'I hadn't really thought about it. What secret entrance?'

'There is a maze of sewers and catacombs beneath the city. From there it is possible to sneak our way right into the dungeons without being seen.'

'Sewers? Gross.'

'It's the only way, I'm afraid. Would you mind waking up the girls and getting them ready?'

'In a second. I wanted to ask you something first, while they were still asleep.'

'Then ask.'

'What happened the last time you fought Sorrow?'

Cloud looked at Tidal seriously. 'That's not the real question, is it?' he said.

'No, I suppose not. I guess what I'm really asking is, do we have any chance of winning this fight? You seem very reluctant to tell us what happened in the last battle, and that means it must have been awful.'

Cloud turned his attention back to the road, watching carefully for potholes and other obstacles that might be hidden by the night. 'It was awful,' he confirmed. 'Mother was the first to go. She was lost before we even knew of Sorrow's existence.'

'You mean she died?'

'She vanished. Her Wing Warrior woke one morning to find she had disappeared. There was no sign of a struggle, and no clue to where she might have gone.'

'How could she have been taken from right out under the nose of the Wing Warrior?'

'I do not know, but he never forgave himself for it.' Cloud seemed to be concentrating a lot harder on the road than he really needed to. His jaw was set in a determined straight line, and his dark eyes were hard and full of anger.

'So what happened once Mother was gone?'

'The infinite vision of the magical Wing Warrior swords told us about the threat of the dark dragon, Sorrow, and we knew Mother had fallen foul of this terrible creature.'

'But wasn't Mother the oldest and strongest of the dragons?'

'She was. And we knew that if she could not defeat Sorrow, then Sorrow was truly the most terrifying and deadly force in the world. We knew we would have to fight her, and we knew we were unlikely to win, so we had to come up with a plan.'

'And what was the plan?'

'Haven't you guessed?'

Before Tidal could answer, something small and wiry came hissing through the air, inches from his head. The thing, which appeared to be a furious bundle of arms and legs, hit Cloud square in the face and pitched him out of the cart into the dirt.

Onyx brayed and stamped his hooves.

'Defend the girls,' Cloud yelled from out of the darkness.

'What is it?' Tidal shouted.

Cloud's reply was choked, as if he was being buried under a squirming, clutching mass of bodies. 'Goblins.'

CHAPTER TWENTY-SIX

Before Tidal even knew what was going on, there was already a goblin in the cart with him. It was a horrible little creature with warty black–green skin and a pointed nose. Black eyes glimmered from beneath an angular forehead, and its mouth was a wicked gash full of razor–sharp teeth.

The tiny monster propelled itself at Tidal in a frantic assault of stick–thin but impossibly strong limbs. Tidal raised his arms defensively, but he was still almost knocked clean off his feet as the goblin powered into him, grasping at his hands and hair.

A second goblin, a third, and a fourth, scurried over the side of the cart, attaching themselves to his clothes, pulling and tearing and biting.

Onyx brayed and bucked, and the cart jostled violently. Tidal lost his balance, and carried by the weight of the goblins hanging on his back, he tumbled over the side, hitting the ground with a bone–shaking crash. The goblins took their chance to swarm over him, and no matter how much he thrashed or screamed or kicked, they wouldn't let go.

'Cloud,' he screamed. 'Cloud, there are too many of them to fight. What are we going to do?'

The horrible wet smacking sound of a sword being used in battle and the terrible yelps of wounded goblins was the only sign that Cloud was still there. Still fighting.

'Tidal,' Sky called, from inside the cart. 'They're everywhere. Help us.'

Tidal tried to struggle to his feet, but the weight of hundreds of goblins kept him pinned to the floor. Their giggling filled his ears. 'I hate you,' he said, redoubling his efforts to get free. 'I hate you, I hate you, I hate you.'

'Tidal, do something!'

He tried to think. The girls were helpless without him and Cloud to protect them.

But what could he do?

He closed his eyes and tried to shut out the pain of the scrabbling, bony fingers pawing at him. If he could just concentrate for a minute, maybe he could do something.

'Where are you?' Glass screamed. 'It's so dark.'

Dark.

It was dark.

Almost like being under the ground.

Tidal had an idea.

'Goblins live in caves,' he shouted. 'They don't like light. Make some light. Burn something.'

'There's nothing to burn,' Sky said.

More goblins were piling in on top of him, clambering over his face and making it difficult to breathe. So this was it. This was how the great adventure was going to end. Eaten by goblins; unable to protect his friends.

He really was just a useless, silly boy. It was no wonder destiny hadn't selected him to be the Wing Warrior. He would have made a worse job of it than Nimbus.

Through the press of sinewy bodies it was just possible to see Sky and Glass standing in the back of the cart. Sky had her arms wrapped around Glass protectively, as goblins crawled over them both. More goblins were hanging on Onyx's harness, swinging their scrawny legs and laughing gleefully. Onyx was stamping his hooves and rolling his eyes and snorting his flared nostrils. Even more goblins were pouring out of the trees around them.

'No,' Tidal growled. 'No, this can't be happening. We can't end up like this.'

Someone loomed over him, and the goblins pinning him down started to scream and run away. 'Get off him,' Cloud bellowed, swinging his sword in dangerous arcs. 'Leave the children alone. You don't need them.'

The retreating goblins were already swarming around again, climbing over trees, rocks, and everything else in a vicious wave.

'Where are they all coming from?' Tidal asked, getting to his feet.

'From the caves,' Cloud said. 'I rescued three soldiers. Now they've come for me.'

'How can we fight them all?' Sky shouted, grabbing one of the goblins and throwing it out into the swelling mass of other goblins.

'We need fire,' Tidal said. 'Light.'

'Light,' Glass whispered.

'Be ready to fight as hard as you can,' Cloud said to Tidal. 'While I try to keep them busy, make your way over to the cart and grab the girls. You must keep them safe.'

Screeching goblins were everywhere, ready to pounce on them all, ready to tear them to pieces. They looked so weak and feeble, yet they were so strong, and so many.

'What then?' Tidal asked.

'Then all three of you run. Run as fast as you can. And don't look back at me. I have to stay here, otherwise none of us are going to get away.'

Tidal swallowed hard. He flexed the fingers on each hand. 'Should I wait for some kind of signal?'

'When they attack again. That's when we move.'

'Light,' Glass said, and she thought about sunshine on a meadow of tall grass.

She thought about the way the moon glowed when it was reflected in a still lake.

She thought about a solitary candle flame, and how it can burn away even the worst shadows of the night, no matter how black and terrifying those shadows may seem.

The goblins pressed closer, giggling and laughing like crazed circus clowns.

'Light,' Glass said. 'We need light.' And when she looked down at her hands, there was light.

At first it was no bigger than a glistening teardrop nestled in her palm, spangling her face with colour; but as she watched, it started to pulse and expand. Soon she had to cup both hands around it, just in case she dropped it or it seeped out of her fingers and escaped into the night. Even then it continued to grow, continued to get brighter.

'How are you doing that?' Sky asked.

Soon it was as if a shooting star had dropped right down out of the sky into Glass's hands, and glowing spears of light began to lance out between the gaps of her fingers.

'What is it?' Tidal gasped.

Glass continued to stare at the pocket of light that was growing out of her hand. The nearest goblins squealed and covered their eyes. Those goblins unlucky enough to be touched by one of the light beams screamed and hurled themselves on the floor where they writhed around frantically.

'Where's it coming from?' Sky asked.

'From me,' Glass said.

And the world exploded.

When the light eventually died away not a single goblin remained. 'Where have they all gone?' Tidal asked.

'Back underground,' Cloud said. 'Back where it's dark, and where they can lick their wounds.'

'Will they return?'

Cloud didn't answer. He was watching Glass, who was staring at a small sphere of white light that was floating just above her open palm and reflecting in her eyes.

'Cloud?' Tidal asked.

Cloud sheathed his sword. Glass's hands were trembling uncontrollably, and there were tears running down her pale cheeks. 'What is it?' she said.

Cloud climbed up into the cart beside her, carefully reaching out for her hand. She let him put his hand over hers, finally extinguishing the light. The silhouettes the light had been casting faded into the greater darkness, draining the world of everything except the night. Glass let out a deep breath.

'Are you okay?' Cloud asked.

Glass looked up at him. It was obvious how terrified she truly was. 'How did I do that?' she gasped. 'I was just thinking about light, and how we needed some, and then it was there.'

Cloud rested his hands on her slim shoulders and smiled kindly. 'There are many strange things happening in the world, Glass. Dragons and goblins are just the beginning. You have a great gift. One you never realised you had.'

'She's a magic user,' Sky said.

'That's not possible,' Glass said. 'I'm not special.'

'You are more special than you realise,' Cloud said. 'And Sky is right. You are a magic user.'

'But how?'

'The magic is coming back into the world. After magic was banned, people forgot it was ever anything more than what was written in the history books. They forgot how to use it, and those things that were magical simply ceased to exist. But Sorrow... Sorrow lived on, somewhere beyond the borders of our land, and when she was strong enough, she came back. She started this. She woke the Wing Warrior armour, and the armour woke Cumulo. With two dragons in the world, it was only a matter of time before the other magical things started to come back. Goblins, sprites, fairies, pixies, nymphs, gargoyles, trolls, ogres, and hundreds of other magical creatures.'

'But why is it in me?' Glass asked.

'It has always been in you. Sleeping. Waiting.'

Glass pressed her face into Cloud's arm. 'I'm scared.'

He stroked her hair. 'You have to be strong. Like you were when the goblins attacked us. Do you think you can do that for me?'

She nodded.

'Good girl.'

'Is she going to be safe?' Tidal asked. 'If she can make light out of the dark, what else can she do? And can she stop it if she needs to?'

'She saved us all. Maybe she does not know how to control her power yet, but I for one feel safer having her here with us.' Cloud climbed out of the cart and released Onyx's harness. 'I'm sending Onyx back home. We will travel the rest of the way on foot.'

'Is it far?' Sky asked. 'I don't think Glass will be able to walk much after all this.'

'Not far. A short way up the path there is a sewer entrance. We cannot take a horse there.'

Cloud led Onyx around, and whispered something in his ear. Onyx snorted, flicked his mane, and jolted into action, thundering away and almost immediately becoming invisible in the dark.

'No, wait,' Tidal said, angrily. 'I'm not going anywhere until we've talked about this. Glass obviously has some strange powers that could be dangerous to all of us.'

'Many people have powers that can be harmful to others,' Cloud said. 'But that isn't what's bothering you, is it?'

'I...' Tidal looked down at his feet. 'You wouldn't understand.'

Cloud leaned close to Tidal's ear so that nobody else could hear him speak. 'Nobody wants to be a hero, Tidal. You may think you do, but believe me, you don't.'

'Who said anything about being a hero?'

'I'm not a fool. First Nimbus faces the dragon when you cannot. Now Glass saves our lives. I can imagine how angry that must make you.'

'I'm not angry about that.'

'But you are, and that's more dangerous than Glass's magic could ever be.'

'I'm not dangerous.'

'You're out to prove something. I don't know if you're trying to prove it to yourself or somebody else.' He glanced at Sky. 'But whatever, and whoever, it is, if you stay on this path you're going to end up getting hurt.'

Tidal kept his gaze fixed on his boots. 'Everybody is making a difference. Even Glass. What good am I doing here?'

'You're here, Tidal. That's enough.'

Tidal finally looked up, bravely trying to meet Cloud's serious stare. He wasn't sure whether he was more ashamed for the way he felt, or for the way Cloud had been able to tell. Either way, he could only match the old Wing Warrior's gaze for a second before looking away again.

'Okay,' he muttered.

'Good, now let's get moving.'

Cloud helped Glass and Sky down from the cart. Glass looked even more fragile than usual, diminished in strength and size. She clung to Sky as though if she let go she might blow away on the breeze. 'She isn't going to be able to walk,' Sky said.

'She has to,' Cloud said, crouching beside Glass. 'You have to be strong. I can't carry you, not even a little way. If the goblins come back... I need to be ready.'

'I'll carry her,' Tidal said. 'She barely weighs a thing.'

Cloud smiled. 'That's good. You're a strong lad.'

Tidal lifted Glass up onto his back. She fastened her arms around his neck.

Cloud looked into the black sky. There was something up there, barely visible. The shadow of a shadow, weaving through the stars.

'Run,' he said, drawing his sword.

There was a shrill scream, loud enough to tear apart the night itself.

'What is that?' Sky asked.

'It's Sorrow,' Cloud said. 'She's followed us.'

CHAPTER TWENTY-SEVEN

Cumulo hadn't liked living in the cave under Sentinel Mountain. It had been dark and cold and damp. As large as it had been, it had still felt cramped to him, and there was nobody there for him to talk to except the bats, and they had very little to say for themselves.

Once he had been released from the confinement of the cave, and he had flown above the clouds, he had made a promise to himself that never again would he live in such a place. He would only ever live above the ground, in a place where he could lie in the sun and flap his wings whenever he had the urge to.

However, despite his promise, here he was, stuck in a tiny dungeon only just big enough for him to curl up in. He knew he had surrendered to the soldiers for the right reasons, he knew it had been the only way to protect Nimbus; but even so, he couldn't help wishing there had been some other way.

There weren't even any bats down here.

He tried to shift around slightly to find a more comfortable position, but his back was pressed hard to one wall, and his head was wedged right up to the bars of the prison gate. It was entirely impossible for him to move anything much other than his eyes.

For the time being he chose to keep his eyes closed. After all, there wasn't much in the dungeon for him to see other than dripping stone walls, damp patches of clinging moss, and bits of old bones. Besides, with his eyes closed he found it easier to think about what the outside world had been like. It had been full of so many colours, so many smells. He wished he had been allowed more time to experience all those strange new things before being brought here.

He wondered whether he would ever be allowed to see the

sun again.

There was a squeak, and he opened one eye to catch the fleeting sight of a brown rat scurrying away down the dimly lit tunnel that led from the dungeon cells to the guard room.

Cumulo sighed. The sigh refused to echo in his cramped room, and fell quickly into stony silence. He truly was alone here, without even an echo for company.

Closing his eyes once more, he turned his attention to the vast collection of memories he had stored away in his brain. Memories that were as strange to him as the outside world had been.

Most of his memories were blurred and indistinct, but every now and again he would come across one that was clearer. It would usually only be a fragment of a memory, like a glimmering pearl sunk in the muddy bed of a fast–flowing river; and finding such treasures only made him more confused.

What were these memories? Why did he have them if they weren't his? And if they weren't his, whose were they? Who had put them there? What was he supposed to do with them?

Perhaps the man called Cloud, the last of the true Wing Warriors, would have answers to these questions.

Cumulo pictured Cloud's face in his mind. It was not difficult, he looked so much like Nimbus.

'I know him from before,' Cumulo muttered. There was nobody there to talk back, but somehow speaking the words made him feel slightly less lonely. 'But how do I know him?'

He dove back into the mess of half–formed memories. He felt that somehow his true thoughts were locked away from him, and if only he had a key of some description everything would be explained.

He remembered the time when he was still in the cave and Nimbus had come to free him. It seemed a long time ago, but it was only a few days. So much had happened since. He had spread his wings, touched the very sky, sat on a beach, spoken with the ghost of Captain Spectre. But back in the cave he had thought he was not allowed to go outside at all. He had thought he was destined for a life without any knowledge of the sun or the wind on his face.

Why had he thought that?

'The wise men,' he said.

That's right. The wise men. Nimbus had asked why Cumulo shouldn't leave the cave, and Cumulo had remembered twelve wise men deep in discussion. They had been talking about keeping a dragon hidden, and a terrible evil rising in the West. He realised now, they had been a war council, preparing for the worst of wars. The war of dragons.

And one man in that council had been Cloud.

Cumulo let a deep growl build in the back of his throat. The memory was unfurling in his mind, like a sheet flapping in a strong wind, becoming fresher and cleaner.

Cloud was sitting at a table, discussing a secret plan that would change the fate of the world forever.

Then the memory was gone, leaving only one thought, and a sour taste in Cumulo's mouth.

It was Cloud who had shut Cumulo under the earth.

Could Cumulo really trust a man who had locked him away from the true wonders of the world?

There was a noise in the guard room. Cumulo opened his eyes. Captain Obsidian was striding down the corridor.

'How do you like your new room?' the captain asked.

'It's cramped,' Cumulo said.

'I'd often wondered why some of the cells down here were so big, with such big doorways and access tunnels. I guess they were built in the olden times, for keeping things like you locked up.'

'Not things like me.'

Obsidian smiled grimly, and placed one gloved hand on the hilt of his sword, as if he expected Cumulo to smash right through the bars of the dungeon and snap him up. His eyes were dark, masking his fear.

'It's okay,' Cumulo said, lazily. 'You won't need your sword.'

'Better to be safe,' Obsidian said, gruffly. There was the very slightest tremor in his voice.

'I'm only here because I allowed myself to be caught.'

'All the more reason for me to believe you could let yourself out whenever you want to.'

'I won't do anything that may cause harm to the people here. Nimbus doesn't want me to fight.'

Obsidian snorted a laugh. 'Am I to believe you are a creature of honour?'

'Believe what you will.'

'Then you will tell me where he is.'

'Who?'

'You know who. We have had word from Landmark. There was a dragon attack.'

Cumulo blinked, but said nothing.

'You are not the only dragon.'

'So it would appear.'

Obsidian gripped the bars of the dungeon. 'Tell me where Nimbus is. I know you only allowed yourself to be caught so he could escape.'

'I did.'

'Was the attack on Landmark part of your plan as well?'

'Do you really believe Nimbus would turn a dragon on his own people? He would not even allow me to defend myself against you and your men.'

'Your friend is a wanted criminal. He has stolen a horse, assaulted my men, laid waste to a mighty fortress. And ran away rather than attempting to clear his name.'

'Nimbus is an honest boy.'

'How can I believe he commands your will yet has nothing to do with this second monster?'

'Because you are not a fool, Captain.'

Obsidian's grip on the prison bars tightened. The muscles in his face twitched, as though he was trying to control some increasing emotion of panic or anger. These last days had been tough for him. He was obviously a good man, with a strong sense of duty; but he was a simple man. Now he was faced with dragons, creatures he had never thought existed. The strain was obviously taking its toll.

'I am sorry,' Cumulo said.

'For what?'

'For my part in your discomfort.'

'I'm not uncomfortable.'

'The magic will change many things. There will be terrible battles, and people will suddenly be aware of powers they never realised they had. Ancient enemies will resurface, and the land will be filled with monsters. A war is coming, and we will need good men like you if we are to survive.'

'Then tell me what I need to know. Tell me where Nimbus is.'

'How would I know? I'm stuck in here.'

'Don't play games with me, dragon. I know you have mystic powers beyond those possessed by mortals. You know where the boy is, and you know what he's planning.'

'I'm afraid I have nothing to tell you.'

Obsidian's jaw was straight. His brow creased with impatience. 'I'll make sure you never leave this place again,' he said.

'If that is to be my fate, then I will live with it, as we all must.'

Obsidian shook his head. 'Then you can rot here. But your friend is still out there somewhere, and I will find him.' A smirk played around the corners of his mouth. 'You should hope I do, because if he isn't siding with the black dragon, then he is against it, and you can't protect him down here.'

'If the boy dies, then hope dies too, Captain.'

Obsidian spun neatly on his heel and strode away. 'If the boy dies,' he said, 'it saves me the job of killing him.'

Cumulo closed his eyes. Inside he was raging, and the desire to smash free of the prison was almost overpowering; but he knew that destroying things and killing people would not help Nimbus.

He listened to Obsidian's footsteps going back down the corridor to the guard room.

He had to be patient.

Cloud had used the power of the Wing Warrior sword to tell Cumulo that they were coming to rescue him. He just had to wait.

Help was on the way.

CHAPTER TWENTY-EIGHT

The sound of huge wings flapping overhead was as deafening as it was terrifying.

'Run,' Cloud shouted.

There was a scream – a bellow of pure rage – and Sorrow swooped down so low the children were all beaten flat to the ground by the powerful wind created by her monstrous wings. They did not see her, but they smelled her deadly breath, and heard her claws scraping through the treetops.

'Get up,' Cloud said, grabbing Sky and dragging her to her feet. 'Keep moving. If we don't get into the sewer she'll kill us all. Without the Wing Warrior sword I can't fight her.'

Tidal was already on the move, with Glass clinging tightly to his back. 'Hold on,' he gasped, as he dived into the thick undergrowth. 'I'm going to get you out of here.'

Cloud could just make out the grim shape of Sorrow turning in the air for a second dive. The dragon's eyesight was so good she would be able to see exactly where they all were. It would be too easy for her to swoop in and pick them up one by one.

She screeched, and rushed down at him. The wind under her wings was as strong as a tornado, and it took all of Cloud's strength not to be blasted off his feet.

'I see you,' she roared, as she approached.

Cloud drew a slow breath. His every muscle tensed, he gripped his sword tightly. Leaves swirled around him. Sorrow was so close he could see the fangs shimmering in her gaping maw. Still he remained perfectly motionless. Letting her get closer. Waiting for just the right moment.

It was just like fishing.

Sky watched, her eyes wide with fear, as the mighty dragon

flew by.

'I see you,' Sorrow screeched.

Suddenly, when she was so close her wide mouth seemed to fill his entire vision, Cloud sprang to one side. It was too late for Sorrow to stop, and she ploughed into a mass of trees. Trunks cracked, and leaves shook down on her.

'Didn't see those trees though, did you?' Cloud laughed, running over to Sky and taking her by the hand.

Sorrow thrashed around in the broken remains of the trees, hissing and spitting.

'I think you made her mad,' Sky said.

'Don't worry about that,' Cloud said, dragging Sky along behind him. 'Run. She'll be after us again in a minute.'

They dashed through the undergrowth, following the trail of snapped twigs and brambles that Tidal had made, and emerged on the other side at the top of an embankment leading down to a vast clearing. In the centre of the clearing, surrounded by jagged shards of glistening rock, was a still lake.

'There is a cave,' Cloud said. 'The sewer water comes out there and feeds the lake. Hurry.'

He dashed down the embankment to the edge of the water, with Sky slipping and sliding beside him. He could hear Sorrow just behind, her great fangs snapping and her nostrils snorting as she emerged from the shattered trees. 'I'll kill you,' she was screaming.

There was the sound of wood splintering beneath the dragon's weight, then the heavy, flat slapping of her wings as she climbed back into the sky.

'Hurry,' Cloud repeated, dragging Sky along the edge of the lake towards an ugly outcrop of stones. 'Just past these rocks.'

Tidal came out of the gloom, running as fast as he could with Glass hanging on his back. 'Thought I'd lost you both,' he panted. 'I can't find the sewer entrance.'

'It's this way,' Cloud said, sheathing his sword and scooping

Sky up in his strong arms. 'Try to keep up. The dragon is close at our heels.'

Pressing Sky close to his chest, he leapt the sharp rocks, landing with a muddy splash in a pool of stagnant water on the other side. Tidal bounded after him, staggering and spluttering, his breath coming in ragged gasps.

There was a cave entrance just up ahead, set in white rock. A sliver of dirty water curled out of the cave mouth, dribbling down through the stones and boulders until it arrived at the circular reach of the lake. They were so close, but Sorrow was already back in the sky, her gigantic silhouette expanding to swallow the universe.

'Keep moving,' Cloud said, grabbing Tidal's shirt and pulling him along.

Sorrow touched the highest point of the sky, stopped, saw where her enemies were, folded her wings up behind her back, and dropped down on them.

With all the strength he had left Cloud threw Tidal and Glass inside the mouth of the cave, and then fell in behind them with Sky hanging off his shoulder. They all hit the ground together as Sorrow landed with a terrific splash outside.

'Cloud?' the dragon hissed. Her voice was thick with menace. 'Come out of there, Cloud, or I'm going to go back to your village and eat everyone.'

Cloud rose. Looking out of the narrow mouth of the cave he could see Sorrow hunched over the rocks, her broad wings folded up in jagged spikes behind muscular shoulders. Her eyes were glimmering wax candles, burned too long.

'Come out,' she said.

Sky grabbed Cloud's hand. 'You can't go out there. She'll eat you.'

The dragon's tongue flicked, tasting the sadness in the air. Her long fangs dripped saliva, and poison puffed from her nostrils.

'She'll kill everyone,' Cloud said.

'If you go out there, she'll kill you, and then she'll go back to the village anyway,' Tidal said.

'Come out, or I will destroy everyone,' Sorrow said. 'Come out, or I will kill... your wife.'

There was a pause, during which time the only sound Cloud could hear was the thundering of blood in his ears.

Fear pricked at his heart with its cruel barbs, injecting him with a paralysing venom.

'Don't do it,' Sky whispered.

'I have to,' he said.

'We need you,' Sky said. 'We'll never be able to free Cumulo without you.'

'But...'

'If you go now, we're all lost. It won't just be the end of our village. It will be the end of the whole world. Please don't go out there. Please.'

Cloud swallowed. He stared at Sorrow, and she stared back. Water dripped from the roof of the cave as though the rock itself was crying for the terrible things that would befall Landmark.

'If I go, maybe it will buy you some time,' Cloud said. 'Enough time to free Cumulo.'

'And maybe it won't,' Sky said. 'Maybe she'll fly right back to the village and destroy everything anyway. Maybe she's already destroyed everything, have you thought of that?'

'But Glass's mother,' Cloud said. 'How can I..?' He wiped his eyes. He couldn't speak any more. The thought of something happening to Strata was almost too much. He knew he had to be strong, for the sake of the children; but how could he be strong in the face of such terrible evil?

'Please. You have to come with us. We can't do it alone,' Sky said.

'I'm sorry. I always feared this time would come. I knew as soon as I revealed my true identity the trouble it would cause.'

'Come out,' Sorrow growled.

'For years I have hidden what I am. To protect Strata. To protect my family. And... And, yes, to protect myself. But when I saw Nimbus fighting Sorrow, wearing armour he should never have been forced to wear, I knew I couldn't hide any longer. My doom was sealed at that moment.'

'Please, Cloud,' Sky said.

'I really am sorry. I can't run from what I am. I have to face her.'

'She'll kill you.'

'She might, but at least you will be alive. You still have a chance to free Cumulo, and stop this before things get any worse.'

'Daddy, please don't go,' Glass said. Her eyes were full of tears that reflected the terror he had hoped would not be visible in his own eyes. 'I'm scared. I don't want you to go to the same place Nimbus has gone.'

'Glass...' He stopped, almost choking on his words.

'Daddy?'

He forced himself to go on. His heart was breaking, but there was only stern authority in his voice: the authority he knew his daughter expected. 'You have to be strong for me. You told me you'd be strong.'

'Come out,' Sorrow said. Her claws scraped along the wet rocks. 'Come out, or I will blow poison into that cave until none of you can breathe.'

Cloud licked his lips. His knuckles were white. 'Okay, Sorrow,' he said. 'I'm coming out, but you have to promise me you won't pursue these children any more.'

'I promise,' Sorrow chuckled.

'You can't believe her,' Tidal said. 'She's nothing but a big, lying lizard. She'll get us anyway.'

'I want you to run on now,' Cloud said. 'Run back into the sewer and just keep going. If she breathes her smoke down here, the tunnels will fill up quickly, so you can't stop, not for anything.'

'We aren't going to leave you,' Sky said. 'If you go out there, we're going too.'

'No. I have to face her alone.'

'I won't let you,' Sky said. 'It's suicide.'

Cloud took hold of Sky's arm and led her to one side. 'Listen to me,' he whispered, glancing over his shoulder at Tidal and Glass. Glass watched him quietly. 'Listen. I need you to stay here, to look after my little girl. She's a magic user, and she's going to need you.'

'Why?'

'She's just discovered something about herself that's going to change her life forever, and I can't be there for her. She's going to need her friends, to help her understand the power she has. Without you and Tidal, she's going to tear herself apart.'

They exchanged a look of such seriousness that Sky knew it was pointless to argue further. 'I'll look after her. I promise,' she said.

'I am growing impatient,' Sorrow said. 'Stop your useless plotting, and come out, Cloud.'

'I have to go now,' Cloud said.

'Daddy?' Glass said.

'It's okay.' He hugged his daughter briefly, not risking holding her any longer for fear he might never be able to let go. 'All of you run along now. I'll keep Sorrow busy for as long as I can.'

'And what do we do?' Tidal asked, hoisting Glass up on his shoulders.

'Follow the sewer. Eventually you will reach a fork in the tunnel. Go left until you reach an iron ladder. The ladder leads right into the dungeons of Crystal Shine.'

'And you think we're going to be able to break Cumulo out?'

Cloud drew his sword. 'I hope you can, because you're all that's left now.'

'Cloud,' Sorrow said, and black smoke puffed in the mouth of the cave. The smell of dirt and rotten vegetation filled the air. 'It's time to play.'

'Run,' Cloud said. 'And don't look back whatever you do. Just keep running.'

'Come on, Sky,' Tidal said.

Sky wiped her eyes with the back of her sleeve. 'Okay,' she said.

A silent look passed between Cloud and Glass. They both knew what chance there was that they would ever see each other again.

Tidal grabbed hold of one of Sky's trembling hands, leading her farther into the tunnel.

Cloud waited until the children were nothing more than echoing footsteps in the deep, and then he turned to face the dragon. Sorrow's eyes glowed like two dying suns as she watched him.

'I'm still waiting,' she hissed.

CHAPTER TWENTY-NINE

A terrifying scream that sounded neither human nor animal echoed across the wilderness, and instinctively Nimbus looked into the purple sky for signs of a winged menace.

'Don't fear,' Guide said, leaning on his walking stick. 'It's nothing that can hurt you.'

Nimbus shivered. Goosebumps had sprung up all over his skin. 'What was it?'

'Just the echo of a spirit passing over. Leaving the world of the living.'

'Coming here?'

'There are new spirits arriving all the time.'

'That one sounded in pain. It didn't even sound human.'

Guide sniffed, then coughed into his cupped hand. 'It was human,' he said.

Nimbus strained his eyes to see as far as he could. They had been walking for hours, but they seemed not to have travelled any distance at all. In every direction there was nothing except the endless expanse of craggy plains.

'Will you help the new spirit?' he asked.

'I need to help you first,' Guide said.

'But we've been walking for so long.'

'It's not much farther.'

'Can we sit down for a moment?'

Guide indicated a flat rock beside him. 'Of course. We have all the time in the world.'

Nimbus sat, resting his head in his hands. 'Why is it so far?'

'Did you expect a journey into death to be easy?'

'I suppose not. But why does everything here look the same? And where are all the other spirits?'

'No more questions now. Rest for a minute.'

Nimbus's eyelids were heavy, so he let them close. A gentle breeze flicked playfully at his curls of hair. When he finally opened his eyes again the Wing Warrior sword was lying on the ground between his feet. His sad reflection looked at him from within the sword's blade. He seemed very small.

'What's that doing here?' Guide asked, agitatedly.

'I don't know,' Nimbus said.

'I told you to leave it behind.'

'I did.'

'Then why is it here?' There was a strange tone in Guide's voice, something more than just annoyance.

'I don't know, I haven't touched it.'

Nimbus reached for the handle of the sword, but Guide rushed over and kicked the sword away. 'No. You mustn't touch it.'

'Why not?'

'That's all in your past now, it doesn't affect you any more. Just think about where you're going, not where you've been. It's no wonder this trip is taking so long.'

'What do you mean?'

'If you insist on thinking about that sword all the time then you will never be able to leave the world of the living behind and we'll be stuck here in this limbo forever, just wandering around like two prize fools. You don't want that, do you?'

'I guess not.'

'Remember, you're dying. It's an all or nothing deal. You can't go picking and choosing bits of your life to take with you.'

'But...'

'Trust me. It's that sword that got you into this situation in the first place.'

Nimbus nodded miserably. 'I know. I don't want the sword any more. I never really wanted it.'

'That's good, very wise.' Guide held out his hand for Nimbus to take. 'Come on.'

'We're going again?'

'I have to get you home.'

Nimbus glanced at the sword before walking on. The blade glowed faintly, like it wanted to show him something almost forgotten, or something that was very far away.

Tidal didn't know how far they had gone into the sewer, splashing blindly through the dirty water, but it was not far enough to muffle Cloud's terrible scream of pain as it echoed behind them.

Tidal stopped, leaning against the damp wall of the tunnel. Glass was still clinging to his back, her breath trembling and full of fear. He gripped Sky's hand as freezing water rushed around their knees.

'Is everybody okay?' he asked. He tried to sound as brave as he could, but his stomach was doing back–flips. In the darkness, the girls were nothing more than terrified breathing; just pounding heartbeats in the earth.

'I'm okay,' Sky said.

'What was that scream?' Glass whispered.

'It was...' Sky began, but she couldn't think of a suitably convincing lie.

'It was nothing,' Tidal interrupted.

'Was that Daddy?'

'No, Glass. It wasn't anything. Probably just an owl.'

Glass was quiet for a moment. Thoughtful.

Rats came scampering out of holes in the walls to ask the children who they were and what they were doing there, but as the children couldn't speak in Rat, all they heard was a series of unpleasant squeaks and chitters that made them feel even more uncomfortable and afraid than they had been before.

'Do you think Daddy could win?' Glass asked, eventually.

Sky and Tidal moved closer together in the dark. Tidal could not see her face, but he could tell that she was crying softly.

He realised then that he had become the leader of the group. Nimbus and Cloud were gone. Now the girls would be looking to him for guidance. For strength. He couldn't let them down.

'Could he win?' Glass pressed.

'Your dad is a true Wing Warrior,' Tidal said. 'There isn't anything he can't do.'

A sad silence descended on the group. Even the rats got bored of being ignored and ran off to find something more interesting to do. The darkness pressed closer. Sky wondered whether there would be anything other than darkness ever again.

'We should keep moving,' Tidal said, adopting a tone he felt best suited his new position of responsibility.

'We're going to get lost down here,' Sky said.

'And it smells funny,' Glass said.

Tidal grinned. 'This is a sewer, think yourself lucky you don't have to stand in the water like us.'

'We need a lantern,' Sky said.

'Maybe Glass can help,' Tidal said. 'Do you think you could conjure up some more light, like you did when the goblins were attacking us?'

Glass gripped around his neck a little tighter. He could feel her heart thudding against his back. 'I don't know how I did that. I don't think I can do it again.'

'Can you try?'

'I don't... I wouldn't know how to. I just thought about light. But I never... I didn't...'

'It's okay,' Sky said, touching Glass's cheek. 'You don't have to be afraid. But you could really help us out here. Would you try to light our way?'

'I don't want to do it again,' Glass whispered. 'Please don't make me.'

'Oh, come on,' Tidal snapped. 'Grow up.'

'Hey.' Sky punched him in the arm. 'There's no need to be like that. Can't you see she's frightened?'

'I can't see anything. That's the problem.'

There was a deep rumbling from the direction of the sewer entrance: The sound of rocks tumbling and thumping against each other. A rush of air came down the tunnel.

'What now?' Sky said.

'I think we should run,' Tidal said.

'Why?'

'I think Sorrow's caved in the sewer.'

'But what about a light?'

'Forget a light. Cloud said to follow the tunnel until we reached a junction. I'll hold on to the wall, you two hold on to me. We'll feel our way out of this place.'

There was another crash as more stone collapsed into the tunnel, completely sealing off the way back.

'I'm not afraid,' Glass said.

Tidal grabbed Sky's hand. 'Good. Don't be afraid.'

He started running as fast as he could, and behind him he could hear Sorrow's throaty laugh: a wicked sound that made it obvious Cloud was no longer going to be able to help them.

They were truly on their own.

CHAPTER THIRTY

Cloud watched helplessly as Sorrow destroyed the entrance to the sewer with great swings of her dangerously large claws. She had discarded him among nearby stones, bashed and bruised but still alive. He knew that wasn't an accident. She was keeping him alive for a reason. She intended to make him suffer.

'You said you would leave the children,' he shouted, when the shards of rubble finished clattering around him.

'I am leaving them,' Sorrow chuckled. 'I am leaving them to rot down there in the dark.'

As she approached, the ground shook and ripples trembled on the surface of the lake. Her talons scraped and sparked on the rocks. Her tongue lashed hungrily. The whole world was cast in her bleak shadow. 'You should be glad they will not have to face the same fate as you.'

'You're a coward,' Cloud spat, bracing himself as Sorrow picked him up.

'You dare to call me a coward after what you did?'

'That was a long time ago.'

'Hundreds of years is but a blink of an eye to an immortal dragon. And I remember everything like it was only yesterday.'

'I did what I had to do.'

'You hunted me, Cloud. When I was wounded, in pain, defenceless. I crawled on my belly, scraping away my scales on the rocks, but no matter how far I crawled, you were never more than a day behind me. Relentless and spiteful.'

'You killed them. All of the dragons and all of the Wing Warriors. What was I supposed to do?'

Sorrow ran her tongue around her fangs. There were fragments of bones and meat between her teeth. 'I had to travel to the very deepest place under the mountain to escape you.'

Cloud wriggled in the dragon's grip. It felt like his insides were going to implode, and it was getting harder for him to catch his breath. 'I didn't chase you far enough,' he wheezed.

Sorrow's eyes narrowed. Her nostrils flared, billowing puffs of smog. 'What kind of man are you? You lured me into your sneaky little trap, let all your friends die by tooth and claw, and then when I was weak and tired, you chased me, and you chased me, and you chased me.'

'My friends knew the risk they were taking when they fought you. And I knew what I had to do to make sure they didn't give up their lives for no reason.'

'Are you sure you weren't just trying to prove something?'

Cloud coughed and writhed. He could taste his own blood in his mouth. 'I had nothing to prove.'

'I think you had everything to prove. After all, you were Mother's Wing Warrior.' Cloud closed his eyes to disguise the pain and shame he felt. 'You never told the children that part of the story, did you?'

'Mother's disappearance wasn't my fault.'

'But how humiliating... a Wing Warrior with no dragon.'

'I woke up and she was already gone.'

'I believe you made an oath, didn't you? You all did. Twelve dragons, and twelve men. Fates intertwined. A knight for every dragon, and a dragon for every knight. Man and beast living together. Dying together.'

'There was nothing I could have done. Nobody knows what happened to Mother.'

'Legend has it that the dragons looked into the hearts of the men who travelled to speak with them, and they each picked the warrior who was most like them.'

'You don't know anything.'

'You then spent every day and night with the dragon who had picked you, learning from them, growing with them, until each man was just as much dragon, and each dragon just as much man.'

'Shut up.'

'Losing the dragon must have been like losing a part of yourself.'

'Shut up, Lizard.'

'You must have felt so useless afterwards, so pathetic and weak. How could you be a Wing Warrior after such a failure? How could you be deserving of such an honour?'

'I looked for her. I would have looked forever if it hadn't been for you.'

Sorrow threw back her head and bellowed a heart–stopping laugh. 'And wasn't I a useful distraction? A perfect target for you to direct all of your hatred and self–loathing at.'

'I had to make sure you would never come back.'

'That was your excuse, how you rationalised your actions. But that's not why you did it. Your pride made you bitter and angry, and pride can be so dangerous, can't it? It can lead a man to ruin.'

Sorrow released Cloud and he flopped among the rocks, limp as a rag doll. There was dust and blood in his nose.

'The boy, Tidal, is the same way,' Sorrow said, lowering her head to speak into Cloud's ear. Her voice had the quality of undrinkable water rolling over sharp stones. 'He is desperate to prove his worth, to impress his friends. It will destroy him as it destroyed you.'

'I'm not destroyed yet, Sorrow.'

'Oh, but you are, Cloud. Just look at you. Destroyed by pride, and vengeance, and...' She sniffed him. 'Fear. So much fear. How delightful. What is it, Cloud? What scares you?' She put one huge claw on his chest and pressed down. His ribs creaked under the pressure. 'What made you become the pathetic thing I see before me?'

'Death,' Cloud gasped. 'Endless death.'

'Go on.'

'The power of the Wing Warrior sword showed me a future that might come to pass. It showed me a lone Wing Warrior locked away in a dungeon. For hundreds of years I thought the Wing Warrior in that vision was me, and the thought of living an immortal life in a cage was too much to bear. I gave up being a hero. I became just a man. It was only many lifetimes later that I had a son and I realised it may have been his fate I had seen in the vision, not my own.'

'A son? Of course. The young whelp who attacked me in the village. You wanted to protect him, so you kept your past hidden. And now he is dead anyway. Dead because you had not passed on your training. How tragic.' The dragon's eyes flashed. 'But as much as I enjoy your misery, I feel our game is coming to an end, and you must tell me what it is I need to know. There is something you have been hiding from me. I have been able to smell it since I woke in the mountains. Something magical. Its power vibrates through the air. My scales are tingling.' She ran one claw down the side of Cloud's face. Her touch was repulsive and dangerous. 'What is it? What are you hiding?'

Cloud closed his eyes and tried to concentrate through the heavy, flat pain in his chest. He had to keep Sorrow talking. The longer she talked, the longer Landmark survived, and the more time Tidal and the girls had to free Cumulo.

He licked his lips. The darkness of the night slowly began to thin out into the cold grey of the morning.

'The disappearance of the dragons was more damaging than I had imagined it might be,' he said. 'The magic became unbalanced, and the vile taste of power turned many of the mages and wizards to thoughts of conquest. They started to tear the land apart. The fort became a strategic vantage point during the civil war, and I could not risk the Wing Warrior armour falling into the hands of a tyrant.'

'So you moved it.'

'I broke into the fort and took it away. I hid it far under the ground, burying it as deeply as I had hoped I buried you. I put it in a place that was haunted by the memory of legends.'

'But why go to such efforts, Cloud? The weapons of a Wing Warrior are nothing without legends to breathe their magic into them. What else were you protecting?' She removed her claw from his chest and moved her head so her snout was almost touching his face. 'What are you plotting?'

Quick as a flash of lightning, Cloud snatched up a handful of dust and shingle, dashing it in Sorrow's eyes. She recoiled with a scream of anger.

Using the last of his failing strength, Cloud pulled himself to his feet and began staggering away. If he could find some cave, some small alcove in the rock, perhaps he could hide.

He looked left, right. He was so faint the world was starting to spin dizzyingly. The rocks became grey and beige streaks in an insubstantial dreamland. Although the new day was fast approaching, everything seemed to be getting darker.

'Cloud,' Sorrow hissed, blinking the dirt out of her eyes. 'That wasn't very sporting.'

Cloud felt the terrible chill of the dragon's shadow fall over him. He kept moving, barely faster than a crawl. Stumbling, scuffing his knees. There was no way he could escape. He was too tired.

Too weak.

'You don't die as easy as the other Wing Warriors did,' Sorrow said. 'I have to admit, you're even more trouble to kill than the dragons were.'

She snatched up Cloud, looking at him closely. Despite everything, he allowed himself a small laughter of defiance.

'Is something amusing?' Sorrow asked.

'The other dragons,' he said, before finally passing out. 'They're not really dead.'

CHAPTER THIRTY-ONE

Tidal looked up. Shattered beams of smoky light filtered down through a metal grille, cutting out parts of his face from the clammy darkness of the sewer tunnel.

A rusting ladder, thick with moss and dripping sludge, was bolted into the wall, and led up to the grille. He squinted, but couldn't see anything. Up there could be a prison, a warehouse, a coal cellar, or a room full of Lord Citrine's finest soldiers.

'This must be it,' he said uncertainly, pulling on the ladder to make sure it wouldn't come away from the wall under his weight. 'We go up from here.'

'Thank goodness for that,' Sky said. 'I'm not sure I could have coped with much more of this sewer.'

'Can we go home?' Glass asked.

Sky took her hand. 'Soon, Glass. Soon.'

'It smells bad down here, and there are rats.'

Tidal climbed several rungs of the ladder. 'Be quiet,' he whispered. 'There may be guards.'

'There's nobody up there,' Glass said.

'I'll go on ahead and take a look.' He carefully climbed to the top of the ladder.

'There's nobody up there,' Glass repeated.

'How do you know?' Sky asked.

'Sometimes I just know.'

Tidal laced his fingers around the metal grille and pushed it open. Above was a small room full of barrels. There were thin shards of light coming through a barred window high up in one wall, and they were occasionally interrupted by the variously shaped silhouettes of passers–by. There were rats everywhere, clambering over the barrels and each other; so many rats that the floor itself seemed to be alive.

'Yuck,' Tidal said, pulling himself up into the room, little realising that most of the rats had just said exactly the same thing about him. 'It's okay,' he called down to Sky and Glass. 'Lots of rats, but no guards. Be careful coming up. It's slippy.'

He shooed the rats away, and they vanished into holes in the walls, tumbling over each other in their hurry to escape. The last pink tail had just disappeared from view when Glass climbed into the room. She was soaked through, covered in mud and dirt, and her pretty hair was matted with grime. It was the first time Tidal had seen her in the light since the goblin attack, and she barely looked like the same little girl.

'What is this place?' she asked, helping Sky up behind her.

'Some kind of store room,' Tidal said. 'I think we're just below street level. See the people walking by outside?' He pointed up at the window as another shadow temporarily blotted out the light.

'Under the ground,' Glass said, shivering uncontrollably.

Tidal started trying to prise open one of the barrels. 'I think this might be like that beer the Landmark garrison drink.'

'And unless you want to end up as useless as they are, you'll leave it alone,' Sky said. 'That stuff is bad for you. It makes you go stupid. It makes people act differently.'

Tidal glanced at her, and he could see from her expression that she was serious. He gave up trying to open the barrel and gave her a smile. 'You're right. We should get on.'

There was only one door out of the room, leading into a wide stone corridor that receded into yawning darkness both left and right. Dirty moisture trickled down the walls and pooled in the cracks of the rough cut flagstones. The smell of sour earth and never–ending misery was overpowering.

'We must be in the dungeons,' Sky said. 'It's so sad down here.'

'People crying,' Glass said, quietly.

Tidal watched her cautiously. He had known her since she was born, had watched her growing up, but he still couldn't shake his increasing sense of unease. He hated to admit it, but she frightened him.

'It's in the air, in the walls,' Glass went on.

'What's in the air?'

'Every tear that's been shed here. It's all remembered. Trapped in the bottomless pits.' She paused, tilting her head to one side. 'And I can hear the dragon too. His breathing vibrates through the stone around us.'

'I don't hear anything,' Tidal said.

'Trust me, he's close.'

'Do we go left or right?' Tidal said.

Glass closed her eyes. After a moment she said, 'Right. There are guards to the left. Four of them. All armed with swords, spears, and shields. They don't like the dragon being here. They just want things to be normal.'

Tidal secretly glanced at Sky, relieved to see she looked just as uneasy as he felt. 'Let's head right,' he said.

Glass shivered, blinked a few times, and then grinned at them both. 'Come on, let's go and see Cumulo. It's going to be exciting meeting a nice dragon.'

They headed down the tunnel, careful not to cause any noisy splashes that would attract unwanted attention.

Down here the only light came from torches hanging in metal brackets on the walls. It was just enough illumination for the children to see where they were going, but not enough to see everything the blackness sought to conceal. There could have been danger lurking at every twist in the corridor.

They passed many sealed doors, many metal gates and barred ways. Sometimes they could see people slumped in the gloom, muttering and coughing. Sometimes they couldn't see anything at all, and that seemed even worse.

'Some of these people have been here for years,' Glass said.

'They don't even remember the sun.'

'Be quiet,' Tidal hissed.

After another fifty metres the tunnel suddenly ended in the largest metal gate they had yet seen.

Cumulo was curled on the other side of the bars with his head resting on his front claws. His big, sad eyes were unblinking. 'I've been waiting for you,' he said.

Tidal smiled sheepishly, trying to disguise how scared he was. The last dragon he had seen had tried to eat him, and he wasn't entirely sure this one wouldn't try the same thing.

'Hello,' Glass said, walking up to the bars. Sky grabbed her arm protectively, obviously sharing Tidal's concern about Cumulo's sharp teeth; but Glass pulled away. 'He won't hurt me,' she said. 'This is Nimbus's friend. Our friend.'

'You must be Glass,' Cumulo said. 'It's a pleasure to meet you.'

'Thank you,' Glass said.

A large brown rat that was scuttling along the edge of the wall stopped for a moment, twitching its nose inquisitively.

There was a clatter from the guard room and muffled voices were raised in argument.

'They're playing cards,' Cumulo muttered. 'They're always playing cards.'

Glass's forehead creased in the slightest of frowns. 'Just think, they can leave this place any time they like, and they choose not to. They must be even lonelier than the prisoners.'

Cumulo wriggled slightly. 'Maybe lonelier, but not as uncomfortable. How do you intend to get me out?'

Tidal grabbed one of the prison bars and shook it. It didn't move. He stopped, looked at Sky. Sky shrugged.

Tidal shook the bar again. It still didn't move.

'Is that the best plan you have?' Cumulo said. 'If it is, you'll excuse me if I don't get too excited.'

'We hadn't really thought beyond getting here,' Tidal said.

'We were relying on Cloud, but...' His words trailed away. He couldn't bring himself to talk about what had happened to Cloud, certainly not in front of Glass. It was too upsetting.

'Cloud would have known what to do,' Sky said.

Cumulo nodded sadly. He didn't need to ask the children what had happened to Cloud; their expressions made it all too obvious that there had been a terrible tragedy.

'Maybe we could steal the key from the guards,' Tidal said, examining the gate's keyhole.

'What if we get caught?' Sky said.

'I could get it,' Glass said. 'I'm small. I could sneak in while they were playing cards.'

'It's too risky,' Sky said.

'Besides, there are hundreds of locks down here, and hundreds of keys for them,' Cumulo said. 'You'd never find the right one.'

'Could you push out the wall?' Tidal asked.

'I could, but we'd have guards attacking us before the dust finished settling. You could get hurt, or I could hurt someone else.'

Tidal leaned against the wall and folded his arms. The corner of his mouth twisted into a sneer. 'Are you serious? These people have locked you down here and you're worried you might hurt them?'

A curl of smoke came out of Cumulo's nostril. 'There are many people I could hurt if I so wished, but if I did, how would I be able to consider myself any better than Sorrow?'

'But these people deserve your anger.'

'I have been locked here because people are scared of me. If I resort to violence, I am exactly what they say I am.'

'But...'

'There is a lot of anger in you. No good can come from it.'

Boy and dragon exchanged a look that said more than words ever could. There was a distinctive change in the atmosphere, like a crackle of electricity. Sky picked up on the sudden tension and quickly jumped into the conversation. 'We need to sneak you out without drawing any attention,' she said.

'And how do you suggest we do that?' Tidal said. 'It's a dragon, not a mouse.'

Glass watched the rat running along the bottom of the wall. 'A mouse,' she said, thoughtfully. 'I like mice.'

The rat stopped, looked at her. Its nose twitched. 'What's wrong with rats?' it was thinking.

'Some rescue party we turned out to be,' Tidal said, bitterly.

'You did your best,' Cumulo said. 'There is little more anybody can ask of you.'

'But our best wasn't good enough.'

'These things happen for a reason. Don't be too angry with yourself.'

'A rat,' Glass whispered. 'If Cumulo was a rat I could put him right in my pocket.'

Sky put an arm around Glass's shoulder. 'It's okay. We'll think of something.'

Tidal watched them silently, chewing on his bottom lip. This was stupid. They had come all this way, escaped from Sorrow, lost Cloud forever, ran through stinking sewers, and after all that... He shook his head. He was so useless.

This was all his fault.

He was the leader. He should have had a plan.

He should have talked about it with Cloud while they were still in the cart. Why hadn't he thought to go through the details of the rescue then? That's what a hero would have done. A hero would never be put in this situation. A hero would never look stupid in front of these girls.

He closed his eyes. Sky was going to think he was a stupid kid. Just a stupid, good–for–nothing, kid.

He should be a better hero than Nimbus ever dreamed of being.

So why wasn't he?

If he had only found the Wing Warrior armour... If Nimbus hadn't lied to him.

Vaguely he became aware of Sky and Glass talking.

'What are you looking at?' Sky was saying.

'A rat.'

'Rats are dirty. Come away from there.'

'I was just thinking how much easier it would be if Cumulo was the size of that rat.'

'Well, yes. It would make things easier. If Cumulo was that small he would be able to squeeze right through the bars and...'

Silence.

Tidal opened his eyes.

The prison cell was empty. Where Cumulo had been, there was now a large space. Glass and Sky were staring at the space blankly.

'Hey,' Tidal said. 'What happened to the dragon?'

Sky pointed. Her mouth flapped open and shut, but no words came out.

'What?'

More pointing.

'What?'

'Cumulo,' Sky said.

Tidal's gaze followed the direction of Sky's pointing finger. 'I don't...'

As he looked more closely into the darkness of the prison cell, he could see it wasn't quite as empty as it first appeared. There was a small animal sitting in the corner, almost completely hidden in the gloom. As he watched, it scurried over and looked at him with tiny black eyes. Its nose twitched.

'Look at that,' Tidal said. 'A rat with wings.'

CHAPTER THIRTY-TWO

Glass put the shrunken Cumulo in her pocket, giggling when he stuck his head out and puffed tiny clouds of smoke at her.

'You can shrink dragons?' Tidal said.

'I guess so,' Glass said, stroking Cumulo's snout.

'But how?'

'I don't know. I was looking at a rat over there, thinking it would be good if Cumulo was that small too, and then he was that small. It just sort of happened.'

'Great.' Tidal threw his hands up in the air and rolled his eyes. 'That's just great. We've freed the dragon, but now he's so small Sorrow will just be able to step on him.'

Sky touched Tidal's hand, but he moved away.

'No,' he snapped.

'No?'

'Don't touch me. This is stupid. We've got a rat–sized dragon. Tell me what good that is?'

'Calm down,' Sky said. 'I'm sure Glass will be able to reverse the magic later. You can reverse the magic, can't you, Glass?'

Glass said nothing.

'Great,' Tidal said. 'See? I told you she would be a danger. I told you she couldn't control her powers, and that could only mean trouble for all of us. I told you that, but did you listen? Did anybody listen? No. Not you, not Cloud. No–one.'

Glass sniffed back a sob. 'I'm sorry.'

'But sorry isn't going to help us, is it? Sorry doesn't save our village from getting stomped by Sorrow.'

'At least Cumulo is out of the prison.'

'Out of the prison and in your pocket. Brilliant.'

Glass wiped her nose on her sleeve. 'I didn't mean to do it. I was only trying to help.'

'Well, do us a favour, don't do us any more favours. Okay?'

Sky stepped between them. 'Stop bullying her,' she said, sternly. 'She didn't mean any harm, and I'm sure we can figure out a way to get Cumulo back to normal. For now, let's just work on getting out of here without being arrested ourselves.'

'Fine,' Tidal snapped. 'But keep the little witch away from me. She can't be trusted.'

He strode off down the corridor, quickly disappearing from view in the dark.

'He doesn't mean it,' Sky said. 'He's just tired and scared, like all of us.'

'He's right though, isn't he?'

'Tidal is never right. Not about anything.'

'I don't know what's happening to me. I'm scared. I can feel stuff going on inside, and it's like I'm being pulled in all different directions. I can do all these things, but I don't know how. Sometimes I feel like me, and sometimes I feel all strange, and it's like I'm someone else in my body.'

'That doesn't make sense.'

'I know, but that's how I feel. I don't like it. I just want to go back to how I was before.'

'Don't be afraid. I'm here, and I'm going to make sure you're okay.'

'But I've shrunk Cumulo, and I don't know how to change him back. I've ruined everything. I should never have come here.'

'My mum...' Sky paused, trying to remember her mother's face. She couldn't. It was too far back in the past. She took a second to control the tremor she felt in her voice, and then went on. 'My mum used to tell me, if a problem seems too big, it's probably because you're looking at too much of it. One step at a time, she used to say. You solved the problem of how to get Cumulo out of the prison. That was something we couldn't have done without you. Next we'll figure out how to get out of here, and then we'll worry about changing Cumulo back. One step at a time, like Mum said.'

Glass tried on a smile that didn't quite mask her mixed feelings of sadness and fear. 'Thanks, Sky,' she said. 'It's dead obvious why Nimbus likes you.'

'What do you mean, "likes me"?'

Cumulo blinked, and licked his nostrils.

Tidal reappeared out of the gloom. 'Are you two coming?' he asked.

'Coming where?' Sky asked, a little distractedly. 'We can't go back into the sewers, Sorrow blocked them off.'

'There must be other routes down there we can take.'

'The sewers are massive, we could be lost for days. We don't have time for that. We need to get back to Landmark.'

'What other option do we have? The guards are still in the guard room. We can't go that way.'

'I've got an idea,' Glass said.

'I think you've done enough damage,' Tidal said.

'At least she has an idea,' Sky said.

'She probably wants to shrink us all, or turn us into frogs, or make us vanish. Well, it's not happening. I'm not letting her use any of her magic on me.'

'I don't know how to turn people into frogs.'

'You didn't know how to shrink dragons either, but you managed to do it anyway. Sometimes you just think things and they happen.' Tidal was starting to back away. 'You could be thinking about turning me into a frog right now. Stop it. If that's what you're thinking, just stop it.'

'I wasn't thinking of using magic to get out of here at all.'

'Let's just hear what she has to say,' Sky said, putting a protective arm around Glass's shoulders.

Tidal shrugged. 'Fine, let's hear the master plan. What do you suggest we do?'

'I think we should just be children,' Glass said. 'That's what we are, after all.'

'What do you mean?'

'I mean, follow me, and do exactly what I do.'

Glass headed down the corridor. 'What's she doing?' Tidal asked Sky.

'I don't know, but we better go after her before she gets herself into trouble.'

They followed Glass to the guard room, moving as silently as wood spirits through the crackling light of the torches. Their hands touched, long enough for Tidal to realise it was not an accident; but not long enough for him to think they were holding hands.

Glass had one ear pressed to the door of the guard room. The gruff voices of four men could be heard coming from the other side.

'We shouldn't have played for money,' one man said, miserably.

'I've lost everything I earned this week,' another said.

'And last week,' a third added.

'Stop being such spoilsports. I'll give you a chance to win it all back,' the last man said. 'It's not my fault none of you are any good at playing cards, is it?'

'So what do we do now?' Tidal whispered, as the men continued to bicker and fight over how unfair it was, and how stupid they had been to waste their money on a card game. 'They don't sound like they're in the best of moods, and I don't fancy fighting our way out.'

'We won't have to fight,' Glass said, pushing open the door.

The guards, who were sat at a round table examining their cards, looked up as the children came into the room. Glass was covered in mud and dirt and sewer slime, and she smelled terrible. She could only imagine what the guards must have thought of her, and her equally smelly companions.

The largest guard sprang up, sending cards flying everywhere. 'What is this?' he demanded. 'Who are you?'

Glass immediately burst into tears. Tidal raised his eyebrows at Sky. 'Great plan.'

'What's wrong?' the guard asked. 'Who are you?'

'Must be some street kids,' a second guard said.

'I want my mummy,' Glass wailed.

'How did you get down here?' the guard asked. 'Are you lost?'

'I want my mummy.'

'Sewer kids,' another guard grumbled. 'Probably ducked down a manhole to get off the streets for a few days and got lost in the dark. That's what they stink like.'

'They could be on the run from the law. We should arrest them.'

'I want my mummy,' Glass howled.

'Arrest them? I don't know about you, but I don't want screaming brats down here. I'm losing money, and I won't be able to concentrate with all that going on.'

The guard who had first jumped to his feet was thoughtful for a moment before speaking. 'You're right. They're just kids. I'll take them up top. Don't look at my cards while I'm gone.'

Glass stopped crying. She looked at the guard with big, watery eyes.

'Come on,' the guard said.

Glass took the guard's hand. She looked over her shoulder and winked at Tidal.

The guard led them up a huge, winding stone staircase, down a maze of identical corridors, and out into one of the many filthy back streets of Crystal Shine. The shining towers of the palace loomed up, a few streets to the North.

'So how did you kids get in anyway?' the guard asked.

'We're not sure,' Tidal lied.

'Well from here on you're on your own. I've got a card game to win.' The guard gave the children one last look, perhaps considering whether he should really leave them alone in the street; then he went inside, closing and locking the door behind him.

The pale sun burned lazily without heat. The alleyway was completely empty.

'This is my first time in the city,' Sky said. 'It's my first time anywhere, really.'

Tidal squinted up at the palace towers. 'It's so big.'

Sky looked around at all the rubbish spilled on the dirty street, and the grime on the walls. 'It's not what I expected.'

'I bet you can see the whole world from up there.'

'But not from down here.'

They both fell silent; both looking in different directions.

'So what do we do now?' Tidal asked, eventually.

Glass took Cumulo out of her pocket. Her eyes narrowed, and her forehead creased with concentration.

'What are you doing?' Sky asked.

'Well, when I thought about a rat, Cumulo shrank to the size of a rat,' Glass said.

'So?'

'So now I'm thinking about an elephant.'

CHAPTER THIRTY-THREE

It was late afternoon when Sorrow descended upon the village of Landmark with the fury of ages.

She swooped down low and fast, and houses crashed to the ground in piles of stone and wooden splinters. The few people who still remained at the village ran screaming as the mighty dragon breathed clouds of poison into the streets and uprooted trees with her terrible claws.

'What will we do?' the people wailed. 'How can we fight this monster?'

Sorrow landed in the village square with a ground–shaking thump. Her head swung left and right, flaming eyes seeking out any person foolish enough to fight back.

There was nobody.

The last of the Landmark soldiers watched in horror from behind their shields as the dragon bellowed and her smoke blackened the sky.

'What do we do?' one of the soldier's said, so scared he could barely speak.

'We hide, and hope that Cloud comes back,' a second soldier said.

At that moment, Sorrow screamed triumphantly and let something human—shaped slip out of her talons.

'I think,' the first soldier said, 'Cloud's already here.'

In the dust, where he had been dropped, Cloud coughed and groaned. There was dirt in his eyes and up his nose, and every part of him ached worse than if he had been pulled apart and then put back together again. He tried to rise, but he didn't have the strength.

'You can't do this,' he gasped.

Sorrow lowered her head. Her tongue tickled his face when she spoke. 'And why not?'

'These people are innocent.'

'You say that as if I should care in some way?'

'These people have never hurt you, not like I did. Take me, but let these people go.'

'No,' Sorrow said, after a thoughtful pause. 'No, I think not. I think, instead, I will destroy this village and everybody in it. And what's more, I think I will make you watch. That would be a fitting punishment for the way you treated me all those years ago.'

'Please,' Cloud said.

Sorrow chuckled deep in her throat. 'Keep begging, Cloud. It won't help, but I like it.'

'You won't be allowed to get away with this, Sorrow. Someone will stop you. '

'Really? And who might that be?'

The air was filled with the thundering of horses' hooves, and as if in answer to Sorrow's question, Captain Obsidian, who had only just that minute returned from Crystal Shine, came galloping down the street with two of his men close behind.

Sorrow tilted her head to one side inquisitively. 'What is this?' she asked.

'Steady men,' Obsidian said, drawing his sword. 'Stay away from its head and claws. Strike for its belly.'

Sorrow reared up and gave a single flap of her wings, causing such a powerful wind that Obsidian and his men were blasted right out of their saddles. The horses turned tail and ran.

'Is that the best this village has to offer?' Sorrow laughed. 'Is there no—one else who will challenge me?'

Cloud watched, horrified, as Obsidian staggered to his feet just in time for Sorrow to swipe at him with her claws. He flew through the air, spinning wildly, and slammed into the wall of a nearby house. When he hit the ground he did not move again.

Any thoughts the other soldiers might have had about continuing to fight were quickly forgotten.

'These people are so weak,' Sorrow hissed. 'So fragile, so easily crushed. Yet you protect them, Cloud. Why do you do that? Why would you die for these people?'

'Because they're good people.'

Sorrow's wings snapped back together as she prowled around the square hungrily.

'You don't need to do this, Sorrow,' Cloud went on.

'I know that... But it's so much fun.'

She threw her head back, and the sound that came out of her was the scream of all the world's victims. A jet of thick smoke gushed from her throat, blasting up into the sky and then drifting down over the surrounding houses. What few green things remained – some grass, a leafy plant – shrivelled up and died, and Cloud began to cough violently. The world suddenly seemed very dark.

And then the world was darker still, as a massive shadow fell over the village.

Cloud looked up. 'Cumulo,' he said.

Sorrow half–turned, but Cumulo, now restored to his proper and impressive size, was already barrelling into her, a roaring mass of talons and fangs. The two dragons rolled together, rending and snapping and biting. Sorrow breathed smoke, and gouts of flame burst from Cumulo. The ground was scorched where they fought.

As the two monstrous titans tumbled and wrestled, smashing flat buildings and fences, Cloud started making his way across the village square, dragging himself with trembling arms, his fingers clenching in the mud, his exhausted muscles groaning with the effort. So intent was he on putting some distance between himself and the dragons that he barely felt it when someone started to pull imploringly at his shoulder.

'Come on,' a voice was saying by his ear. 'Try to stand. You can lean on me.'

He looked up into Tidal's filthy, determined face, and for a second it felt like his heart had stopped beating. 'You did it,' he said. 'You brought back the dragon.'

Tidal beamed, his teeth flashing through caked–on mud. 'Was there ever any doubt?'

'I can't believe...'

'No time for that. You can tell us how great we are later.'

'Daddy!' Glass squealed, launching herself at Cloud and wrapping her arms around his neck. 'You're okay. I knew that mean old dragon couldn't hurt you.' The tremor in her voice made it obvious she had been no way near as confident as she claimed to be.

'I'm okay,' Cloud said. He was too tired even to hug his daughter back, and he sounded no more convincing than she did. 'I'm okay now you're here.'

'We're going to move you,' Tidal said.

Sky appeared beside him: a slight, beautiful creature of calm and purity, moving silently amidst the chaos.

She gently lifted one of Cloud's arms while Tidal gripped the other. 'We can't lift you,' she said. 'You have to help us.'

With their assistance, Cloud half crawled, half stumbled, towards Captain Obsidian, who was now sitting against the wall, completely dazed and in no fit state for a fight.

Behind them, Sorrow growled, slashing out wildly and striking Cumulo on the snout. It was a powerful blow that spun him right around; then he steadied himself, spread his wings for balance, and braced himself just in time for Sorrow to pounce on him. Her weight smashed him down, and her bone–crunching jaws clamped around his neck.

He cried out in pain, his tail thrashing violently. Sorrow was bigger and heavier than he was, and he knew he couldn't win this way. He needed to break free from her grip and keep her at a distance with his fiery breath.

'So you're what Cloud was hiding from me, what he was prepared to die for,' she sneered.

Cumulo twisted and wriggled but he couldn't escape, she was far too strong.

'They pinned all their hopes on you,' she said, toothily. 'And this is all you are?'

With all her strength, she scooped up Cumulo and hurled him into a building. Stones fell down on him, and the wooden rafters broke on his head. Dizzy and confused, he lumbered out of the wreckage, covered in grey stone–dust. His scales glowed blue underneath. 'That was a silly mistake, Sorrow,' he said.

Wreaths of poison hung around Sorrow's vile head, so it seemed that her red eyes floated in a murky shadow as she approached once more.

Cumulo arched his neck and took a deep breath. The temperature dropped a few degrees, as though he was drawing the warmth out of the air. Sorrow hesitated for a split second, then lunged to the attack. Cumulo snapped his head forwards, hacking up a stream of ice crystals that whipped into her face.

He backed away. Freezing cold vapour rose from his nostrils. Where had his fire gone?

He needed his fire.

Sorrow blinked her vision clear.

Now she was mad.

Cumulo showed his claws. His scales continued to glow blue.

Tidal, Sky, and Glass watched the fight from the far side of the square. Sky was clinging on to Tidal's arm, and Glass was clinging on to Sky's.

'Is there something we can do?' Sky said.

'We got him here,' Glass said. 'That was what we were supposed to do. That's what we did.'

'Couldn't you do something to Sorrow? Make her small, or

turn her into a butterfly, or something like that?'

'No. I'm still not sure how I do all that stuff, and if I get something wrong I might end up hurting Cumulo, or someone else. I don't want to make things worse.'

'But Cumulo isn't ready to fight Sorrow. There must be some way we can help him.'

Tidal's concerned expression changed into a wide grin. He looked like a boy who had just discovered a gold mine in his back garden. 'I know a way,' he said.

He ran off, heading for Nimbus's house.

Somewhere else, in a world that existed between worlds, the mouth beneath Guide's hood curled into a cold sneer. 'You don't want to go on with me?' he asked.

Nimbus scuffed his toe in the brown earth. He had never felt so small and lost before, and he couldn't shake the feeling that Guide was laughing at him. 'I don't know,' he said. 'It just feels like I'm running away from something.'

'Running away from what?'

'I don't know.' He knelt down and scooped up a handful of sharp stones. They shone like pieces of broken Glass. 'My sister. I'm sure I heard her. I know you said I couldn't have, but I'm sure it was her.'

'Your sister is alive, Nimbus. You aren't.'

'I might be.'

'But the dragon...'

'I know, I know. But if I go with you, how can I be sure? I could be throwing my life away.'

Guide watched carefully as Nimbus sorted through the stones in his hand. One of the larger stones was round and flat, a mirror in which his sorry eyes reflected.

'You are prepared to risk an eternity on these plains, lost and alone?'

'What have I got to lose?'

'You are talking foolishly. If you come with me, you will be able to see your sister again. You will be able to watch over her as a guardian spirit, and protect her.'

Nimbus looked at Guide. 'What do you mean by guardian?'

'Here, in this desolate landscape, you are neither living nor truly dead. You have no influence over either world. You are just a lost spirit, in torment, and afraid. But if you come with me to the other side, you will be eternally by your sister's side, able to guide her in her decisions.'

'Guide her?' Storm clouds rolled across the sky, an armada of sailing ships on a purple sea. 'Guide. Only people who can't see where they're going need a guide.'

'What's wrong?'

'It's something my sister said.'

'Never mind that,' Guide said. 'We're close now. The way to the lands of the dead are just beyond the next ridge. Do you really want to give up on your sister when you're this close?'

'Isn't it giving up to go on? Shouldn't I stay here and try to find a way back to her?'

'Nonsense.'

Nimbus looked back the way they had come. The Wing Warrior sword was lying on the ground just a few feet away, still glowing, but more faintly now. 'The sword is following me. It wants me to see.'

'See what?'

'I don't know. But my sister said I needed to open my eyes.'

Guide came over to Nimbus and held out his hand. 'Take my hand, Nimbus. You said you wanted me to lead you on this path. Don't run away from me now.'

'I thought I'd opened my eyes, but what if I haven't? What if I'm wrong about all of this?'

'You're acting like a silly child, Nimbus.'

'Glass said I could only save myself from the dragon if I

opened my eyes.' He walked over to the Wing Warrior sword. 'This sword has the power to grant anyone who touches it infinite vision. For some reason it wants to show me something. Don't you think I should see what that is?'

Guide propped himself up against his staff. His mouth was stern and straight. 'Don't make this into an unpleasant situation, Nimbus. Leave the sword alone.'

'I don't think I can. I don't think I should.'

'I won't ask again, Nimbus.'

'I think my sister was trying to tell me something.'

He bent to pick up the sword.

Guide lurched into motion, throwing aside his staff. His hood fell back to reveal his face. His skin was pale, almost unnaturally so, his cheekbones were sharp and well–defined, and he had shining black hair that was tied back in a flowing ponytail. His eyes and mouth were closed, and he approached in perfect silence.

For that one fleeting moment, Nimbus believed Guide was possibly the most handsome man in the world; but as the distance between them closed, Guide's eyes sprang open, and his beautiful face was contorted in a snarling expression of pure evil.

Nimbus recoiled in horror as Guide's eyes flared, startling and red, becoming bubbling pools of volcanic ash and fire; and when Guide's mouth opened, it was as if a doorway into the darkest part of the human spirit had been opened up.

It was obvious that beneath his handsome exterior there was nothing except simple hatred.

His cruel fingers grabbed hold of Nimbus around the throat and clamped down with unbelievable strength. Nimbus tried to scream, but there was too much pressure on his neck, and all he could manage was a pained choke as he was pulled to the ground.

'You wanted to see the truth,' Guide hissed. A wicked tongue – fat and purple–grey – lolled out of his mouth, and saliva dribbled from his sharp teeth. 'You wanted to see the truth, well here it is. This is what I was trying to protect you from. This is the horror of the world. Are you happy now? Are you?'

'You're the poison,' Nimbus choked.

'I am the greatest poison. I am the evil that has slept for many years in the memories of your civilisation.'

Nimbus looked over at the Wing Warrior sword. It was pulsing white light, making a last desperate attempt to be seen. He reached out, his fingers snatching at thin air.

'You can't stop me getting back to my sister,' he croaked. 'I won't give up to you.'

'You're too late,' Guide said. His voice dripped like venom from a spider's ugly mouth. 'You're stuck here now. You're stuck here forever. Once, your father took everything from me. Now I'm going to make sure you never see him ever again.'

Nimbus closed his eyes tight. He knew he could reach the sword. He knew he could.

His fingers touched the cold metal of the blade.

The sword vanished.

Tidal took the Wing Warrior sword from where it was lying next to the sleeping Nimbus. Nimbus's hand moved, and it appeared that he too was attempting to take the sword.

Tidal leaned over the bed, whispering in Nimbus's ear. 'Sorry, Nimbus. You had your chance. It's my turn now. I'm going to finish what you started.'

Nimbus's eyes flickered under his eyelids.

Tidal took the sword in both hands and gave it an experimental swing. It was heavy, much heavier than he had expected, but he was strong enough to use it. His eyes glowed with the prospect of getting the chance to fight and slay the dragon that had been even too mighty for Cloud to defeat.

Finally, this was his chance to be a hero.

'You shouldn't do that,' Glass said, appearing in the doorway. Her voice sounded powerful, ancient and eternal, but small and frail at the same time. It was the voice of a great wizard speaking through the body of a small girl. Tidal was immediately reminded of her ability to shrink dragons or conjure light from darkness.

'Why not?' he said, cautiously.

'My daddy said that every hero needs his sword. You should leave it there on the bed.'

'Nimbus is hardly going to need it, is he?'

'It's not your sword, Tidal.'

'Who says so? Why can't it be my sword? I went down in the cave with Nimbus. If Nimbus hadn't hidden the truth from me, I could have found the armour. I could have found the dragon. And look...' He pointed out of the window. Cumulo and Sorrow were clearly visible, roaring at each other as dust swirled around them. 'I led us through the sewer. I led the rescue mission. Cumulo is here because of me, so why can't I take this sword?'

'We all freed Cumulo,' Glass said, calmly. Her shadow seemed to be getting larger, darker, and more monstrous.

'This is my moment,' Tidal said. 'I won't let you take it away from me. I won't let anybody take it away from me.'

'I can't take it away from you. You're bigger than me.'

Glass was just a little girl, small and weak, and Tidal knew that if he really wanted to he could pick her up in one hand; but somehow she seemed bigger. She seemed so much bigger, in fact, that she was filling up the whole room.

He realised he was thinking about toads. He was thinking about what it would be like to be a toad, and what his voice would sound like if he was a toad, and what Sky would think of him if he was a toad; and he realised it was Glass who was putting those thoughts in his head.

'You aren't going to let me take this sword, are you?' he said.

'No,' Glass said.

'So you're going to let Cumulo get ripped apart by that

monster out there?'

'Cumulo isn't going to get ripped apart.'

'He certainly isn't going to win. Sorrow is much bigger and uglier than he is.'

'He doesn't have to win, he just needs to keep her busy long enough.'

'Long enough for what?'

'Please put the sword back.'

Tidal took one last look at the sword, and then placed it on the bed next to Nimbus's right hand. 'You're right. This is Nimbus's sword. It should stay here.'

'I'm glad we agree.'

Tidal turned his attention back to the dragons outside. Sorrow was being blasted with sparkling jets of ice crystals, and in return she was breathing her black smoke. All the time they were circling each other, occasionally snapping their teeth, or swiping out with their talons. It was truly terrifying to watch.

'Where's Sky?' Tidal asked.

'She's outside. With Cloud and Captain Obsidian. She wanted to stay with them.'

'We should make sure she's okay.'

Glass's shadow shrank back to normal size. 'That's a good idea.'

Nimbus was still struggling to escape from Guide's iron grip when the Wing Warrior sword magically reappeared beside him. It was still glowing, still wanting him to see the truth.

Guide was grinning maniacally, his teeth wet with stinking saliva, his eyes staring wildly.

'You'll be here forever now,' he hissed. 'Here, forever, with me. You'll never see your sister again.'

Nimbus stretched out his arm, grabbing the handle of the sword with numb fingers. He liked the feel of the weapon against his skin, it made him feel safe. It made him feel like he was back home.

'Glass,' he whispered.

'You can't stop us,' Guide said. 'Me, the dragon, my army. We're too strong now. You're too late. This is just the start of my revenge. This is just the start of the suffering your father has brought upon you and your family.'

'Who are you?'

'They called me Crow once. Remember the name, because you will hear it again before you die.'

The sword glowed, and Nimbus closed his eyes against the painfully bright light. There was the sound of rushing water in his ears, and he was overcome with the impression that he was being dragged along by the strong current of an endless river.

Then everything went very quiet, and just like the last time he had held the sword, Nimbus felt like he was floating in the middle of the ocean. For a few blissful moments, moments when it seemed like the world had ended, he was totally calm.

When he opened his eyes again he was standing in a small bedroom he immediately recognised as his own. He was stood by the side of the bed, next to a chair where the Wing Warrior armour had been stacked, but he was also lying on the bed with one hand wrapped around the handle of the Wing Warrior sword.

He smiled, and the other him on the bed smiled too.

'Okay,' he said. 'What did the sword want to show me?'

Around him, the walls began to splinter and fall away, and the other him on the bed disappeared. Now he was standing in a gigantic hall where twelve men were sitting at a table.

'The dragons have done their part,' one of the men was saying. 'The new dragon will come, but somebody must be responsible for protecting the egg until the time is right.'

The room was silent. Eleven of the men were looking at just one. They were all looking at Cloud.

'I can't,' Cloud said.

'Mother is gone. You have no dragon to go into battle with,' the other said.

'Mother's disappearance is my fault. I must make amends. I cannot sit by and watch you all go to war.'

'You have no choice, Cloud. You must protect the new dragon, it must stay hidden, and if things go badly for us, then you must survive us, and be ready for what the future brings.'

'What future have I got without my dragon? I would rather throw myself upon the black dragon's claws than continue this way.'

'There is much you are not aware of, Cloud. We have seen you with a son. He will be called Nimbus, and he will be more than we have ever hoped to be. We have caught glimpses of this future in the mists of possibilities. You would have seen it too, if only you had not been blinded by your sorrow.'

'I will have a son?'

'You know how the power of the swords works. Not all ends will come to pass. But it could be that you are able to keep our dreams alive, even if we perish.'

Cloud was staring at his hands. 'I have drawn plans for a fortress,' he said. 'The greatest fortress the world has ever known. A place for the dragon to be kept.'

The other eleven men nodded, but before anybody else had a chance to speak, Nimbus was slipping away, drifting through layers of reality, and appearing somewhere else.

He was at the top of a mountain, and Sorrow was there, biting and slashing as eleven dragons swooped down at her. Eleven dragons, each one a different colour, a different size and shape.

Nimbus only just had time to realise he was witnessing the death of the last of the dragons, and then he was on the move again. He travelled across rivers, lakes, rocky peaks, and cavernous ravines. He walked with his father who was hunting something, following trails of blood for mile after mile.

'Who are we following?' he asked, but Cloud couldn't hear him.

Then he was standing with Cloud on a mountain road in the rain.

There was no sign of what they were hunting.

'She's gone,' Cloud said, talking to the wind and the rain because there was no–one else to hear. 'I followed her all this time, and now she's gone.' He looked into the sky. 'I am sorry, I let her escape. You all died for nothing. I failed.'

The rain fell harder. Cloud made fists with his hands and hung his head. 'I will make the fortress,' he said. 'I will hide the dragon egg, and I will watch the West. If Sorrow ever comes back, I'll be ready for her, and I will make her pay for this.'

Slowly, the world changed again.

Nimbus was under the ground, deep in the earth. He could hear harsh breathing in the darkness and he knew it was the breathing of Sorrow. She was hurt, weak from the fight with the Wing Warriors.

And she was not alone.

There was someone else with her, stroking her snout, whispering soothingly to her.

'Everything will be okay. You did well. You have rid the world of the dragons. And we can wait. We can wait as long as it takes. You and I, we are the same. We are forever.'

In that moment Nimbus understood what the sword was showing him.

It was showing him what he had already been told, but had never fully comprehended the importance of.

It was showing him it knew everything that had ever happened.

It was showing him it knew the history of every creature there had ever been, even the secret histories that nobody else could know.

It was showing him how he could win.

He jolted upright.

For a moment he was completely confused, then he realised he was sitting in his own bed. The Wing Warrior sword was clenched in his trembling right hand. The armour was neatly stacked nearby, and in it he thought he could see reflections that were not his own. His sheets were soaked with sweat.

'Glass?' he said, already knowing she wasn't there to hear him.

Outside, Sorrow and Cumulo snapped and spat at each other.

Nimbus struggled out of bed, put on the armour, and once more, perhaps for the last time ever, he was a Wing Warrior.

CHAPTER THIRTY-FOUR

Cumulo flew up, twisted in midair, then dropped on Sorrow with all his uncaged fury. Sorrow had already anticipated the move and ducked to the left, snapping her teeth down on one of Cumulo's wings.

Cumulo yelped and pulled back, feeling the skin of his wing tearing. Instantly the colour of his scales seemed to change from light blue to a much deeper blue with flecks of silver–lining. He took a deep breath, to fire another stream of ice and snow, but instead a hot flash of lightning leapt from his jaws, scorching Sorrow's toes. 'How are you doing that?' she said. 'How can you breathe ice and lightning?'

Cumulo grinned cheekily, and then pounced forwards, shifting his weight at the last second to barrel into Sorrow's left side. They fell together, rolling and spinning and clawing. Dust and black smoke spewed around them.

After what seemed to Cumulo like a lifetime of painful nips and scrapes, they drew apart, and as they did so, Sorrow lashed out vengefully. Her claws raked along Cumulo's body, breaking off several of his scales. The broken scales immediately turned grey, shrivelling up and crumbling to dust.

'This can't go on much longer,' Sorrow said. 'You will lose.'

Cumulo moved back to a safe distance. His side was bleeding. The skin of his torn wing flapped loosely. He could barely catch his breath.

'I've got plenty of fight left in me yet,' he gasped. It was a lie, pure and simple; but he couldn't let Sorrow know how tired he was. He couldn't show any weakness.

Cloud, Obsidian, and the children watched silently from near the broken remains of a house. Their eyes were wide and scared.

'You are prepared to die for those people, aren't you?' Sorrow said.

Cumulo blinked. He didn't reply. He didn't need to.

Wordlessly, almost silently, Sorrow launched across the square, butting into Cumulo with her sharp head. He turned away from the blow, losing his balance. Sorrow took the chance to wrap her arms and tail around him in a powerful grip, and then she flew up. Cumulo struggled to the last, but Sorrow's grip was unbreakable as she somersaulted in the air and then drove him into the earth with every ounce of strength she had.

For what seemed like a very long time indeed, she sat on top of Cumulo, breathing in his face as the dust settled.

Cumulo didn't move. His eyes were closed.

Slowly, Sorrow unfurled her body, stretching out her wings and tail elaborately. 'What fun,' she purred. 'It's been such a long time since I had a good fight.'

She clambered down from Cumulo, looking around the village for the next thing to destroy.

She had expected at this point for a ragtag mob of villagers to rush out and stab at her with pitchforks, or perhaps for Obsidian and Cloud to make one last brave defence in which they would most certainly be killed. What she hadn't expected was a fully armoured Wing Warrior to be standing at the edge of the square.

'I thought I killed you,' she said, slightly annoyed.

The Wing Warrior put down the visor of his helmet with one gloved hand. In the other hand, despite its obvious weight, he was holding the Wing Warrior sword. The blade of the sword glowed brightly.

'You're different,' Sorrow said. 'Bigger somehow. Strong enough to carry the sword.'

'Yes, I'm different,' the Wing Warrior said.

'It's no matter. I beat you once, I can do so again.'

'Let's find out.'

Sorrow's wings snapped closed. She champed her mouth

hungrily. 'I'm going to enjoy this,' she said, and rushed at the Wing Warrior.

Casually, without any apparent urgency, the Wing Warrior drew a line in the dust with the blade of the sword, took a few paces back, and braced himself.

His heart was thundering painfully. The dragon's black clouds fell over him. He held his breath. He was only going to get one shot at this. He had to do it right.

As Sorrow crossed the line in the dust, the Wing Warrior sword flashed brightly, and the Wing Warrior angled the light into her face. She reared up with a scream, pawing at her eyes, exposing her underbelly. The Wing Warrior knew this was his only chance, and he ducked under the dragon's flailing limbs, driving the blade of the sword deep between two of her thick, black scales and leaving it there.

Sorrow howled, swinging her claws wildly and catching the Wing Warrior around the side of the head, knocking off his helmet. The Wing Warrior – who without his helmet was just Nimbus, just a boy – staggered under the force of the blow and dropped into the dirt. His vision swam out of focus. 'Got you,' he grinned, through a mouth of blood.

'Got me?' Sorrow laughed. 'You think sticking me with this little sword can kill me?'

'No,' Nimbus said. 'But the sword was glowing. The sword has something to show you. Something you forgot.'

Sorrow shook her head. 'I think I hit you a bit too hard. You're talking in riddles.'

Nimbus let his eyelids flick closed. 'You'll see,' he muttered, as he fell unconscious. 'You'll see it all.'

Sorrow looked at the crushed body of the little boy. 'Silly,' she growled.

She plodded across the square. Cloud put his arm around Glass protectively. Similarly, Tidal put his arm around Sky. But while Cloud stared down the approaching dragon defiantly, Tidal looked away, gritted his teeth, and hoped that what happened next wouldn't hurt too much.

'I'm scared,' Glass whispered.

'It's okay,' Cloud said. 'I'm here. Don't be afraid.'

Sorrow was almost on top of them now, all snarling menace and sharp teeth. Her claws flexed; her neck arched.

Captain Obsidian, who was barely able to see straight, and whose ears were still ringing from when he had been blown off his horse, prepared himself for a desperate last stand. 'Are you fit enough to fight along with me?' he asked Cloud.

'I don't think there will be any need for that,' Cloud said.

Sorrow hissed, her head shot forward, and then she stopped. A light come on behind her eyes, and she recoiled in fear from something that wasn't even there.

'No,' she snarled. 'No.'

'What's happening?' Obsidian asked.

Cloud smiled grimly. 'The Wing Warrior sword gives whoever holds it the power of infinite vision. Sometimes it shows you what you have no wish to see.'

Sorrow shrunk away, saying over and over again, 'No, no, no.' The sword in her belly glowed with memories. It glowed with images of what had been, what was, and what might yet come to pass; and those images gradually took shape in the shadowy recesses of her mind, unfolding like a play she had no choice but to watch.

In the play, Cloud was sleeping in a temple at the top of a mountain while Sorrow watched him.

But in the play she wasn't called Sorrow; and in the play her scales weren't black.

It was cold, but Sorrow liked the cold. Everything smelled fresh and crisp, like new snow, and there was sleet in the air. It was calm and quiet, but Sorrow felt a deep despair in her heart.

Recently there had been a change in the magic forces of the world. Evil energy – more than there had ever been before – was growing like poisoned ivy in the far reaches of the land. Sorrow had felt it happening slowly, over the course of many years, and now she had a sense that the ivy was ready to stretch its vines into the world of man, choking all that was good.

The dragons and the Wing Warriors had protected the lands of men for a long time, and they had often thought there was no threat they could not overcome; but Sorrow knew this threat was different. This threat could destroy them all.

Still feeling sad, like something was dying inside her, Sorrow walked out onto the balcony of the temple. As she left, she took one last look at Cloud, little realising it would be the last time she ever saw him as a friend. There were thin streaks of cloud in the pale sky. There were no birds.

'What is this terrible thing that is coming to us?' Sorrow asked, looking at her golden claws.

'That would be me,' a handsome man standing at the edge of the balcony said.

'Who are you?' Sorrow asked, more intrigued than alarmed by the stranger's presence.

'I am Crow,' the man said.

'You are a very magical thing,' Sorrow said.

'I am a necromancer. I channel living energy into death. There is no other like me.'

'Why did you come here?'

'I am building an army. It is almost complete, except for the two most important pieces. I need a general, and I need a messenger.'

'What kind of messenger?'

'There are storm clouds before the storm, there are the living before the dead. I need a figurehead, a banner bearer who will announce my arrival to the world.'

Sorrow flexed her golden wings. 'And who will be this banner bearer you require?'

'You will, of course.'

Kevin Outlaw

'I'm afraid that is impossible.'

'Perhaps I can convince you otherwise?'

'You cannot.'

Crow moved quickly, without seeming to move his legs at all, and appeared right next to Sorrow. She barely had time to be surprised before he had thrust a vicious black dagger into her belly, sticking it between two of her golden scales.

Sorrow jolted, spasmed horribly, and dropped to the ground.

'The blade I have just stabbed you with has a poison on it,' Crow said. 'It is a very rare poison, and takes a very long time to make. It has taken me many years to produce enough for this encounter with you.'

Sorrow tried to scream, to make some sound to warn Cloud of what was happening, but she couldn't. It felt like somebody had stolen her voice.

Crow smiled with wicked delight as he continued. 'The poison will fill your body, and then you will be able to breathe a thick smoky poison of your own.'

'You can't do this,' Sorrow gasped. Her beautiful golden claws were turning black.

'Furthermore, once this poison has finished running through your blood, you will completely forget your life here. You will be truly evil, and a puppet under my control. Then I will turn you on your dragon friends, and you will destroy everything you love.'

'But why? Why me?'

'You must understand, you are the perfect subject. I am the necromancer. I turn good into evil, and day into night. You are Mother, the first dragon, the mother of all dragons. You were life, and now you will be death.'

Sorrow coughed and wheezed, and her last kind thoughts dissolved like whispers in the wind, heard briefly then forgotten.

'Now,' Crow said, triumphantly, 'you will be Madam Sorrow.'

Sorrow stood. Her eyes were red, and her tongue flickered. 'I am Madam Sorrow,' she said.

Then the play finished, the curtain fell, and Sorrow was back in the village of Landmark.

But she wasn't called Sorrow any more, and her scales weren't black.

Cloud's breath caught in his throat, and a complicated series of emotions swelled within him: Love, hate, despair, happiness, anger. An ugly human mess of feelings, all directed at the golden–scaled dragon before him. 'I don't understand,' he gasped.

But he did understand. He understood all too well. Sorrow had not defeated Mother.

Sorrow was Mother.

The dragon groaned and slumped in the dust. Her golden sides rose and fell in time with her heavy breathing.

As he looked on helplessly, a deep needling pain found its way through Cloud's ribcage and began stitching the dragon's suffering to his own thundering heart.

'What happened to her?' Sky asked.

Cloud shook his head. There were tears in his eyes, and a hurt so deep inside that he did not think there was any blade in the world sharp enough to cut it out.

'What's going on, Cloud?' Tidal said.

The mighty dragon's eyes closed. Her wings twitched and then collapsed in on themselves. Her great strength had failed her completely.

'I thought she was gone,' Cloud whispered. 'All this time.'

Glass tugged at his hand. 'What happened to her, Daddy?'

As if her little voice had broken some kind of spell, Cloud looked down at her, and wiped his stinging eyes. 'She has remembered who she really is,' he said.

'Is she Mother?'

Cloud nodded solemnly. 'The beginning of all dragons. I should have realised.'

'Is she dying?'

'I think so.'

'But why?'

Cloud looked back at the dragon, clutching one hand to his chest. 'She has been a terrible creature for many years. Now she knows just how terrible, and I think her heart has broken. Evil is blind. It is that way for a reason.'

He took a step towards the dragon, but then stopped, and looked instead at the small crumpled figure of his son, lying sprawled out in the dirt. He felt himself being pulled in two directions at once, and didn't know what to do. How was one man supposed to suffer such loss and pain?

Mother had been his closest companion, a great and important part of his life. But Nimbus... Nimbus was his life.

He turned away from the dragon, and crouched beside his son.

Behind him, Cumulo stirred and got to his feet. He shook his head groggily. His scales were red, and puffs of hot smoke came out of his nose.

He looked at Mother, and a terrible wave of sadness rose inside him, casting a shadow over his heart. Then he saw the small body of Nimbus, limp and awkward in his father's arms, not moving, not breathing; and the wave of sadness came crashing down, crushing his heart completely.

From the way Cloud was holding the fragile body to his chest, crying hopelessly, Cumulo already knew Nimbus was dead.

Strata came out of one of the nearby houses, from where she had watched the whole terrible ordeal, and she stood beside Cloud. Her eyes glistened wetly, but she refused to cry. For years she had hidden the truth about Cloud's true identity, and she had told the same lies that he had told. She had supported his choices, and played the dutiful wife even though she knew his heart could never truly be hers; and now, because of the lies she had buried under more lies, her son was dead. Nimbus was dead, and it was as much her fault as it was Cloud's.

What she felt as she looked at the brave and broken remains of her only son was beyond her abilities to express in actions or words, so she did nothing, and she said nothing.

And she fell apart alone.

'He saved us all,' Cumulo said, when it became apparent nobody else was going to speak.

Strata wiped her eyes with her sleeve. 'He shouldn't have had to,' she said.

'He chose to fight.'

'But he didn't choose to die.'

'I'm sorry I couldn't protect him.'

'Protecting him wasn't your responsibility.' Her gaze darted towards Cloud. 'This is what happens when parents fail their children.'

Cumulo paused thoughtfully. His head was sore, and his brain was still muddled, so the idea he was having took slightly longer to form into words than it might have done normally. 'But Mother has returned,' he said.

The golden dragon's breathing was slow and awkward. Her eyes were closed. 'She is dying too,' Cloud said, coldly.

Cumulo padded over to Mother. 'My Lady,' he said quietly. 'Mother, can you hear me?'

Mother opened one eye. 'I can't do it,' she said. There was pain in her voice, and not just physical pain. There was the type of pain that can only be caused when a spirit is wounded. 'I cannot do the thing you are about to ask of me.'

'You are Mother, the first life force. You created all the dragons. You must be able to help him.'

The village was quiet. Cloud watched the two dragons talk as he cradled his son's body in his strong arms.

'I am the golden dragon. I have the power to bring new life... It is beyond my talents to restore a life that has been taken away.'

'You must be able to help.'

'I cannot.' There was a pause, almost long enough for Cumulo to think that Mother had nothing more to say. Then she added, 'But you are different.'

'Me?'

'When we were fighting, I saw it in you. I saw my children.'

'What do you mean?'

'Somehow, you are all of them. All of my children that have gone before you.'

'She's right,' Cloud said. 'We did it. But we never expected it to happen this way.'

'What do you mean?' Cumulo repeated.

Cloud spoke softly, stroking the hair away from his son's forehead. 'After Mother vanished, the remaining dragons feared the worst. They worked together to produce a single egg. No dragon other than Mother had ever produced an egg, and we didn't even know if it would work. Each dragon put a part of themselves into that egg, as a safeguard for the future.'

'And that was my egg?'

'You were gifted with a piece of each dragon's memory, so that they would all live on through you. But somehow, because of what we did, you don't just have their memories. You have their unique abilities too.' He paused. When he finally spoke again, his words were barely even audible. 'It doesn't make any difference though. There was no dragon who could bring the dead back from the other side.'

Mother coughed violently, and her sad eyes rolled up under her eyelids.

'Mother?' Cumulo whispered.

There was a moment of silence, a moment that seemed as long as all the time there had ever been, then Mother coughed again and swivelled her great head to look at him.

'I saw it when we fought. You have all the power possessed by dragons. They gave it all to you.' She blinked carefully. 'Come closer, I will tell you a story.'

Cumulo leaned nearer.

'In my life, I have laid eleven eggs, and each has hatched into a dragon. All of those dragons were good at heart, if sometimes misguided, but there were two of which I was very proud.' The ancient dragon paused, fighting for breath. 'Earth was a beautiful green dragon, whose breath had the power to make dead things live again. But her power was limited to plants and trees.

'Many years later there was another dragon. We called her Snake, because she had no wings. She was very young when she died. When I...' There was another pause, pregnant with misery.

'You mean, when Sorrow killed her,' Cumulo said, helpfully.

Mother managed a grateful smile before she continued. 'Snake had only just begun to learn her powers. She could heal the wounded, the sick and the dying. Hers was a great gift, and we believed that one day she would be able to do what Earth had only dreamed of, and bring dead people back to life.'

Cumulo simply stared at her, not quite comprehending what he had been told.

Mother's breathing started to get heavier. 'It will not be long now,' she said. 'Soon I will pass out of this world, so listen carefully. If you have the strength of all dragons, then you have Earth's superior knowledge and you have Snake's superior ability. If you are a combination of them both, and also every other dragon, then you are the greatest of all dragons. Eleven dragons in one body.'

Cumulo looked at Cloud, then at Nimbus. 'Do you think I could do it?' he asked Mother. 'Could I bring him back?'

'He's your friend. If you cannot then no—one can.'

'But how do I do it?'

'That, you will have to figure out for yourself. Just promise me this, if you do figure it out, don't bring me back.'

'Why?'

'Because I remember my life as Mother, bringing magic and life into the world, and I remember my life as Sorrow, bringing nothing but pain and suffering.'

'I... understand.'

Mother smiled kindly, despite the pain. 'Your friend is waiting,' she said. And that was the last thing she ever said, before her heart stopped beating and her eyes went blank.

For a moment everything was silent. Nobody spoke. Nobody knew what to say.

There were tears streaming down Cumulo's face. If he cried until forever, he would still have tears left to shed.

He looked at the fallen Wing Warrior.

Nimbus's eyes were closed. There was blood in his hair, and down the side of his pale face. He looked strong, dignified. He looked every inch the hero he had always been destined to be.

He also looked dead.

'I don't know how to do this,' Cumulo said.

He turned his thoughts inwards, trawling back through the half—formed memories the great dragons had given him, searching through the skills they had gifted him with before he was ever even hatched.

The inside of his head was still so murky, so dark and strange. The memory he needed, the small snippet of knowledge that could bring Nimbus back to life, was like a glimmering firefly in that gloom. Every time he tried to focus on it, it flew away; every time he drew near, he suddenly realised it was somewhere else entirely.

'I don't know how to make it work,' he said. 'I have no guide. I wish Mother was here.'

His scales were red.

He could smell the smoke in his own nostrils.

Nimbus was perfectly still, as a dead person was expected to be.

'He's so brave, and I'm going to let him down. I'm going to

let everyone down.'

The colour of his scales thinned out into the cold blue of a midwinter morning.

He studied Nimbus's face carefully.

The boy was at peace, and Cumulo suddenly doubted if bringing him back was the right thing to do. There were strange forces at work in the world, and Sorrow was just the beginning of the trouble. If Nimbus was brought back then he would have to assume the role of Wing Warrior, as was his destiny. He would have to stand against the evils of the world, risk his life time and time again. He would have to defend this land. Perhaps he would have to watch the people he loved die, and even faced with that horror, he would have to fight on. His work would never be done, and he would never be allowed a moment's rest.

But he was resting now.

There would be other people who could fight the war that was coming. There would be...

Cumulo looked off into the West. There was nothing there now, but he could imagine there was. He could imagine the pain, and suffering, and death, and blood.

It would be a living nightmare.

Many people would stand up and fight, and many people would die. The people would look for a hero, but no hero would come.

Cumulo knew then, Nimbus should not die. This boy was the hero the world needed right now.

This boy.

This knight.

This Wing Warrior.

'Stand away from the body,' Cumulo said, and then he breathed into Nimbus's mouth. Two long, slow breaths.

'Please wake up,' Sky whispered.

Glass gripped Cloud's hand tightly. 'It's going to work,' she said. 'I told him he wasn't supposed to go anywhere without me.

I told him we had to stick together.'

Tidal remained silent, his lips drawn into a thin line. His eyes glittered in the harsh daylight, giving away none of his thoughts. Strata's expression was equally unreadable.

Nimbus jolted upright with a gasp, sucking oxygen into lungs that had not been working for the last half an hour. The silence of death was utterly shattered as everyone in the crowd shrieked, and cried out, and burst into applause.

Sky broke down in floods of tears, slumping against Tidal, who gripped her firmly.

'Told you,' Glass whispered, her voice full of triumph. 'I told you.'

'How do you feel?' Cumulo asked.

Nimbus ran a hand through his hair, and blinked his vision clear. 'Alive,' he said, shakily. 'I feel alive.'

CHAPTER THIRTY-FIVE

Tidal sat on a rocky outcrop, not far from the broken remains of the pier, with his feet hanging out over the still ocean. The sunlight glimmered on the surface of the water, reflecting like gold, and a single white bird bobbed and weaved above him. The world was peaceful and still, so very different to the crazy world of just a few days ago.

He picked up a broken shard of rock and threw it out into the sea. It made a satisfying plop as it disappeared, deep down into the cold underwater realm where the terrible thing was.

'Where are you?' he muttered.

The white bird continued to circle in the sky. Two men on the beach were building a new boat, hammering and chopping and sawing. There were three more boats out on the water, each manned by fishermen who had not yet given up the search for those people who had gone missing during the tidal wave.

'I know you're out there,' Tidal said. 'You took a bite out of me. I know you're real.'

He scratched his chest. His cuts were almost completely healed, but they itched a lot.

A single bubble rose to the surface of the water where he had thrown the rock. For a moment the bubble shimmered in the sunlight, and then it popped. It made a peculiar hissing noise.

'I don't know what you are, but you're mine. I found you. Nimbus can have his dragon, Nimbus can be the Wing Warrior. But he's not taking this away from me.'

Another bubble rose and popped. There was another strange hissing sound.

'I will be a hero one day,' Tidal said, confidently.

Another bubble.

Pop.

But no hiss this time. This time a gurgling, slimy voice. 'Of course you will.'

Tidal's heart started to thump in his chest. He pulled his feet up, just in case something should leap out of the water and grab his toes. 'I knew you were there,' he said.

He thought he caught sight of something large and snakelike moving in the deep.

A flurry of words came bubbling up. 'I'm here. I've been waiting for you.'

'You ate those fishermen,' Tidal said.

'I eat lots of things.'

'You tried to eat me.'

'If I had wanted to eat you, I would have.'

'You bit me.'

'That's true. I needed to know who you were. There's no better way to find out about someone than tasting their blood. Everything's in the blood, you know.'

'No, I don't know.'

'I've tasted your dreams, your fears, your hopes. I can help you.'

'I'm going to stop speaking to you now.'

'Why?'

'Because you scare me.'

'We could help each other.'

'I don't want to help you.' Tidal stood. 'I'm going.'

'Okay. You run along now. Just remember, I'll be waiting for you. If you change your mind, I'm always here.'

'I won't change my mind.'

'Talking to yourself?' Sky asked, walking down the shore past the ugly pier wreckage.

Tidal cleared his throat awkwardly, and kept his eyes fixed on the point where the bubbles had been rising. 'I was talking to the water,' he said.

'Why?'

'Because there was nobody else here.'

'I suppose that makes sense.'

They were quiet for a moment, standing close, but not that close: not close enough to touch.

'How are the injured?' Tidal asked.

'Recovering well.'

'And that soldier from the fort?'

'Hawk's fine, although he says he has no intention of ever returning to his position as watchman. And we've had word from Flint Lock that the other sick soldiers are recovering too.'

'That's good news.'

'Everything's getting back to normal.'

Tidal laughed unpleasantly through his nose. 'How can you possibly say that? Nimbus is a Wing Warrior now. He flies around on a dragon. Flint Lock and Landmark are in ruins. There are goblins in the woods. Not just old stories, real goblins. Glass is a witch...'

'She's not a witch.'

'What else do you call it?'

'She's not a witch.'

'You keep telling yourself that. And keep telling yourself that everything's the same.'

'We're still the same.'

Tidal saw something glint in the water. He could still hear that hissing, gurgling, bubbling voice in his head. 'I'm not so sure,' he said.

'But at least we're still together,' Sky said. 'So come on.'

'Come on where?'

'We need to get ready.'

'Get ready for what?'

'The party, Silly.'

Tidal rolled his eyes theatrically. 'Of course, the party. Nimbus's big event. How could I possibly forget?'

***

Captain Obsidian stood in the great ceremony hall of Lord Citrine's palace. He was in his full ceremonial armour, which he had only ever worn once before, and his heart was pounding as he waited at one end of the long red carpet.

At the other end of the carpet, sat on a high–backed throne, was Lord Citrine, a rather slim but handsome man with yellow hair, who looked too young to be the lord protector of the lands of men. His beautiful wife was sitting beside him in a similar, but less elegant, throne. She was wearing a flowing silver gown with flowers in her hair and diamond circlets around her wrists. Her skin was pale, and her eyes large, and she was as close to a stone sculpture as any human could be.

Captain Obsidian licked his lips. He had been drinking a lot of water, but his mouth still felt dry.

'Captain Obsidian of the Landmark garrison,' Lord Citrine said, in a commanding voice that suggested strength beyond his age. 'You may approach the throne.'

Obsidian swallowed. Rows and rows of spectators, lining the carpet on either side, watched him quietly.

This was it. His moment.

He started walking up the carpet on wobbling legs. Beads of sweat formed on his face. When he reached the throne he dropped to one knee and bowed his head.

'Captain Obsidian,' Lord Citrine said. 'You have shown great courage in the defence of our lands. You have performed acts above and beyond the call of duty in my service, facing not just one but two dragons in deadly combat.'

Obsidian mumbled something, which might have been, 'It's my job.' As if anybody could seriously be expected to believe that fighting dragons was part of a normal working day.

'As such,' Lord Citrine went on, 'I am giving you the greatest honour it is within my power to give. From this day forward, you are no longer a captain, you are a guardian of the realm, and will take up immediate position here at Crystal Shine, where you will have a command of two thousand men.'

Obsidian was caught completely by surprise. 'Guardian? Two thousand men?' The words were clumsy, half–stuck in his throat. 'But that's... I can't...'

Lord Citrine smiled a warm and open smile. 'You are fully deserving of the position.'

'But... My garrison. Landmark.'

'A new captain will be appointed to assume your role as captain of the Landmark garrison.'

Obsidian's men were watching. Men he had played cards with, trained with, hunted Nimbus with, fought Cumulo with. They looked happy for him.

'That's very kind of you,' he said, awkwardly. 'It's what I thought I always wanted...'

'What you thought you wanted?'

Obsidian swallowed again. He could barely believe what he was about to say. 'I'm afraid I can't accept the position you're offering me.'

'You... can't?'

'I mean, that is to say, I would like to take the position.' He paused, thinking it through before speaking. 'It's a great honour, but I would like to, if I could, if it would be all right with you, stay with my men. We've been through a lot together recently, and I think it would be for the best.'

'You wish to stay in the village?'

'The way I see it, Crystal Shine is well protected, there are more than enough good men here. But Landmark... I think I'm needed there. The world has become more dangerous, and a place like Landmark cannot stand alone against that danger.'

Lord Citrine nodded. 'You are a good man, and now you have the opportunity to be a great man. Don't turn down that opportunity out of a sense of duty.'

'Landmark needs to be rebuilt. The grass and trees are already starting to grow again, but it will take a lot of work to put the homes of the people back together. It is my village, and rebuilding it is my responsibility. I would like to stay there, even if it means I am just a good man, and not a great one.'

Lady Citrine spoke then, and her voice was as beautiful as she was. 'We must all do what we feel is right.'

Lord Citrine raised an eyebrow at her. She nodded slightly, so slightly the motion would only have been noticed by the most observant members of the crowd.

'So be it,' Lord Citrine said. 'You may retain your position as captain of the garrison.'

Obsidian rose. 'Thank you, My Lord.' He turned smartly on his heel and walked back down the carpet. He was still a captain, with no more power than what was his when he walked up the carpet, but he felt stronger than he had ever felt before.

He felt good.

He felt better than good.

He felt great.

'And now,' Lord Citrine said, 'the main reason we are gathered here today. Nimbus, Wing Warrior, will approach the throne to receive the thanks of the people he has saved.'

The crowd looked on expectantly.

Meanwhile, in a large room down the corridor from the hall where Lord and Lady Citrine were waiting for him, Nimbus was looking at himself in a full–length mirror. He was wearing the Wing Warrior armour, and trying to adjust the various plates to fit him a little better.

Cumulo was hunched in the corner, breathing as loud as a rumbling volcano.

'Have you been to Sorro... I mean... Have you been to

Mother's burial mound yet?' Nimbus asked, sitting his helmet on his head awkwardly.

'Not yet.'

'You should. They found a good spot for her, down under the mill on the hill. The sun shines there for the longest part of the day, and golden flowers have already started to grow.'

'I will go soon, but not yet. For me, the sadness is still too fresh, and I have not been hatched long enough to understand the emotions I feel when I think about her death.'

'Seeing the grave might help.'

'Perhaps. But today is not a day for dealing with grief. Today is your day.'

Nimbus adjusted his chest guard. 'This armour is too big,' he moaned.

'You're already growing into it.'

'I'm going to look a fool.'

'You will look like the hero all these people know you are. Lord Citrine is going to recognise your birthright as the last true Wing Warrior. You are part of a legend that dates back many hundreds of years. It is a great honour.'

'It is an honour, but I cannot help being afraid of what it means. The people will turn to me now, whenever there is a problem, and Sorrow is just the beginning. There is a greater threat.'

'You mean Crow, the man from your dream?'

'Yes. He is terrifying beyond imagination. Handsome on the surface, but different underneath. Full of hatred that is just looking for a way out to hurt people.'

'But as terrifying as he may be, we will stand and face him. Together.'

'Together.' Nimbus looked hard at his reflection in the mirror. 'You really believe in us, don't you?'

'And you don't?'

'I don't know. Captain Spectre said I should.'

'You've seen Captain Spectre?'

'No.' Nimbus looked embarrassed. 'I spoke with him, but I couldn't see him. He said it was because I didn't believe enough.'

Cumulo nodded. 'I suspect the next time you meet him, you will see things more clearly. You are somewhat changed from the boy I first met in that cave.'

There was a timid knock and Glass poked her head around the door. 'They're waiting for you, Nim,' she said.

'Okay.'

Glass waited for a moment. She looked the same as she always did, but Nimbus was acutely aware she was different now, in a way that was not immediately obvious. Some unimaginable and destructive power had awoken insider her; a power he could never hope to understand. She was a magic user.

'Hurry up,' she said, turning to leave. 'Just because you died twice, that doesn't give you the right to keep people waiting.'

'Glass,' Nimbus said.

'What?'

'Thank you.'

She grinned, the same way she always grinned, and for that single moment, at least, Nimbus felt that everything was going to be okay.

'You know what?' she said. 'In that armour you kind of look like Daddy.'

'I do?'

'A little bit.'

She closed the door behind her.

Nimbus adjusted his shoulder plates, and strapped on his sword belt. 'Well,' he said, 'there are a lot of people out there waiting to see a Wing Warrior. I guess, whether I believe it or not, that's me.'

He took a last look at himself in the mirror, standing next to his dragon friend.

Already the armour didn't seem so big.

THE ADVENTURE CONTINUES IN...

THE UNICORN RIDER
- Book Two of The Legend Riders -

Nimbus has defeated the black dragon, Sorrow; but his problems are only just beginning. Glass is losing control of the magical energies coursing through her body, and Nimbus must quest into the realms of the dead to find a unicorn, the only thing that can save his sister's life.

But there are powerful enemies who want the unicorn for their own reasons: The necromancer, Crow; the all-seeing cyclops, Carnelian; and the immortal Vampyr. And while Nimbus walks the path between life and death, his best friend Tidal chooses to take a dark path of his own.

There is danger on all sides, and this time Nimbus won't have his father, his friends, or his dragon to help him...

www.thelegendriders.com

Printed in Great Britain
by Amazon.co.uk, Ltd.,
Marston Gate.